COUNTERFLOOD

Also by Kit Thackeray

Crownbird

COUNTERFLOOD

Kit Thackeray

WILLIAM MORROW AND COMPANY, INC.
New York   1979

For Joey, who never missed a year –
and Jenny, without whose company this
book would have been finished a
damned sight quicker.

COUNTERFLOOD

Prologue

The tiny high-pitched whine filled the stifling darkness. It was the only sound, and it came and went uncertainly, like a motor on the wind, hesitating, then surging onwards with renewed confidence.

Tenuous as the sound had been, when it stopped there was nothing to replace it. The night air was still and empty, as if waiting breathlessly for something, anything, to happen. Heavy on the horizon, a full moon cast a jaundiced light on an untold acreage of *cerrados*, scrubby trees, and a small collection of houses made from stones, plaster board and corrugated iron.

The room was small, without furniture. The moon's meagre light showed shapes, nothing more. There was the shape of the room itself, four walls, a ceiling, a closed door. There was the shape of a bed pushed hard up against the wall furthest from the door. And on the bed was the shape of a figure, lying still under a single sheet.

The mosquito made a delicate landing at a point midway between the sleeper's right ear and mouth. Senses alert for the slightest movement, it sank its proboscis into the skin, piercing with ease the fragile cell walls, eager to gorge itself on the blood within.

But the blood wouldn't come.

The mosquito was a creature of instinct, and it drew no conclusions. Only one thing was certain: the smell of blood was strong on the air. Easily, it moved down onto the right wrist, stopping momentarily on a simple bracelet bearing the name Noélia. But the smooth dark skin still failed to yield a drop of blood.

When the sun rolled molten up the eastern sky the mosquito was still there, blindly persevering, no wiser after the fruitless night.

And the girl on the bed had been dead for seven hours.

Chapter 1

He met Emmanuel Nigra by chance, and it was also by chance that he became rich. As many of the men with medals will confirm, life is so often a matter of being in the right place at the right time.

In all the vastness of Brazil there were, to his knowledge, only two spots called Rochedo; doubtless others exist, for the word means simply 'rocky'. They share things in common, these far-flung Rochedos: unremitting heat during the day, clouds of tireless biting flies, and a river. And the rivers, too, share a feature: they flow past banks that have been persistently rifled for over half a century in the search for alluvial diamonds.

He saw that there were six *garimpeiros* still digging. For over twenty long years they had sifted the butter sand along the river's north bank wherever it looked promising, and their workings stretched upriver and into this, the latest of the seven thousand sunsets some of them must have seen reflected in the sand-polished metal of their spades. To walk up that riverbank was not a question of distance but of time, and little by little the vegetation had crept back to reclaim the land the men had searched. The sieving itself was a drawn-out process done in the shallows at the river's edge. First the sand was coarse-sieved, lifted in and out of the water and spun dexterously to gravitate the heavier stones to the centre of the mesh. After each sieving there was an inspection. Then the ritual was repeated until the time came for the last sieve with its fine wire mesh. Finally the

3

garimpeiro would turn the contents of this ultimate tray onto the accumulated mound of sand that rose up out of the still, warm water like a child's castle. There was a wet slop as this golden, sandy pancake flopped out onto the pile. Then the man would sink to his knees in the water, and bend towards the results of his labours like a Muslim on his mat. If there were a diamond, it would be right in the middle. But usually there was nothing; or worse, some of the stones that the men called *forms,* shards of almost indestructible matter, that at some moment in prehistory could have been created on the periphery of the same upheaval that pressured diamonds out of carbon. There were many of these *forms,* and they took their names from the minds of men who lived in solitary hope surrounded by nature. There were slim, black fragments called fingers, globules of calloused quartz called tears. And rainbow stones, chips of citrine and garnet, pigeon's eyes and dog's teeth. But there was no word for the real thing except *diamante.*

The *estrangeiro* was of medium height, and blond. He came to the town one liquid evening, the noise of cicadas running shrilly through the air, and perhaps because he was tired, or perhaps because he'd often thought of diamonds, he stopped in the evening light by the river, and looked along its winding course towards a westering sun.

The stranger listened to the distant gurgle of the water as it sucked thickly round the dark-skinned calves of these patient men. Perhaps in the past, he thought, Rochedo had been a thriving village, once when the diggings were fruitful. Now there was just a small bar by the river, and the empty sockets of doors and windows in houses without people. Three distorted trees of a species he did not recognize stooped over a clearing that might once have been a market place. Their misshapen limbs were wrongly swollen, like men from another planet caught snooping, pretending not to be there, frozen in guilt. Rochedo suffered the sun and the shrill cicadas with latin lethargy, and children and chickens ran with naked bottoms, black, pink and feathered, from shade of palm to shade of orange. The few families left were almost all negro or mulatto, and regardless of origin they stuck together. Except for Nigra.

4

Dogs watched sleepily as the blond man turned, hefting his kit easily, the profile of his arm and shoulder corded with muscle. He moved off the track, heading towards three broken houses that lay, pastel-daubed, on a promontory above the water. The foliage had grown thickly about them, and he had to stoop to enter the first doorway, brushing aside the sweet-smelling branches of fig, and pausing to accustom his eyes to the gloom. To his right there was a door and he stepped towards it, hitting a loose plank and stumbling noisily into the room. At first he didn't see the old man; he was lying unmoving in a corner on a makeshift bunk. A rat scurried past the broken ends of a jagged floorboard and disappeared. The sun grinned redly through the window. The stranger knew that some of the nicest views are seen from the least likely places, and he paused to take it in. Then, behind him, the old man coughed.

The young man reacted instinctively. Before the cough had died away he spun and crouched, a long knife glinting in his right hand, his bag held protectively to guard his flank. Then he saw the source of the noise and slowly relaxed. With a thin exhalation of breath he sheathed the knife and looked at the old man.

Sometimes it's obvious when someone has only a short while to live. Nigra seemed to be nothing, just a bony framework covered by a translucent diaphragm of pale brown vellum.

During his time in Rochedo he had been an outcast, because he wouldn't join the others' little co-operative. He preferred to work alone, the way he always had done for thirty years on the Rio Mequens and then here. Subconsciously he had gravitated nearer towns as his age increased. But he had no idea how old he was: he was *bastardo*, and had always laughed when he said it. Nigra was nearly a white man, but not quite. His hair was grey, in parts pure silver like aspen bark dusted with snow in a high place, his eyes a leached blue as if faded with the years. And his skin had the faintest touch of colour that was more than just the sun.

His voice cut the silence with surprising strength.

'Are they working?'

The blond man looked out into the evening, and now saw

5

no-one at all. The river flowed quietly and the banks were deserted. He thought he heard distant music from the bar.

'No,' he said at last. 'There's no-one out there.'

Nigra nodded, and motioned him to sit, but there was nowhere except the floor, and the other man remained standing.

'I am Nigra,' the old man said at last. 'They think I'm mad.' Without waiting for a reply he went on: 'Who are you?'

The stranger bent, and pulled a hammock out of his kitbag. The kitbag was of faded green canvas, the type that sailors have, but the hammock was bright yellow. It spilled into the room like a huge daffodil. On two facing walls there protruded metal hooks. That they should be the right distance apart for a hammock was no random chance: in the interior of Brazil it is the agreed dimensions of the hammock that govern room sizes. With his *mata* slung, the younger man half reclined across it, legs dangling, eyes travelling the river through the window.

'I'm called Kees,' he said, and his voice was gruff with dust and fatigue. He went on, not wanting to give the wrong impression. 'Kees Kuyter. If you tell me where I can get some food, *chefe*, I'll make you supper.' But the thought of moving again immediately was unwelcome, and gratefully he lay back and closed his eyes.

The old man watched him, his own eyes so sunken and bright that he did indeed look a little mad. But after his fashion he'd worked out a philosophy to live by, and he knew that there were many people more insane than he scattered throughout the world. It was enough that the God in which he had always meant to believe had sent him someone at the end. To live alone was one thing. To die alone ...

The old man closed his eyes and could see Kuyter's face clearly in his mind. It was a strong face, weathered with small lines round the blue eyes, the face of a man in his prime. Beneath the set jaw a pale ridge of scar tissue ran like a necklace. Where he had come from, this man, to find Nigra at the end? How many long kilometres? The old *garimpeiro* opened his eyes suddenly to be sure he wasn't wandering, but the strong brown legs still hung from the hammock, reminding him of how he had once been, bounding over the face of the country

6

like an antelope, tireless in the fiercest heat. 'Age,' he thought, 'has stalked me cunningly, and deserves a clean shot.' Every time he had looked over his shoulder the mounting years lay hidden behind his pride, until gradually the pretence became obvious, as he slowed faster and tired more easily. But he didn't want to die, not unremarked, unmourned. Perhaps he could influence the life of this man, even from his deathbed, so that when the centipedes were feasting the name of Nigra would live on, and travel far with the strength of another. A tremor ran over the old skin and died away. He had, after all, one last die left to throw.

'Who thinks you're mad, Nigra?' Kuyter had rested for thirty minutes and was now sorting untensils from his bag.

The old man gestured upriver. 'My *amigos, os garimpeiros.* At least they send food from time to time. I can't ask for more.'

Kees moved closer to where he lay, and thought he could feel the wasted body radiating its small reserves of energy hotly out into the air.

'Nigra,' he said. 'You're sick and should have medicines. I'll help you, but you must tell me what is wrong. Have you had this illness before?'

For the first time the old man moved his head and looked up.

'*Mãe de Deus, gringo,*' he said. 'You would help me with medicines?'

Kees nodded.

Nigra coughed, turned, and spat onto the wall. The mucus hesitated, then started thickly towards the floor.

'Boy, I am grateful for your help, but I am not ill, I am old.'

This was so true that Kees tried to reassure him. 'Not so old,' he said. 'Tell me. Tell me your age.'

Nigra laughed a little. 'When I am gone, make a cut and count the rings. I have never observed passing years, just the passing water. And now it's not important.'

Kees was at a loss, and stood there undecided. If he left, the old man would die sooner or later, and if he remained there was little enough he could do to change that. But if he were to stay just for one night, and talk to him, perhaps it

7

would cheer his passage, keep his mind on other things as his life stole to its close.

'Nigra,' Kees asked. 'Are you too old to eat a chicken?'

Kees made a fire outside the window, and that way he was able to talk with the old man while he turned the bird. He had walked up the twilit road to get it, and a woman had despatched her young son to find one in the near-dark. The boy certainly knew where the birds roosted, because he'd plucked one out of a nearby orange tree like a noisy feathered fruit. An indignant uproar from the darkened branches soon died down, and then the hen was held up for inspection. He'd nodded, and the boy silenced its clucks with a dexterous wrist movement. Then he paid and walked back down the track.

He gave Nigra the breast, the most edible part. The rest of the bird felt as if it had spent most of its life in training. But the old man ate very little, and afterwards Kees fed him wild figs, which grew up on the other side of the house, and hot *café zinho* without which Brazil would collapse completely.

They talked till late into the night. Emmanuel Nigra had many stories of the great outdoors, and he told of how he came to leave home, of his sicknesses, the first diamond.

'Two carats,' he said. 'Just another grain of sand on the river bank. And I found it.'

His eyes brightened at the memory. 'Who knows from where it had come? It was buried in the sand by a nameless river that flows into the Branca. Out of the countless mountains of earth in Brazil, I had found a diamond. And not by luck. By patience and the eye.'

By the eye, he meant the knack prospectors have for picking a site. But this amounts to a blend of luck, experience and some practical knowledge of geology.

Kees climbed into his hammock and watched the stars through the window. He could have dreamed of diamonds, but more and more now his sleep was troubled and he found his mind rifling through the years, filling the night-time hours with faces from the past.

He had been born in Amsterdam thirty years previously, to

8

a mother who loved him too much and a father who was seldom home. When he was twelve his father had died trying to pilot a jet through the stormy skies above Indonesia. Twenty-three had perished with him, and the *Telegraaf* asked in banner headlines: 'Djakarta Disaster – Pilot Error?'

The family - Kees, his two sisters Yfke and Annemiek, and their mother - had left Holland for New Zealand, and in a waterside house at Howick, Auckland, started to build a new life. His mother was South African and for her the language was no problem, but it was in New Zealand that she found her son had a flair for languages too, because English came to him easily, and Maori as well.

At seventeen, Kees got a friend of the family in the RNZAF at Whenuapai to arrange an indulgence passage for him on one of the planes going to Singapore and Thailand. That ticket to Bangkok had cost just fourteen shillings and tenpence, some two dollars, an administrative charge for a seat meant for the relatives of Service personnel. After that, the years fled in the great melting pot of the Far East, and he'd signed on a tramp out of Hong Kong called the *Borua*. In Paramaribo, Dutch Guyana, he heard his native tongue again and jumped ship. And then another new continent lay before him, inviting him to come closer and hunt out its opportunities. Once again there were ventures and partnerships that flared and broke up. That these things would come to nothing, he had somehow never doubted. And so he drifted as the months turned into years.

Kees woke and looked about him. He felt vaguely sad, but could not discern the reason. His hands gripped his single blanket tightly, and he forced himself to relax, shifting slightly as the hammock swayed. Once he used to wake up disoriented, wondering where on earth he was. Out in the night the river moved through the darkness, round the next bend and on to an unseen destination. A dog barked. Rats scurried. Kees breathed deeply and sank back into an uneasy sleep.

The next day Nigra was worse. Kees found it difficult to leave him, not that he was ever asked to stay. He fetched the old man

9

water to wash in, and carried him outside to do his ablutions. It seemed he weighed less than the kitbag.

At midday Kees went down to the bar to ask what should be done. The women were shy with him, but one of the Negroes answered his questions.

'Nigra is old,' he said. 'There is nothing to be done.'

'And when he dies?'

There was a muttered conversation about priests, and then the Negro said: 'He is not one of us. I have never seen him in the church. When he dies he must be buried.'

Kees thanked him and walked out. In the street there was a ruined chapel; its bell had fallen onto the beaten earth and the sky showed through the roof. He walked by, scuffing the dirt with his shoes, and thinking that perhaps Nigra had better places to commune with the Almighty inside his head than a priestless chapel in a broken town.

The next day the end was imminent. But the old man's mind was clear and sharp to the last.

'Kees,' he said. 'You are young and impatient, yet you have waited to say goodbye to me. *Muito obrigado, amigo,* it is more than many would have done.'

The Dutchman felt his eyes on fire for the old man, and wished he could have known him better.

Nigra made a great effort and moved his body on the bunk.

'Kees,' he muttered. 'I told you of Santa Clara. There was a mission there to the Indians, but they built the road to the east and the country is as it always was. Perhaps some Indians remain, there is no-one else. Behind the ruins of the mission there is a path leading away from the water. Follow it upwards and you will come to a flat rock that sticks out over the trees like an eagle's beak. I used to go there with a girl, a young *indigena* from the village ... they thought me mad in those days, too.'

He reached out a hand, and Kees took it. Single tears squeezed themselves reluctantly from his eyes as he saw the other man fighting and losing. Somewhere in the moonlight outside a dog was howling.

'Kees.' Now the voice was so quiet he had to lean over to

hear him. 'Everything I ever had is there at the Eagle's Beak. Think of Nigra. I was once young, like you.'

Kees buried him the next morning, and made a cross from broken planks. He took the heaviest stones he could find and laid them on the grave to keep out the scavengers. Then he packed his kitbag and set out for the road he had left a few days ago.

Outside Rochedo he found his way blocked by four men. He started to push past them, but they stopped him.

'So Nigra is dead,' their spokesman said.

'Yes,' Kees agreed. 'Dead.'

'What did he give you before he died?'

'He had nothing to give.'

The *moreno* made a signal, and two of them grabbed the Dutchman's arms. They ripped the pack from his back and scattered its contents all over the ground. After a feverish search they found nothing.

'Where are Nigra's stones?' the man snarled. A fist caught Kees round the face, another in the stomach. He fell to the ground, and the *moreno* issued instructions in rapid dialect. The four men set about stripping him, and one of them thrust a foot into the small of his back and ripped his trousers off. Kees could see nothing but the dirt of the road, and then they pushed him along the ground, and he felt his body slide over something hard. He recognized the shape of his Puma knife with its twenty-centimetre blade and managed to reach for it with one hand. But still he couldn't move. They forced his buttocks apart, and he felt hard fingers probing his body, searching nails ripping the flesh. Bile rose in his throat, then the pressure relaxed, and the men stood up. He kept the knife by his side, praying for a chance to use it.

The big man leant over him as he lay there on the ground, and reached down to spin him over. As Kees rolled the knife was freed from the weight of his body, and he brought it up and across. It slashed the *moreno*'s windpipe so cleanly that at first he thought he'd missed. Then the blood came. The man rose to his full height, hands clutched to his throat as a gout of red pumped its way thickly through his fingers and smaller droplets spattered through the air. Before the man to his left had recovered from the shock, Kees jabbed upwards with the point and felt it slide along bone before it found the soft spot and disappeared into the rectum. He gave the man the full eight inches, and pulled it out at an angle. Then he gained his feet. The two men that remained were opposites in every way, one fat and one thin. The thin one decided to leave his knife at his side and run. Kees let him go. The fat one had no choice. He squared up like a cornered animal, lips drawn back, watching his opponent's knife. He was still watching when it sank into his gut, and his hand clutched feebly as he sagged to the ground. When Kees turned round there was just one other body at his feet. The big *moreno* had carried a lot of blood, and now it was all over the road. The other man had hobbled off as best he could into the trees.

Kees packed up his gear slowly for the second time that morning, and wiped the knife clean. It made him think of the *Borua*, and another night a long time ago in the streets of Wanshai. Fully dressed again, now dirty and blood-stained, he started up the road. He was walking bow-legged, but at least he was on his feet. As he went he tried to keep his mind on other things, hoping he would avoid the reaction to what had happened. He thought about Nigra and of what he'd said. 'Everything I ever had is there at the Eagle's Beak.' What had he meant? Happiness? A girl? Or a cache? The latter was extremely unlikely: the old man had died with nothing. Surely if he'd had stones stashed away he would have returned there to get them and convert them into cash. But no sooner had the thought of going there occurred to Kees than he found he couldn't leave it alone. He took out his map. As the crow flies, it was only twelve hundred kilometres to Santa Clara.

If Brazil's western frontiers had ever reached the Pacific, then possibly there would have been a hotel at Santa Clara, a church, petrol pumps and shops. It may still happen, but not this year nor the next. Santa Clara has always been nothing, and nothing has changed. Other towns have flourished briefly near the

western borders; to the south, Vila Bela, also known gran-
diosely as Mato Grosso city, lies forgotten in the shadow of
the Bolivian hills. The great road that was to have linked it with
the north-west was bulldozed through the *cerrados* hundreds
of kilometres to the east, and it was Campo Grande and Cuibá
that had boomed. The road to Vila Bela is grassy and long,
the population black and insular. The Rio Guaporé provides
water, fish and a means of travel, but the town and its people
comprise a forgotten outpost.

The only alien life near Santa Clara was the squatters. There
is a great drive to populate the Brazilian jungle with poor
whites from the parched north-eastern states. It is not that
they have no rain at all in Goiás and Piauí, just that when it
comes it does so in unreasonable quantities, wears away the
tired soil, and leaves it to the mercies of months of baking
sun. The result is terrible erosion. So the emigrants pack up
their meagre belongings and travel with other families who
are prepared to share the cost to the fabled lands of Amazonas,
Rondonia or Acre. After a week or more living and sleeping in
a truck they arrive, and are allocated a patch of virgin jungle,
the title deeds to which are based on U.S. satellite pictures,
provided with seeds, and advised to clear and cultivate the land
by the method known as 'slash and burn'. The men and
women cut down the primary rain forest, burn the timber and
plant crops. The first year is reasonably successful; the wood
ash fertilizes the earth and supplements the humus. The second
year the crops diminish, perhaps providing no surplus for
seed. By the third year the families may have to move on to
find another site to slash and burn.

For the earth that appears to support such luxuriant growth
supplies little more than water and humus from the trees' de-
composing leaves. The rain forest is not as it seems. Over
millions of years it has been forced to adapt, to draw its sustenance in ways unknown to an European oak, whose roots
may stretch further than its branches through a thick, brown,
life-giving topsoil.

Some of the hopeful *pobres* who arrive in the northwest
squat on tiny plots of land fringing the huge parcels bought

unseen anually by businessmen from the industrial east. If they remain undetected by the owner or his agents and improve the land, then, after some years, if they are not forced away by hired *pistoleiros*, the land becomes theirs.

When Kees walked into the small community of Boa Paz there was little sign of life, but he heard the chatter of children and found school in progress in a small grass-roofed building near the edges of the ever-present jungle. A truck driver had told him of the existence of the settlement three days before, but even as he approached the schoolroom to seek a bed for the night he found it hard to believe. In terms of remoteness Boa Paz was the end of the earth.

There were about eighteen students in the school hut, boys up to the age of ten and girls a little older. They all looked round when the blond man walked in, relaxing blue eyes in the welcome shade, and he smiled and wished them *Bom dia*. They answered in chorus, except for one voice, the teacher's. It was a deep, musical voice, with laughter in it and a lot of warmth. 'Are you looking for someone particular?' it asked, and then she came into his line of sight between the blackboard and one of the timbers holding the place up. He looked at her for several moments, and she held his gaze. He saw the blackboard out of the corner of his eyes, and irrationally memorized a sentence about chickens and their genders, *'Galo é o masculino de galinha'*.

The children whispered and the flies buzzed. Sweat dribbled between Kees' shoulder blades. Things would have been a lot easier for him if he had never met Noélia at the village of Good Peace.

She told him she had never known her parents; an unwanted girl child, she had been left naked near the small wooden crosses that marked the last resting place of three Catholic priests in the mission garden on a small tributary of the Rio Mequens. Her proximity to the dead had saved her life; the Fathers had found her and raised her with the help of Zenilda, a Negress who had worked for the order since her husband's death fifteen years before. When Noélia was ten the Indians on

14

the river took a terrible revenge on the mission and its occupants for two of their kind who had been raped and killed by hunters. The priests had all died, and she only escaped because Zenilda hid them both in a cramped cellar under the kitchen floor. After that Noélia had stayed with the family who looked after the church-run Indian museum in Porto Velho. She went to school near the great Madeira River and learned the ways of a frontier town; Porto Velho was fifty hours by bus from the nearest asphalt road, and then only in the dry season. Eventually she had become a teacher, and then travelled with a young geologist, perhaps her first lover, into the Serra dos Pacaas Novos. Somewhere along the line she had met Manoel Machado, the squatters' leader, and agreed to stay for a time and run a school.

Kees arranged to sleep the night in Boa Paz, and before slinging his hammock he met the squatters. They were a tough and outwardly cheerful breed under the iron leadership of Machado, but beneath it all they were insecure and frightened, isolated from the world.

All that is asked in return for hospitality in the remoter areas of South America is news – second hand, third, hearsay, it doesn't matter. Any words from the traveller are absorbed instantly and voraciously by those who have made their lives on the frontiers of civilization. Though weariness urges sleep, and one's mind registers less than nothing at the thought of some dusty, eastern town, the mention of which has set them afire with nostalgia, one look at the waiting circle of eager faces tells the traveller he has no option: who could deny these people, who have not even a radio between them, one evening with the stranger from faraway places and his talk of the outside world?

Late that evening Noélia made Kees *guaraná*. Not the fizzy replica on sale in the east, but the real thing. She took a stick of the stuff, as hard as oak, about six inches long and the thickness of a stave, and ground some of it into a powder using a metal file. *Guaraná* seeds come from an Amazon tree, and they are dried and compressed before being sold. A glassful a day, it is said, practically ensures longevity.

Noélia mixed up the powder with sugar and water, and Kees drank it.

She laughed. 'Do you like it?'

He didn't have the heart to tell her he'd had it before. 'It's good,' he told her. 'When do the dreams start?'

'No up or down with this,' she said. 'You just stay where you are longer!'

It was his turn to laugh; he felt lightheaded. But it was her, not the drink.

'Where are you going?' she asked.

'I don't think you'd know it,' Kees said. 'It's almost not on the map. I don't really know what I expect to find there. Once there were missionaries, but now ...' He shrugged. 'Santa Clara, it was called.'

She started excitedly, and fingered a locket that hung round her neck. And then, over the next hour, she told him of the missionaries and her early childhood. Never before had he seen anyone as beautiful as Noélia; her eyes had a slight slant to them, and her hair hung to her waist. Her body was a light brown, lithe and supple.

'You're beautiful,' he told her, and she smiled her thanks. He knew he could talk plainly to a *morena*, where he could have wasted months with some *branca*, determined to protect her blue jewel while the world passed her by.

'Do you have a man here?' Kees asked her.

She shook her head. 'No.'

He laid his hand lightly on her shoulder. True to her blood, the skin was softer than the finest chamois. All the creams in the world could never give a European woman's skin the unique quality of an Amerindian's. Noélia was part Indian, and thus Eurasian, combining the best of the two races rather than the best of two people.

They kissed, and he felt her fingers strong on his shoulders. She folded against him for short periods, occasionally moving her hands to his chest, trying half-heartedly to push him away. Perhaps, like a man on a long night drive who toys with death when he closes his eyes for seconds at a time, she too felt the need to keep awake and in control, not to succumb. But she was fighting a losing battle, because she wanted him as much as he wanted her. By the yellow light of an oil lamp he stripped her of her skirt and shirt. The only other garment she wore was a pair of thin black pants, cut in a sharp vee like a Rio bikini. They revealed her buttocks, firm and brown, and cut across her hair so that it spread out in a triangle to either side of the thin elastic. And then he took those off too, and ran his hands lightly over her entire body.

She leaned against him, and he heard her whisper, '*Gosto muito de ti*'. Then his shorts were falling to the floor, and he felt her take hold of him. He laid her down on his sleeping bag on the floor, because a hammock can make a mockery of the most ardent attempts at love. She thrust her belly upwards, and her flesh opened moistly to accept him; and then he became aware of something further, something he had never experienced before. Noélia was moving the muscles inside her body in a slow, sure rhythm, gripping him, pulling, controlling. Gradually he stopped his own movement and lay quietly on top of her. His blood pounded in his ears and he felt like a man who has just discovered great wealth: stunned into immobility. She opened her eyes, black and deep as the holes between the stars. She kissed him and pulled him to her, while deep within her loins muscles he had never heard of stroked and caressed him, rippled and relaxed. She was older than all his years, and knew when his moment came though he uttered not a sound, and neither of them moved. Strangely, he felt robbed and manipulated. He had lost the initiative. And he felt tired, more drained than he would have believed possible.

But Noélia had all the answers. They lay for a short time, and then she began to stir under him. He protested: it was too soon, there was no chance. But she knew a point on his spine, and another at the base of his tired flesh. Amazed, he felt himself reacting, swelling, bursting. With it came an inane pride in his power of recuperation. This time, he vowed, he would do it his way.

Noélia's breasts were perfect cones of coffee brown, her skin as smooth on the tongue as caramel. And her progenitors had passed on to her an ability to please, an instinct for love that made her unique in his experience. All that first night he lay with her, absurdly pleased and sated after a long thirst. He had been in the right place at the right time.

Tomorrow he would be another day nearer the Eagle's Beak. He thought of Nigra then, as he lay beside the girl. Of Nigra lying dead, and of what he might find in the rocks above Santa Clara. And then he drifted into sleep.

The path up from the river was steep and ill-defined, but he pressed on, anxious to reach his goal after two weeks of travel. Behind him the river wound away into the sunlight, and the crumbling walls of the mission looked like a graphic representation of his own faith in God. Bird calls sent shrill news of him up on the hill, and for a moment he thought he could smell frangipani, and see the lop-sided grin of a friend called Billy as they whiled away the dark hours of a Borneo night betting limp Straits dollars on the calls of the toc-toc birds.

Gradually he came out of the vegetation onto an area of broken orange rock. He walked crabwise across its sloping shoulders and down into a small gully. Below him, Brazil stretched towards Bolivia. And above rose the rock that Nigra had described. The resemblance to an eagle's beak could not be seen from all angles, but the name was apt, because its shape was jutting, predatory, dominating its territory; so apt, in fact, that any other name would have seemed laughable. Kees sat and looked about. The scene was one of beauty and stillness, and he tried to imagine where a man might have hidden something up here, and why he should have hidden anything of value and then continued in a life of toil and poverty.

Wondering just a little what had prompted his unlikely journey, Kees started to climb the rock. Though steep it was easy, and soon he was sitting on the forehead of Nigra's eagle. As a young man, with his life flowing strong in his veins and stretching ahead of him, perhaps Nigra too had shinned his way over this rock. Kees moved slowly forward. And then he realized, was certain, that Nigra had been there.

He knew he was going to find something, even before he put his hand into the cavity, as surely as if the dead man had spoken. The hole was like an eye socket in the bird's skull. He dropped a stone down in case of snakes, but nothing moved, and he reached in. His fingers groped round a square rough object and he lifted it out. A rusty tin. He wiped the top with his sleeve, and it fell apart. A small label in English and Chinese landed face up: 'London and Hamburg - China Black'. His nostrils distended for the lingering smell of tea, but only rust was in the air that morning.

He turned the remains of the tin upside down and a small canvas sack fell out. Inside its weather-weakened folds was a roll of brittle yellowed plastic that contained two pieces of paper. One was a remarkable drawing of a young Indian girl, and he stared at it closely for the girl's eyes were familiar. They were like Noélia's. He tried to fit it all together. Nigra had had a *namorada* here, all those years ago. Was it she who had laid an unwanted girl child of mixed blood on the mission steps? Questions leapt to his mind. Had Nigra ever seen his daughter? Perhaps he'd left before her birth, and the woman, wishing to erase all memory of the union, had then abandoned the child. He opened the other piece of paper. On it was a sketch of the mission, with a priest standing outside; underneath were words in simple Portuguese: 'Father: if you are reading this, then perhaps you can also see an Indian girl called Tutá, and a child born or unborn. If the child is born of mixed blood, then it is mine, and I would ask you to help them in any way you can. She brings you good payment. I am Nigra who was prospecting on the river. I ask pardon for what I have done before God.'

Kees reached further into the roll and picked out a metal tube, sealed and dully shining with the eternal sheen of aluminium. Once again he saw the last yellow pancake flopping out of the sieve, the men crouching, probing thigh-deep in the black shallows beneath the heaped butter-sand banks. How could the girl have ever been expected to find this cache? Kees supposed that during their visits to this place they had come to know the contours of the rock fairly well. Then something else struck him. Nigra had spoken of the mission ruins: Had he then been back once, more than once, adding to his hoard, nurturing some impossible crazy dream fostered by years of

19

solitude? 'Mad,' he had said. 'Even in those days they thought me mad.'

Certainly it was the act of a strange mind to perpetuate the memory of a brief encounter with a primitive girl from a pre-historic tribe. Kees shook his head. The girl was handsome in the drawing, and Nigra had been lonely. He turned seven stones in his palm. It had taken two weeks to reach the Eagle's Beak, fifteen minutes to become rich. But his elation was muted, and carefully he pocketed what he had found. When he turned away from that place, where a man now dead had salved his conscience and a gesture had become a shrine for memories, he already knew that though he had removed the stones it had not made an end to their story.

Kees spent a moonlit night in the mission ruins trying to think things out. Ghosts did not worry him at all. The next day he returned to Machado's village to see Noélia, and late the next evening, with sweat still damp between them, he told her about Nigra, and what he had deduced of the man's past. She lay there with him quietly, and then disengaged herself and opened the locket around her neck.

She kept very still as the tiny sepia photo appeared in the gloom, and she held it up for inspection, a picture of a man with black hair and a thick moustache. Even allowing for the changes that twenty years' prospecting can make to a man, Nigra was barely recognisable. But Kees nodded, and squeezed the locket shut. Tears appeared in Noélia's eyes and began to roll softly down her face. Kees felt his feelings for the girl heighten with each inexplicable twist of destiny.

'The diamonds are your birthright,' he said eventually.

'But he gave them to you as he was dying. You travelled far and found them. They are yours.'

Two days later he left the squatters' village on an eight-wheel drive Mercedes timber truck carrying four ironwood trunks. The girl left with him.

They returned to Porto Velho and caught the river boat to Manaus. Three days. They were good. Through late-evening pinks and golds the boat glided in from the wide Madeira to small inlets with precarious wooden jetties built high enough to top the floods. There was always a crowd to meet them, and hands of bananas and clusters of oranges tumbled down into the waiting arms of the third-class passengers, their deck space a riot of coloured hammocks from the Fortelezan looms on the Atlantic seaboard. As the steamer slowed down, women in dugouts with one or more of their brown-skinned infants aboard paddled recklessly towards it, calling for food for their children. Often they were showered with orange peel and laughter, but sometimes a loaf of stale bread or some old clothes found their way into the river where they were eagerly salvaged from the canoes.

Later, by moonlight, Kees held Noélia in strong arms, feeling the softness of her through her thin dress. Once a lone *vaqueiro* urged a line of cows across a creek, his calls echoing eerily over the watery landscape. Then a cloud took the moonlight and the scene disappeared. On the river there was a sense of timelessness. The engines throbbed and the water lapped. The Dutchman felt the diamonds secure, reassuring, and the girl, twenty years an unknown, newly intimate. If he felt any presentiments about the immediate future he pushed them to the back of his mind. Like the boat, it was easier to travel with the waters than against them.

In Manaus Kuyter went to see Pieter Schalter, a distant relative of his mother. Noélia sat quietly by his side as he made calls in strange tongues and sent carefully worded messages to people he knew in other lands. At last Kuyter had three options open to him for the disposal of the stones. The best seemed to lie with a German dealer in Argentina. Kees shrugged and saw no hardship in a journey south with Noélia. For both of them it would be a voyage of discovery. He insisted on shopping with the little money they had between them, and bought her clothes and a small duty-free camera. The next day they took their leave of Pieter and started out, in a roundabout way, for Buenos Aires.

At Campo Grande, in the centre of the Mato Grosso, they stayed in the Rio, a cheap, noisy hotel, and ate in a good restaurant called the Boi nos Ares. The name was a *jeu de mots* on their destination: with roughly the same pronunciation as the city's name it managed nevertheless to mean in Portuguese 'beef in the air'. But this seemed nothing in a country where *puxe* on a door meant 'pull' and taps were marked 'Q' and 'F'; though the water from the taps in their room flowed neither Q nor F, but somewhere in between.

The next morning when he awoke the first thing he saw was Noélia, sitting motionless in front of the mirror. He approached her, but she turned away. 'What?' he insisted, and turned her round. One eye was swollen and puffy. He looked at her critically for a moment but it just seemed like an insect bite. Swellings and rashes came and went in the tropics, often with no hint of explanation. He smiled.

'People will say I have to fight you for favours,' he told her. 'It's just a bug bite. It won't last forever.'

She cheered up after that, and they went by cab to pick up an old Ford that Pieter had arranged for them to borrow. But by lunchtime Kees felt strangely fragile, and both he and Noélia went to bed. Their lovemaking was desultory, and afterwards he slept a little, feeling flushed and heady. The heat of the day built up right through the afternoon, and by five Kees could stand the claustrophobic room no longer. The boats down to the Argentine ran every two weeks, and the thought of staying in Campo Grande for that length of time to catch the next one was not appealing. He woke Noélia and helped her pack her few belongings; within the hour they had paid the bill and were driving out of town on the new road to Corumbá and the Paraná River.

They had barely been on the road two hours when the first wave of dizziness struck. He felt himself break into a sweat as it passed, and a throbbing set up in his head. He slowed as if to stop, but he had never suffered illness in his life and to admit that there was a disease that could force him down in the space of a few hours was more than he was prepared to do. Yet the thought of Manaus and various fevers nagged him, and he asked Noélia to reach into his case for their small bag of medicines. Malaria? Nearly every week of his adult life he'd taken prophylactics. The headlights seemed to vary in intensity as the road leapt ahead in a series of long sweeps. His hands slipped on the wheel and he started to tremble. Vision blurred, the car tilted. Someone screamed. Was it him? Now the road was high above them, ramping into the night sky. The lights revealed sloping orange banks, the tops of stunted trees. The wheel twisted to life, wrenching its way out of his hands. Violently they floated, fell, rolled and stopped. He tried to relax his arms but they wouldn't. The girl. She was leaning forward onto a suitcase. His case. It had been in the back. No, medicines. It was all coming back. Slowly he pulled her upright. She was shocked. Of course. 'Noélia' - a grinding whisper, desperately loud - 'Are you hurt?'

Shaking of the head. The eye still swollen, then hidden by hair. God, what had happened? How had it all come to this? He looked at the bank they had just plunged over. He felt the fever rising inside his head to strike him down from within. It was as quick as that.

'Noélia.' Concentration. Nothing. 'Darling.' She looked at him, reached out a hand. 'I am sick. Need help. Leave me here and find a doctor. Back. Back along the road.' He fumbled. 'In my bag. Money. You know. Take it all.' The shivering was not to be denied. 'Noélia,' he tried, and he could see by her eyes that he was talking, although he couldn't properly hear the words. 'Take these. Your father's *picuá*. Put it safe, inside, like he would have. You will be a - *garimpeira* – until I get better.'

Then he realised that you didn't go up or down with a fever, just in and back and away.

Chapter 2

The door of the small room swung open and sunlight sliced the darkness. A man entered, beating orange dust out of his trousers with sharp blows from his left hand. In his right hand he carried a brown leather bag, much scuffed and worn, a little like the man himself. Behind him came an old woman dressed in black, her head bowed on her chest with age or arthritis or grief, or a tragic mixture of the three. The man pulled up short when he saw the girl on the bed. She had been beautiful and even death had not taken that beauty away. She had Amerindian blood, he noted, a pretty oriental bone structure like Nambiquara, or, to be more specific, Mamaindé. The man was a doctor and knew something of the western tribes. It was only when he moved nearer that he saw the other side of her face. The left eye was puffy and swollen, almost closed. The doctor felt the distorted flesh.

'Romana's sign.'

Involuntarily, his voice whispered the exclamation. Deftly, he pulled back the sheet and looked at the girl's body. She was wearing a red dress, torn in many places but of good quality, none of the rubbish one found so often on young women forced into prostitution. On her right wrist was a cheap bracelet inscribed with a name. The doctor leaned forward: Noélia. Then he pulled the dress up and laid a hand on the girl's stomach while the old woman crossed herself. But the stomach, like the rest of the body, was slim, too slim perhaps, wasted by fever. It was difficult to tell. Idly, he traced a finger over the heart area. The answer would be there, of that he was sure. His professional curiosity was roused. Abruptly he recovered the body with the threadbare sheet.

'When did she come to your house, *Senhora*?'

'It was last night, *Senhor*. My son found her in the road. It was all we could do.'

'Where is your son now?'

'He works at the meat factory.'

The doctor looked at the shape of the girl.

'Did she have anything with her, *Senhora*? Besides the bracelet? Papers? Money?'

The old woman's lips writhed briefly over toothless gums. Then she crossed herself again.

'*Nada, Senhor, nada.*'

The doctor nodded absently. 'I will take her to the town. This is no place for a corpse.'

The body fitted crosswise into the open back of a Ford Ranch Wagon, looking like a roll of carpet. Before the doctor left he leaned out of the window and addressed the woman.

'If you find anything, *Senhora*, - identification, something that may have dropped to the ground . . .' He gestured vaguely and looked through the blue-tinted windscreen at the scrub, the poor houses, the orange track. 'You have nothing to fear. She died from *chagas*. And I will be seeing the *policia*.'

With the doctor gone and his dust settled the old woman walked tiredly back to her house and poured a small cup of *cafézinho*; the pungent aroma of Brazilian coffee seemed to continue percolating in the very air. With fingers like the gnarled roots of the *mandioca* that was her staple diet she took out an expensive hide purse from the folds of her dress and opened it. In a trance, still unbelieving, she counted out the bills one by one until there were five hundred and fifty *cruzeiros* in front of her on the table. The only other thing was a photograph of the dead girl standing high above the water on the roof of a river steamer. With her was a man, blond hair cropped close. They were looking at each other with the knowledgeable, tender eyes of lovers. On the back of the photo was written 'Noélia', and some words in a foreign tongue. The Kodak paper was date-stamped February.

The old woman put the photo to one side and let her eyes linger once more on the money. God would forgive her: it was not a bad thing that she had done. The girl had died of *chagas*, the kiss of death. And that death, like any other, was final. From where she had gone not all the money in the Mato Grosso could bring her back.

After leaving the old woman, Dr Lani paid a brief visit to the police post and took official custody of the body. He also took a *cafézinho* with the lieutenant on duty. Eventually, if anyone were interested, the results of the autopsy would be on file and a copy would find its way back to Terenos. Afterwards he drove fast along the black ribbon of tarmac towards Campo Grande. Beside him on the big bench seat a holdall bounced around and two gun cases stood drunkenly upright, the covered barrels pointing through the window at the sky. On the floor were a pair of muddy boots, chains for wet ground, a cool-box containing twenty kilos of good marsh deer and half a dozen agouti.

He had spent the weekend on a friend's *fazenda* near the town of Aquidaduana, to the extreme south of a vast area of swampland called the *pantanal*. The Aquidaduana River was the most southerly of the dozen or so large rivers and countless tributaries which flowed west, draining the huge, swampy basin, until they joined the Rio Paraguai and the Brazilian border. The Paraguai flowed south to Asuncion, and from there across half a continent to Buenos Aires and the sea.

The doctor glanced at the Seiko on his wrist; as he looked the digits clicked over to read 7:35, so he had done fairly well in spite of the unscheduled stop. He had only called in at the surgery at Terenos to give a colleague a package of drugs, and it was there that the old woman had persuaded him, against his will, to see the girl. Normally in rural Brazil it would be impossible for a poor family to get a doctor to call. However sick the man or woman, they would make their way as best they could to the nearest road, there waiting for hours or even days for someone to stop and give them a lift to the nearest town. Many times it was the *motoristas* driving huge transcontinental Mercedes trucks who would take pity on the hunched figures at the roadside and brake their way down the gears to offer help.

The doctor glanced over his shoulder, away from the sun's glare: the body was lying in the shadow of the cab, wedged firmly in position. He was still not sure what had prompted him to go with the old woman. Perhaps it was the terse way his colleague had treated her, but a glance through the surgery door had been enough to explain his attitude: early though it was, the queue spilled into the street – and these were the living, they were not beyond help. The old woman spoke of a dead girl, and when all was said and done what could be done for her?

But she had also talked of the girl as a 'lady'. Whether this was because she'd had possessions which the old woman or her son had conveniently neglected to mention, he wasn't sure. But in any case if someone of good family were missing the police would soon know. And if not, then the body would serve to demonstrate autopsy aims and procedures to the students, especially if, as he suspected, the girl had died during or just after the acute phase of *chagas*.

The car swept past the big Bordon abattoir where the woman had said her son worked. The doctor had once made a visit there to see the machinery of slaughter in operation. He had started in the stockyards and watched as the cattle were herded through special gates until they could only move in single file into a high, sheer-sided concrete canal. Traps were lifted and dropped from above and, like boats filling a lock, the cows had been split into groups of a dozen or so; above them, a man on a boardwalk leant over into the canal and galvanized the slower animals into involuntary action with an electric prod. Pipes countersunk into the concrete sprayed the livestock with insecticides and detergents until, bedraggled and afraid, they presented themselves at last for death.

It was here that the doctor had been fascinated. He had thought that in a new slaughterhouse a modern way of killing would have been devised. But there, almost invisible in the blackness where the living production line fed itself into the bowels of the building, stood a huge Negro wielding a sledgehammer. Sometimes (because of an inconsiderate movement by the animal) it took six blows to fell a beast, and then it was hoisted high off the ground by a hook thrust through a back leg and slung on a wire to hang and bleed.

The doctor shook his head sadly as he turned into Avenida General Rondon. It was important that his students acclimatize themselves to death. Those who eventually came to work in the interior, rather than joining some relative's select practice in São Paulo, would see plenty of it. It was important, too, they realize that death was no respecter of age, beauty, rank. The girl in the back had been beautiful, and she had died young. Her body was slim and brown and desirable, but microscopic creatures carried in the faeces of a two centimetre long bloodsucking *barbeiro* had infected her, proliferated in her constant warmth, eaten her heart out. He would watch their faces, the doctor thought, all those city boys and girls doing their year in the mato. He would watch their faces as the knife went in, and all that they had ever held dear in life was cut to pieces so that man could learn, one day, to protect himself, and understand the obscure diseases of the tropics.

The Ranch Wagon swung in towards the entrance to the Clínica, Campo Grande's biggest hospital. An armed and uniformed policeman called out *'Bom dia'* as he recognized the doctor, and then the big car was heading down towards the mortuary.

A man dressed in a light blue coverall consulted a piece of paper, then slipped it neatly under the spring of a clipboard. It was Wednesday, not that it made much difference. Work was work, even in the stiff house. He consulted an index hanging on the wall, and moved away down the line of cooled cubicles until he came to the indicated number. Leaning slightly, he pulled the drawer out from the wall until it jutted well out into the room. The corpse was sheeted, but around the small right ankle was a paper card giving all known details of the deceased. The attendant untied the card from the ankle. The skin was cold, but not icy to the touch; the thermostat maintained a temperature at which organic deterioration was halted. Then he moved a trolley alongside, slid the body sideways onto it, and pushed the empty tray back into the wall. Next he weighed the body, wheeling the trolley onto a metal plate set in the floor. The scales were adjusted to register only the weight in excess of fifteen kilos, the trolley's weight. He noted the new figure, remarking that the girl had lost almost nothing during her short stay. This was quite usual, though regulations still stipulated the double weighing. Humming softly to himself, he wheeled the trolley through the swing doors and down the white-tiled corridor to the autopsy room.

The student doctors, now in their third year, were already gathering when Wilson Alviera started to prepare the body. The autopsy room was tiled, like the corridors, but in pale green, and six stone slabs, like shallow baths on pedestals, were arranged in two rows. Along one side of the room were cabinets and benches for the tools of the trade, and a pair of large sinks. A power drill and attachments lay ready. Wilson Alviera had been doing the same job for thirty years and had worked in most of the principal cities of Brazil. He was a single man without aims or imagination, untroubled by the thought that one day it might be him, face up and buck-naked, dead on the slab.

The students drew closer as he removed the sheet and man-handled the body into position on the table. The girl's skin was damp and cold, and had taken on a greyish tinge, but she still retained a serene quality that gave her presence even in these extreme surroundings. One of the femal students came closer to look at the dead girl's face. Wilson Alviera glanced up; strangely, there was a similarity between the living and the dead. But he dismissed the thought immediately, and slapped his hand down sharply on the corpse's thigh. The student flinched, and Alviera put his face close to hers and hit the leg again. The noise was not the same as a slap on living flesh; the sound was dead as well, like a heavy stick hitting plasticine. Alviera took the student's hand and pulled it down until it was resting just above the dead girl's breasts.

'Never be afraid of the dead,' he told her. 'They have no feelings.'

The student tried to remove her hand, but he held it and moved his face closer still.

'When I was young they told me "Kiss the flesh, Wilson, kiss the dead flesh, and you'll never be scared again." And it's true, *moça*, it's true. If you can kiss the dead, they'll never come to play their games in your mind.'

Abruptly, he laughed and let go of her hand. Then he covered the body with the sheet and moved on to the next table.

The student backed off, rubbing her hand on her skirt, and was watching Alviera preparing another body on another slab when Dr Sebastião Lani entered the autopsy room. The doctor's *'Bom dia'* in a loud voice had the effect of momentarily silencing the chatter of his dozen students before a chorus of voices returned his greeting.

Without preamble he switched on the lights that illuminated the autopsy table and opened a drawer containing apron and gloves. Purposefully he donned both, and adjusted the apron strings for a comfortable fit before turning to face the students. Like the man controlling the opening curtain at a theatre, he pulled the sheet from the body, and there was silence.

He paused and looked around. The students seemed to get younger every time he saw them. But they were the doctors of tomorrow. Quietly, he spoke.

'*Senhoras, Senhores.* Today we have the sad case of a girl taken in her prime.' He gestured to the table with a gloved hand. 'It is probable that only one month before she died she was uninfected and healthy. That is how quickly her illness killed her. It is a disease that is widespread in South and Central America, and one for which there is no effective cure. I speak of *chagas*, named after its discoverer, Carlos Chagas.' He motioned the students closer, and they moved in to form a little circle of living cells around the dead nucleus on the slab.

'Before we go further, who can tell me something of Chagas' disease?'

He looked around from face to face and met the eyes of a short, stocky young man with spectacles.

'*Você.* What is your name?'

'Borba, *Senhor.*'

'Borba. *Bem.* Well, what can you tell me of this illness?'

The young man blinked rapidly, and started to talk just as fast in a surprisingly deep voice.

'*Chagas* is a parasitic infection caused by the protozoan flagellate called *Trypanosoma cruzi.* It infects animals and men, and wild animals in the south of the Estados Unidos.'

'Right!' said Dr Lani. 'Now, how is the disease transmitted?' He swung around to a dark-haired girl at the foot of the table. 'You, young lady. What's your name?'

'Arruda, *Senhor.*'

'Well, how would you go about catching *chagas?*' He permitted himself a faint smile. 'That's always supposing that you wanted it in the first place.'

The girl started to speak, but Lani interrupted her immediately. 'Speak up, girl, speak up. I can't hear you. Now, start at the beginning.'

The girl spoke up. 'In certain areas, bugs infest the walls of people's houses and suck blood while the occupants are sleeping. They defecate on the skin, and when the victim scratches the bite sometimes faeces get into his bloodstream and that person gets infected.' She tailed off as she saw Lani slowly shaking his head. 'That's if the bug was carrying the parasites in the first place.'

The doctor gestured her to silence. 'That's the sort of generalization that everyone on the street should know. About as much fact as a Paraguayan newspaper.' The students laughed, and Lani went on. 'Transmission of *chagas* is by *Triatomine* bugs. There are eighty or so different species. Here in Brazil we are concerned mainly with two: *Panstrongylus megistus,* and *Triatoma infestans.* As adults they are about two centimetres long, with a cone-shaped nose. They have wings but rarely fly. And as the young lady said,' he smiled across the table, 'they bite the inmates of infested houses, often on the throat, nose, lips and eyes. Thus its euphemistic name the "kissing bug".'

He stopped and looked down at the body. Almost paternally

he moved the girl's face from left to right, so that they could all see the left eye, swollen and closed.

'Infection is established when faeces containing the organism contaminate the mouth, nose, eyes or the wound made from the bite of the bug itself. The organism multiplies at the site of the inoculation causing a "chagoma" or swelling. If this occurs at the eye' – he pointed to the dead girl's face – 'we get Romana's sign.'

He took his hand from under the girl's head and turned to the cupboard behind him, speaking all the while. 'After local multiplication, the organisms disseminate by means of the bloodstream and multiply in other organs. Their noticeable preference is for the heart.' When he turned back to the students he was holding a large scalpel in his right hand. 'Today we will go through the normal autopsy procedure, and on the way we can see if my diagnosis has been right. Only about ten per cent of patients die during the acute phase of *chagas*. By acute, I mean the initial stage, up to about one month after infection. Pointers to correct diagnosis are a history of exposure to the bug, skin lesion, fever, and trypanosomes in the bloodstream. However some patients may have no symptoms, and acquiring the disease will go unnoticed. Not enough is known for statistics to be available. There are some drugs which can help if the infection is detected within days or weeks, but in general ...' he shrugged his shoulders. 'There are so many unknowns. In one hut in the north-east thirty-seven per cent of bugs carried the infection. Seven thousand were captured in the hut. They feed between every five and thirty days taking between five and three hundred milligrams of blood. Bites are usually painless, but can cause fever. Another name for them is the "assassin bug".' He looked up to catch the students' eyes. 'Yes, they eat each other too, and cross-infect that way.'

At last he leant forward, and the knife caught the light. 'We are like wood-ants in the jungle, with some of these diseases, with no conception of the size of the problem we are attacking.' The scalpel pricked the skin behind the angle of the dead girl's jaw, then stopped. Lani looked up at the students thoughtfully; their faces reflected a variety of emotions from curiosity to outright abhorrence. One girl wore the blank expression of a person who has temporarily vacated her mind and plans to return later when things are better.

'Most people,' the doctor was saying, 'die, in the final analysis, from cardio-respiratory failure of some description, and the lack of oxygen to the body during this failure manifests itself in several ways. Look for swollen legs, and squeeze them. The flesh will be soft and soggy. The same goes for the area above the natal cleft.' He gestured to the girl's fingers. 'Look for purple colouration under the fingernails, on the lips and ears. These are all indications of heart failure.'

Before he had even finished speaking, Lani had drawn the scalpel down from the girl's jaw across to the little ridge beneath her sternal notch, and then down in a straight line, swerving slightly to bypass her umbilicus, until the blade stopped against the bony rise of the pelvic girdle. Working quickly, he duplicated the first part of this long incision so that the cut extended from the angle of the jaw on both sides of the face. Then he cut swiftly through the pectoralis major and lifted her breasts away from the ribcage.

At this point there was a sound of muffled vomiting, and one of the girl students hurried from the room with a handkerchief over her face. It was had to tell whether she was fleeing the mutilation or the gagging, sickly-sweet smell. Lani called to one of the attendants across the room.

'Barboza.' He jerked his head urgently in the direction of the door. 'It's important that she comes back when she feels better.' The man nodded and disappeared.

Lani started to work more slowly now, and to describe what he was doing. 'Next we reflect the skin of the neck back to the level of the lower jaw. Cutting against the inside of the jaw, we penetrate the floor of the mouth, free the tongue, sever the back of the pharanyx and the upper gullet, and dissect the tissues off the front of the cervical vertebrae.'

Now the face of the girl was no longer human, and somehow it was easier to watch. Lani reached for the rib shears and started to cut through the costal cartilage close to the ribs. 'I have done only five thousand autopsies,' he said. 'There are those who have performed twenty or thirty thousand.' The shears crunched, and he talked over the sound. 'It's of paramount importance to fix the mind on the scientific aims of what you are doing, otherwise ...' he shrugged slightly and added: 'I cut the cartilage because, unlike the ribs, they will leave no jagged edges to tear my gloves.'

When the sternum was out, the doctor opened the pericardial sac. It contained a quantity of pale yellow fluid. 'At this stage note the size of the heart,' Lani explained. 'Later we will be making microscopic examination of various sections and I dare to predict that we may find this girl's heart has literally been eaten away.' He pointed with a gloved finger. 'Slides here and here might show you what looks like a beam that has been riddled with beetle. In due course a rotten beam breaks. Likewise, it becomes a physical impossibility for a heart thus infected to function flexibly as it should.'

In one fluid movement he took hold of the tongue and neck tissues, and pulled the heart and lungs out of the chest through the left side of the body, placing the organs behind him on the bench.

'Now the pleural cavity. Look for the fluid or pus.' There was a pause, during which the sound of other activity in the room seemed to the students to be borne faintly on the wind from an impossible distance. Then they heard Lani's voice again. '... an amputation knife,' it was saying, 'to cut behind the oesophagus, aorta, and then the intercostal blood vessels.'

They watched him cut the diaphragm at the junction with the ribs, allowing the liver and abdominal organs to enter the lower thorax. He kept talking now, engrossed in his work. 'We cut through the peritoneum and omentum behind the caecum, thus freeing the colons, the bowel being transected through the sigmoid colon and removed.'

Afterwards Lani could not remember at exactly which stage of the proceedings it was that his knife scraped something hard and patently inorganic.

'For the small intestine we cut through the root of the mesentery,' he heard himself saying, and once again his knife strayed and came up short against an obstruction where no obstruction should exist.

Easily, with no outward sign of the tingling curiosity he was feeling, Lani concluded in the abdomen and went on to the brain. Ear-to-ear incision just below the vertex, the scalp reflected forward to just above the eyes and back to the occipital notch, the roughly circular cut, dropping slightly on either side to approach the ears. The familiar whine of the saw, the smell of burned bone, and splinters of the stuff flying all over the table. A hammer and chisel just to finish the job, and there, revealed for the first and last time, was the dura mater, the last protection afforded by nature to what had once been a human female's guiding force. In this small, grey light-starved cavity she had learned to think and hope and love.

Lani cut the dura mater precisely along the line of the bone cut. It parted easily under the steel. Then he lifted the brain and transected the upper cervical cord. He had almost forgotten the students, and they had almost forgotten him. They all looked at the girl's brain and the mutilated body.

Lani placed the brain gently by its recent housing and faced the students. 'For now, that will be all. If you feel that the procedure you have seen is something that you personally could never do, remember this: it's always worse to be a spectator. I could never stand to watch an autopsy – even today.' Abruptly he turned to the sink in a gesture of dismissal. Somehow it had not gone well.

'My God,' he thought to himself. 'Have I really done that five thousand times?'

Ten minutes later, with the students out of the way and only one other table in use at the far end of the room, the doctor positioned himself so that he effectively blocked the dissected body of the girl from view. Quickly, he thrust two gloved fingers into the vaginal orifice. *Mãe de deus,* but there was something there. He gripped it, found a tube, and slid it out of the purplish flesh. He had it in his hand when a voice behind him said:

'Have you finished, Doctor?'

Lani froze momentarily, then continued moving his hands as if inspecting something on the body. Without turning, he replied:

'Nearly, Alviera. *Obrigado.* Give me five minutes.'

He sensed the attendant moving away, and relaxed slightly. He noted that his heart was beating abnormally fast. Quickly he transferred the tube to his pocket, stealing a quick look at it on the way. A stainless alloy. About eight centimetres long. Might have been made for ... what? A short cigar? The *garimpeiros* called tubes like these *picuás.* They varied in size and design from little film-tins to plastic fountain-pen bodies, and the *garimpeiros* kept them in much the same way.

Lani took off his gloves and apron, unaware that Alviera was watching him strangely as he left the autopsy room. Minutes later, safely in his office with the door locked, the doctor withdrew the *picuá* from his pocket and placed it in the sink in the corner of the room. It was tightly sealed with a screw cap, but he thought twice about submersing it. Instead, he washed his hands thoroughly with a strong soap, and wiped the tube with a disposable towel soaked in disinfectant. At last, barely able to contain his curiosity, he pulled the blinds, quickly sat down at his desk, switched on the lamp and unscrewed the cap.

Cottonwool. Gently he eased it out into the air. More cottonwool: he reached for a toothpick and stuck it into the white fluff, twisting the wood until it caught. The second ball of cottonwool joined the first on the table. Lani looked into the tube, holding it close under the light, and a long sigh slid through his lips. Gently he upturned the contents into his palm. A single stone rolled out like a piece of sea-worn bottle glass against the pink flesh. The doctor put it on the blotter and reached for the toothpick again. In two minutes the *picuá* was empty, and there were seven stones on the desk.

Lani sat there thoughtfully. He fought down an insane impulse to leap up and see if one of the stones would scratch the window. Instead, he put them back in the *picuá.* They were, he supposed, diamonds. Of their value, he had no idea. It never occurred to him that they might be hopelessly flawed, inferior or without value.

Diamonds. Lani's mind began to race. Automatically he tidied his desk and put the *picuá* safely in the button breast pocket of his shirt. It would be no good trying to get rid of them in Campo Grande. These were surely stones such as were never found by the *garimpeiros* even after twenty years of digging and sifting along some fever-ridden stretch of waterway a thousand kilometres on the other side of nowhere. No, he would take his find to the city. To the biggest city: São Paulo. There he would make a sale.

The doctor switched off the lamp and opened the blinds. He would go to the Lanche bar on Rua 13 Maio, and drink a bottle of ice-cold Antarctica. And he would think this out further. He got up, unlocked the door and left the room, feeling the *picuá* as a reassuring lump hard against his chest.

In the mortuary Alviera was tidying up. He pulled the girl's body into a big plastic-lined bin on wheels, which would go immediately to the furnace. The legs stuck out awkwardly, but he pushed them down and shut the lid. The only thing left to do was to hose down. The strong jet of water cleared the blood and bone grist until the slab was clean and shiny. Ready for Dr Vilela, Alviera remembered, at 3:15.

Chapter 3

The red and white Beechcraft appeared suddenly over the
Fazenda Sabaca two hours before lunch, taking everybody by
surprise. As the aircraft slid down onto the grass landing strip
about a kilometre east of the main house, things started to happen quickly. Joaquim the gardener hurried into view, shooing
two assistants before him. Within seconds, all three were busy
sweeping the lawns with straw brooms. A bevy of young girls
armed with mops attacked the already gleaming tiles on the
patio floor, and a group of *vaqueiros* who had been smoking
quietly by the high wooden fence of the corral unshouldered
their *cordas* and ducked back into the branding pen.

Simultaneously, Oscar spun out of the house, doing up his
shirt as he went. He got momentarily caught up in some washing strung up to dry between two trees, but the line broke under
his onslaught and the garments fluttered damply to earth behind him. He headed straight for the Ford parked in the shade,
but changed his mind at the last moment.

'Levy! Levy, *Cristo*, bring the horses, man, the Coronel is
here!'

There were sounds of frenzied activity from the stables
abutting the house, and in an amazingly short time a small man
appeared limping between a proud Carthusian mare and an
even larger black thoroughbred stallion. Oscar hoisted himself
into the mare's saddle and spared Levy and his two grooms a
grimace of thanks. Then he wheeled away and broke into a
flat run for the airstrip.

Coronel Castro Silveiro Falco chuckled as he tethered the Beechcraft. He had radioed ahead to say he was on his way from Cuiba, and that Dona Tereza would not be with him. He had neglected to mention that he was only twenty-five minutes away at the time. He could imagine the scene down at the house now: Joaquim polishing the grass and Gabriel branding anything that moved. Though fifteen minutes ago, from a considerable height, there had been none of that frenetic activity.

He straightened, a tall man with piercing grey eyes and a matching moustache he had once grown to make himself look older, and now would never shave for fear of losing some intangible aspect of his distinction. The eyes narrowed, and came to rest on a head that appeared to be bouncing along the ground towards him. Then a pair of shoulders lifted it above the horizon, and Oscar crested the rise with the two horses flank to flank and flat out in an unconscious assertion of skill.

'A good seat,' the Coronel thought to himself. 'If the world were just a matter of horses, Oscar would be king.'

He walked out of the shadow of the aircraft, and waited erect as his son drove down on him with twelve hundred kilos of horseflesh. Oscar swung out of the saddle, and seemed to tread air for at least five yards. Then father and son were embracing, the air was full of the smell of horse sweat and aftershave, and the dry lifeless taste of the aircraft cabin was gone.

'A good trip, *pai*?'

A frown crossed the Coronel's brows, but he answered negatively. 'As these things go. How is the *estrangeiro*?'

Oscar smoothed the mare's flank and handed the stallion's reins to his father. 'He's a little better. Been bathing in the river. He's like a fish.' He laughed. 'Gleide told him about piranhas.'

The Coronel smiled. 'So?'

Oscar swung into the saddle. 'He just laughed and caught some for her that evening. He's called Kuyter, by the way. His last name. Oh, and Dr Lani was here at the weekend. He's had a look at him.'

Both men were now in the saddle, but neither made a move for home.

The Coronel looked at the sky he had so recently left. High as a kite, a black speck stroked the wind for favours.

'Is he German?'

'He seems to be from everywhere.'

'Yet he must be from somewhere.'

'You must talk with him, father. He is a strange man. Dangerous, perhaps.'

'But not to us.'

'No, of course not to us. He is grateful.'

The stallion snorted and the Coronel laughed.

'Fuego seems to think little of human gratitude.' Then his voice grew quiet. 'Amerigo Lind will be with us soon. Our negotiations in America have proved useless. We will have to seek another solution.'

Oscar felt a throb of pride as his father spoke. Not so long before the old man would never have confided to him who was coming to the ranch and who wasn't. Even now his knowledge was far from complete. He knew only that his father and a consortium of landowners had been trying to obtain control of large tracts of mineral-rich land in the Mato Grosso, and that these efforts had been thwarted by an American called Totm. Maybe things were changing, Oscar thought; it was certainly about time. If a man was old enough to sire sons among the ranchworkers' daughters, then surely he ought to have a say in the running of the place. But up to now the foreman managed the ranch in the Coronel's absence, and Oscar had been left to amuse himself as best he could.

He was so immersed in his thoughts that the black stallion got a good twenty yards clear before he could wheel and give chase The two horses raced across the *prado*, Oscar furious at having been tricked. Damn, it happened every time: no wonder he never got to run anything around the place – he hadn't inherited enough plain, mean, animal cunning from his old man.

The foreman watched the two horses gallop onto the track and jump the cattle grids. Then he started the Ford and headed up towards the plane to pick up the Coronel's bags. He passed the two flying horses and waved, bumping off across the rough pasture and onto the strip. He didn't look round because he knew who would win the race, and because really it aidn't matter. Father or son, the foreman had as much pride in the Fazenda Sabaca as either of them, and to his way of thinking it was the best ranch in Brazil, and thus the world. It was good to work for a winner, and the Coronel had been one all his life. Maybe one of these days Oscar would be one too. The foreman smiled a little smile. One of these days.

Kees viewed himself dispassionately in the large wall mirror of his room. The muscle had fallen from his legs during his illness, the shape of his skull pushed out around his eyes; he pressed thumb and forefinger into the corners of these organs in an effort to ease the lingering headache that the bright sunlight had given him. Naked, he straightened and paced the room, trying with even footsteps to sort out the confusion that he still felt. This was the Fazenda Sabaca, and he had been found delirious five days previously, wandering kilometres from any road. He reached the wall, seeing himself once more in the mirror, gaunt, etiolated.

But that would pass. It was the state of his mind that was driving him mad, the enforced idleness and the unanswerable questions banging round inside his head: what had happened to Noélia, and where were the diamonds? In delirium his recurring nightmare had been the thought of her walking out on him, selling the stones in the city and taking another man. But really he didn't believe that. Yesterday some of the *vaqueiros* had come in, having been to the place where the car lay wrecked in the *mato*. But it was empty, they said, and someone had stripped it of wheels, battery and seats. Oscar had radioed the police in Aquidaduana, but it was hopeless. No-one was about to start a search for a *cabocla* girl in a country where thousands died or disappeared without trace every year.

He was so engrossed in his thoughts that he didn't hear the knocking at the door. Gleide, the house girl and his self-appointed nurse, ventured in and saw Kees standing quite still looking at the wall. She let her eyes run over his lean body, then coughed softly.

He turned and saw her, and she drew back at the sight of his

41

face. The eyes, hollow from fever, were now filled with a terrible fear. Slowly the look faded. Aware of his nudity, the man reached slowly for a towel and wrapped it round himself.

'Gleide,' he said. 'I didn't hear you. You look beautiful today.' A little of his old self returned. 'You save my life and now you torture me with thoughts of things I cannot have!'

The girl laughed. She had grown used to this man in a back-to-front fashion; first the intimate procedures of washing him and tending him like a nurse, or even, Gleide had sometimes thought, a wife. She remembered the day he'd arrived. He had been found during a roundup, wandering with a high fever along a rough track that petered out in the vast areas of swampland that stretched to the Bolivian border. The Fazenda Sabaca was huge, and the Coronel often said it was the size of a small country. The *vaqueiros* had brought him in, and in the absence of both the Coronel and his son told the woman in the house to take care of him. At first there was fear that disease would spread among them, but Joaquim, the ancient gardener, had pronounced the sickness 'malaria from the north', and everyone had relaxed. Shortly afterwards Dr Lani, a friend of the Coronel's, called on them on his way back to Campo Grande; he had visited the *fazenda* to go hunting, and gave Gleide medicines for the man, together with advice on how to tend him. Now, with the memory of these intimacies already remote, she had to make do with his teasing.

'*Senhor* Kees,' she told him, 'The Coronel is here and asks you to join him for lunch. Here.' She picked up a bathrobe belonging to Oscar. 'Put something on.' She giggled. 'Have you no shame? Walking almost naked in front of a young *moça*?'

Kees swung into the robe as she held it for him, roughed up her hair, and kissed her on the cheek before she could turn her mouth to intercept his.

'I'd better get dressed. When's lunch? Now? *Agora mesmo*?'

She searched for a nuance in his voice, a hidden meaning. Would he like a delay? But sadly there was none.

Gleide was a simple girl, one of the *vaqueiro*'s daughters. Her father, unable to support the new addition to the family, had asked the Coronel to accept her into the household. Now she was the Dona Tereza's personal servant, and under the feudal system of a great ranch, a legally adopted servant of the *fazenda.*

As she left the room, telling him to hurry, she wondered what sort of man this *estrangeiro* was. At the beginning her friend Camilla had said that he must be German, but when Gleide asked her how she knew the other girl just coloured and left the room. In any case, some of the things he said in his sleep were easy to understand, and helped explain, perhaps, his lack of desire. The name, for example: Noélia.

Gleide closed the door behind her and thought that Noélia must have been beautiful to earn the love of a man like that.

Lunch was an informal affair attended by the Coronel, Oscar and their manager Gabriel. Kees shook the Coronel's hand and thanked him for the hospitality shown him over the past week, and then he sat down beside Gabriel and serving girls brought chilled Brazilian wine and avocados from the huge tree around which the house seemed to be built.

'*Bem!*' the Coronel pronounced, sipping the wine. 'Well, it's good to be back on the ground.' To Oscar: 'I see the cats are working in the northeastern sectors.'

Oscar nodded. 'Yes, we've got the new one going. You should see that chain!' He spoke to Kuyter. 'You must come and see the clearing operations. Two cats pulling a chain, links like your chest. *Cristo,* but the ground shakes!'

Gabriel said, 'Carry a gun all the time up there. You never know what's going to be flushed out.'

The glasses were refilled, and a whole fillet steak appeared on the table, about eighteen inches long and covered in a succulent sauce; beside the meat, a big bowl of *feijão,* Brazilian black beans. Salads arrived, and cubes of black radish.

The Dutchman helped himself at the Coronel's invitation, and settled down to the serious business of refuelling his depleted resources.

'If it's O.K. with you, Coronel,' he managed between mouthfuls, 'I think I ought to leave in the morning.' He smiled down the table. 'Not that I want to leave, you understand, but –'

The Coronel wiped his mouth carefully with a huge linen napkin embroidered with the brand of the *fazenda*. '*Senhor*, you should not leave in the morning, I insist you rest some more. This is a cattle ranch of some few hectares. One mouth more or less to feed will make no difference. We'll have a little talk after lunch. I am interested to hear your story.'

Oscar added, 'My father's right. You must rest, and if it's the matter of the girl that's troubling you –' He stopped, unsure how to go on. 'I was going to say that when you're stronger I'll come with you, and we can ask in the settlements along the road. Most of the land is ours, and they will answer my questions. A stranger would simply make them suspicious.' He cut into a piece of steak. It gave way to his knife easily, the tender to the keen.

Kees nodded and thanked them. Inside, he knew they were right. He still got dizzy standing up quickly. But the next morning, he vowed, he would hold Oscar to his promise.

It was late afternoon when Dr Lani nosed his car into the out-skirts of São Paulo. He had deliberately taken two days over the drive from Campo Grande, using the dirt road via Água Clara with its interminable wooden bridges to Três Lagoas in order to see the Paraná River dam. Now the long run down the Castelo Branco highway was over, and another ninety minutes should see him in the city centre.

São Paulo was more than a city: in every sense of the word it was a megalopolis. From miles to the west one could see the yellow smog bank that lay like a greasy cloth over the whole vast agglomeration of concrete. Deep in the shaded, airless canyons transecting the heart of the city several million cars, most of them Volkswagens, added to the pollution, and the fumes from these and a myriad other machines tickled the throat and stung the eyes.

For the city was filthy and overpopulated, a concept of civilization run horribly amok. In 1540 it had been the site of a solitary Indian mission school; at the turn of the century, a town. Now it was the biggest city in the southern hemisphere,

44

with an urban population of twelve million that was rising fast. Visitors from London, Cape Town or Sydney would probably be awed at this reinforced-concrete creation, their senses bludgeoned by its sheer scale. It would take a New Yorker to look up and around, to note the way the buildings seemed to lean and fall in relation to the passing clouds, to breathe the familiar smoky air and feel an environment not alien to him.

Strangely, the city knew how to be beautiful. Lani had been there before, though he made several mistakes on the way in and finished up driving down the long descending sweep of the Avenida 9 de Julho. The sun had gone, but red shafts of light still caught the higher buildings, and lit a part of the municipal theatre. Pedestrians in black ant-like columns hurried over fragile footbridges that were slung like careless hammocks from the belly of a road slanting high across the Praça Ramos do Azevedo. Lani eased towards the left-hand lane as the highway dropped down among the buildings; unsure of himself, he missed the correct turning and took the next road on the left to bring him into Santa Ifigênia. From here he was able to make another left into Ipiranga and find his hotel, the Lider.

The next morning he ate the breakfast which had been brought to his room at nine o'clock, and looked out over that part of the skyline that was visible from the third floor. Down below, the Avenida Ipiranga was still in shadow, and even on Sunday a solid phalanx of VW taxis was stretched across the eight lanes, waiting raucously for the lights, like a patchwork steel quilt. The doctor raised his eyes. The sky at the end of the street was a creamy brown, like *café* with too much *lait*. Gradually, as he tilted his head back, the colour changed until overhead it was clearly blue.

Sunday in São Paulo. Lani left a small package in the hotel safe and walked out on to the street with a 'What's on?' pamphlet from reception and an empty mind. His throat was sore, and he found himself trying to breathe shallowly to avoid taking in too much of the polluted air. Suddenly anxious to be off the sidewalk, he bought a paper and wandered into a Lanche bar. The place was empty. He ordered coffee, two *quibes* and some slices of lime. After wasting an hour he became restless and strolled up the street towards the Praça da Republica. Here, to his surprise, he found an extensive open-air market in full swing under the trees. Everything was for sale, from old copies of *Life* magazine containing advertisements for products no longer made and in-depth interviews with the young Ginger Rogers to coins from all over the world, and impressive stacks of pristine but worthless banknotes: the old Brazilian cruzeiros, inscribed *'Os Estados Unidos do Brasil'*. As he worked his way to the centre of the *praça* the paths became lined with pictures, many of which depicted the primaeval Amazon jungle in eerie greens and greys. Suddenly he thought, 'These people, artists and shoppers alike, could get in a car and drive to Porto Velho or Belem to see the real thing.' That was the amazing realization: it was all half a continent away, but still very much Brazil. And how many of them ever would? Not too many. Suddenly his attention was caught by a flash of purple. He veered towards it, and came upon a big stall littered with semi-precious stones. It was all from Minas Gerais, he supposed, and brought to the city for cutting, polishing and selling. Idly, he picked up one of a matching pair of bookends. They had been cut from an entire amethyst nodule, and one side was flat and polished with a rich deep colour that caught the light. The other had been left as a slightly concave jagged clump of translucent crystals; they must have weighed over five kilos each. Lani was tempted. In spite of the reason for his visit, he found it hard to resist the feel of the stone.

He beckoned to the owner. *'Ametista?'*

'Sim, Sim,' the man nodded, *'Tudo. Ametista mineira.'*

'Quanto é?'

The man didn't hesitate. 'One hundred and eighty cruzeiros.'

Lani shook his head, not in disagreement, but in disbelief. One hundred and eighty cruzeiros, about twenty-five U.S. dollars. He knew nothing of stones, but surely this was cheap.

The stall-holder was looking at him. Lani replaced the amethyst and tried a long shot.

'Supposing I had something to sell, here in São Paulo,' he said. 'Something of great value. Where would I go?'

The other man came nearer, and started polishing the book-

46

ends. They sparkled in the sun. 'You mean gemstones of quality?'

'I mean,' Lani began, 'Yes, I mean stones of great value.'

The man looked at him, and then through him down to where traffic snarled round the *praça*. After a while he said, 'I can take you somewhere. But later. You must meet me here later with a sample of what you are selling.'

'I could do that,' Lani told him. 'But I must have some assurance.'

The man took him by the elbow. 'My friend, you can take what precautions you like, leave a letter with a picture of me, if you must, to ensure against your return. They have my photo in the *Prefeitura* attached to my trading permit.' He chuckled. 'You are right to be careful, but really there is no need. I shall take you tonight to the house of a rich man. That is all. Either you will do business or you will not. Not everyone is a gangster.'

Lani felt foolish and amateur in the face of the other man's amusement, but he managed a smile. 'Well you must forgive me. I come from a distant town and this place ...' he gestured around him. 'Anything could happen here.'

'My friend, nothing ever does. For two centavos I'd go and pick *cacau* up the coast. Shall we say six p.m.?'

'Six, yes, six would be fine,' Lani told him. There was a silence. 'Till later then. *Até logo.*'

'*Até logo,*' agreed the man.

Lani walked back towards the hotel trying to reconstruct the conversation in his mind. The man had said that nothing ever happened in São Paulo when there was in fact an alarming homicide rate. Once he glanced back and saw the bookends glittering in the sun. In a way he wished he'd bought them.

At ten past six Lani and his contact started their drive through the suburbs of São Paulo. The stallholder ran a Brasilià, yet another breed of Volkswagen, and the doctor soon lost his sense of direction entirely. The two men said little, and in half an hour the car pulled up in a wide tree-lined street outside a pair of imposing black iron gates. The driver got out and pressed a button on the pillar to the left of the gates, subsequently exchanging a few metallic words with a talkback system. Then there was an electric hum and the gates swung open. The doctor craned his neck as they swept into the drive of the house, and once again evoked a deep chuckle from the other man.

'Don't be so nervous, my friend. If you don't know where you are, *não tem importância*. Perhaps Senhor Bretas will give you his card when you leave.'

They parked the car and got out. Two tough-looking *morenos* escorted them up the steps to the front doors, the whites of their eyes glinting in the near darkness. Inside the house another Negro led them along a parquet-floored corridor and into a small study. The door had scarcely closed before it opened again and a young man entered wearing a business suit. His black-rimmed spectacles reflected the lamplight.

'Amorim? Would you be so good as to wait here?'

Lani's companion nodded and sat down, while the new-comer led the doctor through another door that he had failed to notice. This opened onto one corner of a huge open-plan studio. In the dim light Lani got fleeting impressions of zebra skins, climbing plants, wrought iron and water. But his eyes were drawn to the far corner of the room which seemed to glow with a bright nucleus of light. Between them and the light, Lani realized the strange visual effects were caused by the surface of an indoor pool. The two men advanced to the opposite corner of the room, carefully skirting the pool, and then the doctor was on his own and face to face with the man whom he supposed must be Senhor Bretas.

Bretas half rose to his feet. 'Ah! *Senhor* ...?'

'Lopes,' Lani told him.

The other man extended a hand in welcome. '*Sim, sim, Senhor* Lopes. My name is Bretas. I'm glad to see you are here!' He sank back into his chair. 'A small something, perhaps? Brandy?'

Lani nodded. In this house brandy would be brandy, not the national imitation.

Bretas snapped his fingers and a trolley appeared out of the gloom, wheeled by one of the servants. A few moments later Lani allowed some of the most delicious Armagnac he had ever

48

tasted to trickle smoothly down his throat. He determined never to buy the local product ever again, and reached inside his shirt for the envelope. The liqueur had already made him feel unusually optimistic, and he nearly tossed the small package on the desk. Instead, he passed it to Bretas who took the three stones Lani had chosen to bring out of their wrapping.

There was a silence lasting three or four minutes while Bretas adjusted the diamond light. The whole desk seemed enveloped in a blue aura making a small lamp to the left seem ridiculously dim and red by comparison. Bretas smoothed each stone between thumb and forefinger and nodded to himself. Then he fixed a glass into his eye and brought the stones into its sphere. After an intolerable wait he looked up at Lani.

'What do you know of these stones, *Senhor*?'

'They're diamonds,' Lani told him. 'Of gem quality.' He had done a little research in the library at Campo Grande, and in any case, now was not the time to admit ignorance.

Bretas nodded. 'They are diamonds,' he conceded. 'Are these all you have?'

'No,' the doctor told him. 'I have others.'

The jeweller sighed impatiently. 'How many you have in your package could make a difference to the overall price.'

Lani remained cautious. 'If we strike a bargain, I can bring the rest here tomorrow night.'

Bretas was patently not interested in cloak and dagger. He pulled a small pair of scales towards him and released the pivot so that it rose and fell gently on its knife-edged agate mounting.

'The total world production of diamonds is about fifty million carats annually,' he said quietly, apropos of nothing in particular. 'About twenty-three percent of that harvest are gem quality.'

He picked up a minute weight with a pair of tweezers and put it on the scales, and continued expounding diamond statistics. 'In the cutting we expect to lose fifty or sixty per cent, and for the finished article there is a fairly well-regimented scale of prices dependent upon cut, colour and quality until around the fourteen carat mark; thereafter prices tend to be more negotiable.'

Now he was weighing the second stone.

'In mining operations one has to dig and process one hundred million parts of rock to find one diamond. The best mine in the world, in South West Africa, still processes four and a half million parts of rock for one of diamond. And when all is said and done, we measure a diamond in carats, and there are one hundred and forty-two carats in an ounce.'

He sat back and contemplated the doctor. 'Are your other stones the same size, *Senhor*?'

'No,' Lani told him. 'Two are much bigger.'

Bretas nodded. 'Well, you may think I am talking against myself when I give you these facts. But that is not so. You have here three stones of about five carats each, that's four hundredths of an ounce. Remember, I said we lose fifty to sixty per cent in the cutting. And without polishing a window and looking more closely I cannot be certain of their quality. So much for that side of it. There is another.'

He stopped and sipped his brandy. Lani, who at one stage of the proceedings had begun to feel extremely rich, was now beginning to worry about the hotel bill. He realized that Bretas played upon people as others might a violin. It crossed his mind that if he was on the point of being swindled, it couldn't possibly happen in nicer surroundings.

Bretas continued. 'I won't ask you how you got these *brutos*, *Senhor*, that is none of my business. I take it, however, that they were acquired in some way that is untraceable. Bought from *garimpeiros*, perhaps, or left to you in a will?'

'Perhaps,' Lani told him, feeling an almost uncontrollable urge to snicker.

'Am I safe to assume that no great robbery was involved?'

Lani nodded. 'You can assume that.'

'*Bem*. Then I can offer you seven hundred and fifty dollars in the rough for each stone of five carats, and proportionately more for the others you mentioned, subject to examination. If you accept I will give you cash, and there our contact must cease. We are both aware of the attitude of the government, I think. Now, if you require time to think it over ...'

Lani's brain was working furiously, and it came up with the

magic figure of at least forty thousand cruzeiros, tax-free, in the pocket. But maybe the stones were worth more. Perhaps he ought to shop around.

As if reading his mind, Bretas added, 'I must point out that the price I pay on occasions such as these varies little. If you feel it is on the low side, perhaps you are forgetting my considerable overheads and the problems involved in finding private buyers for the finished parcels.'

But even before the man had finished speaking Lani had decided to take the offer. They made arrangements for the delivery of the other stones, and then Bretas went to a safe and extracted packets of money that reminded his visitor of that afternoon at the market in the Praça da Republica.

After the doctor had left the jeweller sat there for a few more minutes in the centre of the shining light, toying with his little purchases and one stone in particular. He had paid about two per cent of their final worth, and was thus not displeased. Perhaps *Senhor* Lopes – Bretas chuckled inwardly at the name – would have been happy with even less. But that wasn't likely. The man had been of good education, and hardly on the brink of starvation. Abruptly, he turned off the inspection light and got up. Diamonds made such devious detours in their journeys from the earth to the wall safes of the rich. And his house on the Avenida Catarina was but one of them.

Chapter 4

All through Sunday Kuyter made enquiries in the roadside settlements, asking countless families if they had seen a young girl of Noélia's description. He didn't even have a photograph of her; whoever had stripped the car had done a predictably thorough job and taken the luggage as well. He contacted the first-aid posts in four villages, and **the** police in Terenos. There, had he but known it, he missed by ten minutes the policeman who had signed over the girl's body. His replacement was not in a happy mood, and stifled a yawn as Kees asked him to check the records to see if anyone had been reported hurt. The policeman poured himself coffee and neglected to offer any to his visitor. The records would indeed be checked, he said, and if the *Senhor* would care to return later in the week ...?

Kuyter walked outside and swore. He wished he hadn't persuaded Oscar that he would be better off by himself, and swung once more in to the cab of the Chevvy pickup that the Coronel had placed at his disposal. Five miles further on he nearly passed a small group of derelict-looking houses set back from the road on a shoulder of land. There was nothing to them, just a group of little box shacks, plasterboard and sheet iron, set like tatty coloured dice on the threadbare baize of the land. Kees hesitated, then pulled off the road. It was about the only feasible place left to try unless Noélia had got a lift further on towards the city. He parked the wagon, got out, and stretched. Two children huddled together for safety watched him curiously from beneath a ragged banana palm, and an old dog walked towards him, then thought better of it and retreated growling under a house. Kees stretched again and approached the nearest hovel. The door was ajar, so he called 'Anyone in?' There was no answer. He was about to move on up the hill when he heard shuffling steps behind the door, and it slowly swung open. An aged woman peered up at him, shielding her eyes against the light.

'May I enter?' he asked her. 'It's hot out here.'

The crone said nothing, but stood slowly to one side. Kees accepted the gesture at face value, and walked into the room. He sat gratefully on a wooden bench along the farthest wall and looked about him. It didn't take long, because there was nothing to see. The tiny room contained two benches, a table, and three upturned crates which had been pushed together to represent a work surface. Several old copies of *Manchete* lay in front of a small wood-burning stove, its heatproof mica window flaked and brown after decades of use.

At the beginning of the day Kees had engaged in polite conversation with people before explaining what it was he wanted. But after half a dozen stops he'd given that up as a waste of time. Without preamble he came to the point.

'About a week ago I was taken ill on this road, and I crashed my car. There was a girl with me, and she left me to go and get help. Since then I have been unconscious with fever. And the girl has disappeared.'

The old woman's eyes slid away from his, and she walked over to the stove and started to get things together for a meal. Kees went on talking to her back.

'She was young,' he said, 'and *cabocla*. Half-breed. Had you seen her, then you would remember.' The old woman clattered the pans and ignored him. Kees felt annoyance, but he controlled it. 'Old lady,' he said evenly, 'I am asking you a simple question. If you can answer me then I'll be on my way.'

The old woman started to turn round, but her chance to answer the question slipped away. There was the sound of running footsteps, and a brawny young man in his mid-twenties burst into the room. He started to say something about the car

53

parked between the houses, and then his eyes caught sight of Kees and he stopped dead. Whatever else he may have been, he was no actor. The face showed recognition, then fear and guilt. Quite suddenly, the atmosphere became tense and Kees stood up. Mother and son looked at each other, unable to speak but trying to decide on a course of action. Even allowing for her diet and the life she had led, Kees thought, if this was her son she must have had him late in life. Then the man advanced to the middle of the room and spoke.

'You better get out. We don't want strangers here upsetting the women.'

Kees relaxed, hands by his sides. 'Before I go, maybe you'd like to tell me where we've met before?'

The same look of guilt revisited the man's eyes. 'Out,' he said, '*Pronto.*'

Kees took a pace towards the door. 'All right,' he said. 'But I should tell you I'm a guest at Fazenda Sabaca. And I'll be back later, not with the nice friendly cop from Terenos but some of the hard boys from the *Policia Militar* barracks in town.'

It was the old woman who showed him what was coming. Her hand jerked involuntarily upwards as if simulating the blow, and Kees moved quickly to one side and felt wind as the fist sliced past his neck. Off balance, the man leant forward and Kees pivoted and hooked him in the windpipe with his right hand. For good measure he stamped hard on the exposed right foot, twisting his heel as it landed and feeling the man's skin tear and the toes flatten. There was a bull-like roar, and the Brazilian turned to face him, tears streaming down his face, arms swinging as he tried to land a blow. But he never did, because the Dutchman kicked him hard in the crotch.

For a part of a second the two men looked at each other in absolute silence. Then the pain arrived, and a grunt that shook the frail fabric of the house. The Brazilian fell to the floor, vomited convulsively, and curled into a foetal position. He clasped his genitals, and his body rocked to and fro in its agony. Gradually his noises died away till there was just a heavy silence punctuated by groans. The frieze came slowly to life as the old woman bent over her son making little clucking noises, and Kees sat down again on the bench. The action had lasted some fifteen seconds.

After a minute, he addressed the old lady again. Already he was sorry about the figure lying on the floor, but in his present condition he was in no state for a prolonged brawl with a man who looked as if he chopped ironwood for a living.

'*Velha*, if you will tell me what you know, I will leave you here in peace. Come,' his voice hardened, 'you have seen my face in a photograph. The photograph was in her bag. How did you come to see inside her bag?'

The old woman turned her face up to the stranger sitting above her. The loose skin around her face moved in anguished ripples over the line of her jaw, and she cradled her son's head protectively. She realized, fatalistically, that this was trouble of the worst sort, and that there was no way out. Having come to terms with the situation she decided quite simply to tell the truth.

'My son found her in the road, *Senhor*. She was very ill. We put her on a bed in the other room. We looked in her bag to see who she was. We found the photograph and some money.' The old woman withdrew one of her arms to cross herself. Her son groaned, and started to sit up. Kees listened to her story with dread.

'Well?' he forced out at last. 'Where is she now?'

The woman went on in the same monotonous tone of voice, devoid of expression.

'In the morning I got a doctor to come here. I was lucky. He filled in the paper for the police, and took her away to the *Clínica*.

'Then ... then she's in hospital?' Kees felt relief flooding through him like a drug.

Now the man spoke. His voice was low and harsh, his face turned to the floor.

'You won't be screwing that any more, *bastardo*, unless corpses turn you on. The worms'll be eating the soft parts now.' He forced a chuckle and coughed. 'She was nearly gone when I –'

The voice stopped abruptly when Kuyter's shoe exploded into the nerve centre between the jawbone and ear. Horrified, the old woman fell across the body crying, 'You've killed him, you've killed my son!'

Kees was pale with anger. His voice shook. 'If I see him again, I will kill him. It's true what he said? The girl is dead?'

The woman nodded mutely. Blinded with remorse, Kees stumbled out into the sunlight.

Revisiting the police post at Terenos, he managed for a small fee, to extract the information that it had been a Dr Lani from the *Clínica* who had taken charge of Noélia's body. That made sense: it had to be the same Lani who had treated him at Sabaca, the friend of the Coronel's. By now Kees was like a man in a trance, following his nose without really being aware of what he was doing. But during the drive to Campo Grande he managed to pull himself together, and by the time he entered the city he was well in control and behaving almost normally.

In the mortuary at the *Clínica*, Wilson Alviera was another man with something on his mind. Today he prepared bodies, swabbed them down, and even talked to them without the jocular bonhomie other staff in the hospital were used to and which had led them to earmark him long ago as 'corpse-crazy'. In reality, Wilson Alviera was thinking of what he had seen Dr Lani take out of a dead girl's abdomen the previous Wednesday. He also had a vivid picture in his mind of the doctor sitting at his desk behind locked doors, looking closely at some objects he had extracted from a small metal container. Alviera had only been able to see that by standing in a flowerbed and surreptitiously peering through the doctor's partially-drawn blinds. Now Lani had gone away for a few days, and Alviera was beginning to think that he had missed his chance to convert what he had seen into a little ready cash.

Not far away in the hospital reception Kees found out that Lani was not expected in until Tuesday morning. He also learned that although Lani had for many years held a practice in the town, he was now the hospital's senior pathologist.

Tiredly, he walked out into the afternoon to start the long drive back to Sabaca.

On Tuesday morning Kees left the Fazenda Sabaca for the last time, in the company of Oscar who had offered to run him to the city. The Coronel seemed to have taken a liking to him, and forced him to accept some money which he promised to return as soon as he was able. On arrival in Campo Grande he rang the *Clínica* and was put through to Lani's office. He identified himself as the man Lani had treated at Sabaca, and wondered if he might meet the doctor privately that evening for a further consultation. The doctor agreed readily. He was feeling in fine form after his long but profitable trip to São Paulo. He suggested seven p.m. at his apartment in the Rua Mirando Leão.

At seven o'clock, the steps leading to the front door of Lani's apartment were in shadow. The apartment itself was on the ground floor and separated from the road by a high wall. Between wall and building were a selection of thick-leafed tropical shrubs that no-one had ever remembered to prune.

Wilson Alviera was unsure what he was doing there, crouched in the shrubbery. But once the idea of trying to profit out of Lani's activities had occurred to him, he had been unable to get it out of his mind. Tonight he'd intended simply to confront the doctor and tell him that he had seen everything and that his silence was for sale. But what exactly had he seen? Was Lani in fact doing anything illegal? Irresolute, Alviera had run out of courage, and ducked into the bushes to rehearse a little more fully what he intended to say. He was on the point of trying again when a man he'd never seen before walked up the steps and knocked loudly on the door.

Comfortably seated inside the doctor's living room, Kuyter didn't take long to come to the point. His nerves were vibrating, and pleasantries would have been more than he could take.

'A short while ago,' he started, 'you took the body of a young girl from Terenos into the *Clínica*. You must have picked her up on the way back from Sabaca. All I want to know is what happened to her.'

The doctor paled and moved to a small drink cabinet in the corner of the room. The atmosphere in the house seemed unaccountably stuffy and he opened a window.

'Before I answer, *Senhor*, may I ask what she was to you?'

Kees' voice dropped away till it was little more than a flat whisper. 'If it's all the same to you, doctor, I loved her. She was with me when we crashed. It was she who went for help.'

Lani exhaled slowly and looked at his visitor. The last time he had seen him, the man had been in a high fever. Now he was on his feet again, and Lani could see that he was no ordinary white drifter. From a lifetime of reading faces, living and dead, the doctor knew he was looking at a man who was answerable to no-one. Playing for time, he asked: 'You knew she was ill?'

Kees shook his head angrily. 'If I'd known she was really sick do you imagine I'd have been driving off through the *mato*? Now for Christ's sake tell me what happened.'

Lani hesitated. Then, 'I took her to the *Clínica*. That's all. I'm sorry. Later she was cremated.'

Kees' voice changed subtly. 'But before she was cremated, doctor. You know,' he encouraged. 'You're a pathologist. You said she was sick, so sick she died. What was it, *Senhor* Doctor? What did she die of?'

Lani could feel his composure falling away under the persistent questioning. With far from steady hands he offered a cigarette, anticipated the slight shake of the head, lit one himself, and sat down. Behind him the drinks remained forgotten in the cabinet.

'Chagas,' he muttered. 'She died of chagas. Her eye, you must have seen it: Romana's sign. The crash, the last run for help – her heart collapsed. We, that is my colleagues and I, found the heart tissue to be paper thin. She was being eaten alive.'

Kees felt the anguish he had been fighting for days start to burn holes in his stomach and throat. Through an opacity of tears, feeling nauseated but knowing it had to be done, he asked the final question.

'She was carrying something that was ours, doctor, carrying

it here.' He gestured between his legs. 'Either you have it, or it was burned, or I have to make another visit to the man who found her on the road. Which is it, doctor?' The voice rasped with urgency. 'Tell me which it is?'

For what seemed like a long time, Lani tried to say that whatever Kees was referring to must have been cremated with her body. But his eyes kept falling to the ground, and he knew he'd just be wasting his time. For the first time in his life he was guilty, and someone far stronger than he was probing that guilt. He realised what it must be like to be taken by the *Policia Militar*, and his voice broke at the thought.

'Diamonds,' he said, 'Yes, I found them.' Kees moved slightly, and the doctor, having started, found it impossible to stop. 'I found them, and I sold them. Mother of God,' he cried out suddenly, 'What would you have done in my place?'

Kees shook his head hopelessly at the information he had extracted. He didn't doubt for a moment that the doctor was telling the truth. 'The name,' he said at length. 'The name of the place. Where did you sell them, and for how much?'

Lani recomposed himself, and somehow contrived to look as if his professional ethics were being threatened. 'You must realize I can't tell you that,' he said desperately. 'I gave my word and I'm not in the habit of breaking it.'

Kees was in front of Lani before he stopped speaking. Angrily he gripped the doctor by the shirt front and pricked his chin with the point of his knife.

'As you're a connoisseur of knives, my friend, you'll know how much damage this could do in the hands of someone who didn't care about the consequences.' His voice cracked out in the other man's face. 'You'd better tell me right now just who's got those diamonds or you'll get more that just your bloody word broken!'

The sharpened steel indented Lani's throat. Suddenly the man sagged forward, and Kees had to snatch the blade away. He looked at the doctor's face: it was white, and very frightened.

'So, now,' Kees said. 'The name of the place. Where did you sell them, and for how much?'

When he had learned all he could about Bretas and the

house on the Avenida Catarina, Kees stood up to leave. At the top of the steps he turned and said:

'One more thing. Don't be tempted to contact Bretas and tell him I'm coming, or before God I'll come back and kill you for what you've done. You of all people should feel no love for him. Those stones are worth fifty times what you received.'

Without waiting for an answer he turned and walked away into the night.

Beneath the open window of the doctor's apartment Wilson Alviera listened to the visitor's receding footsteps. Several things had become very clear to him, but one in particular: the doctor had found diamonds, and they were worth a fortune. Certainly he could never hope to get the stones from the dealer, Bretas, in São Paulo. But getting them away from one man, the blond *gringo*, if he were successful, that was a possibility. And it underlined the need to keep Lani from contacting the dealer. Sure in his own mind as to where he stood, Alviera mounted the steps to the apartment and knocked on the door.

Chapter 5

Night was pouring thickly into São Paulo's concrete hulk as Kees arrived outside Bretas' house on the Avenida Catarina. Earlier in the day he had reconnoitred the building, noting the linden tree whose branches draped across the high perimeter wall, and the long balcony that started on the western side and apparently ran right round to the back of the house. At seven o'clock he had started back towards the building from his *pousada* in Ifigênia, dressed in rubber-soled shoes, dark trousers and a dark grey tight-fitting sweatshirt with long sleeves. In a bag over his shoulder he carried a waterproof and various items that would later help him to force entry. Not far from Bretas' home he stopped and telephoned the man's number. The voice answering the phone was tough and uncultured. Kees asked for *Senhor* Bretas and gave his name as Dr Kiefmann. Bretas would be unlikely to refuse a call from a doctor, even one he'd never heard of. When the man came on the line Kuyter played the charade right through to the end. 'Carlos?' he called happily. 'Federico here. I've made it at last. How are you?'

When Bretas had interrupted and explained that he was not in fact Carlos Bretas, but Ramon, Kees apologized profusely for having dialled the wrong number and replaced the receiver. Now he knew that at least his man was in.

By eight he was outside the house, hidden in the darkness across the street under the shade of one of the innumerable trees lining the *avenida*. By eleven no-one had entered or left, and there were some signs of activity on the top floor. Kees passed a little time wondering which room might catch the morning sun and where Bretas was likely to sleep; and he thought, too, about the Negro *capangas* mentioned by Lani. At eleven forty-five there were no lights on at all in the building, and he settled down to a long wait. At one point it looked like rain, but the wind dropped and the presence of the night closed in around him again like a warm blanket. He dozed fitfully, back to the tree.

At two-thirty in the morning he crossed the road and climbed into the lower branches of the linden tree. In seconds it absorbed his shape, and only a slight agitation of the foliage marked the moment when he quit the tree's shelter on the other side of the high stone wall.

He ran swiftly around the perimeter of the lawn, and then angled in towards the corner of the garages. Without breaking his stride he ran at the garage wall and leapt upwards. Momentum carried both his hands over the ridge of the gently sloping roof and the rest of his body followed smoothly. Still moving fast, he ran four steps along the roof and jumped for the balcony balustrade. It was only five feet away but considerably higher than the garage. Swinging from side to side, he managed to pull his body up and sideways until he was lying on the balcony floor on a thin strip of concrete outside the balustrade. He paused to collect himself, and then moved fast over the railings and into the shadow close to the wall of the house.

The balcony seemed to stretch forever in front of him, perspective narrowing its breadth. On silent feet he started along it, a tiny flashlight in his right hand.

The first three rooms were empty, and he was approaching the fourth when light came flooding through the window. Cautiously he peered round the corner and looked in. A girl of about eighteen had just entered. Quietly, she closed the door behind her, took off her dressing gown, revealing a flimsy nightgown over a good figure, and got into bed. The light went out.

Kees eased his way past and hesitated. The girl's nocturnal walkabout might mean that there was some man in one of the other rooms who was very much awake, though no lights had gone on. In the end he waited for five minutes, crouched on the tiles, then went on to where the balcony swung right at the corner of the house.

This was the north side, and thus got good light all the year round. Immediately he knew he'd found one of the main bedrooms. The moon shone slightly through the windows, and he could see the scale of the room with its big canopied bed like a monstrous howdah set in a well in the centre of the floor. Someone was there all right, but it was impossible to say who. Kees walked past the big room towards the end of the balcony. There were just three other rooms in all, two empty bedrooms and a bathroom. It was the bathroom that interested him most. Its windows were louvred in metal frames. He knew from experience that by bending the metal tabs at the end of each pane one could easily slide the individual sheets of glass out of their slots. With infinite care he set to work.

The complete frame held six panes, and after extracting the first he was able to put his hand through and operate the lever that moved the other five. When they were all open it was easier to work on them, and he pressed on until all six were stacked on the ground at his feet and the frame was empty of glass and easily big enough to let him through. It was then that he made his first mistake. As he lifted himself to enter the house, his foot touched the little stack of panes. The top one slid off the others and dropped onto the tiles. In the night silence the noise was deafeningly loud. Kees hesitated, then slipped quickly through the empty frame and unlocked the bathroom door from the inside, in case he needed to retreat fast. He moved through the room and out onto what appeared to be another balcony on the inside of the house. A slight luminosity spilled out beneath him, showing that he was on a gallery overlooking a huge open courtyard which seemed to incorporate most of the luxuries in life, including a swimming pool and solarium set amidst a selection of carefully nurtured tropical flora.

In a crouch, Kees worked his way back to the door that should lead off to the big bedroom. Silently, he turned the knob and pushed it open. Three inches. Six. A foot. Nothing stirred. He slipped into the room and eased the door gently shut behind him. He was just about to move again when a blaze of light flooded his eyes; half-blinded, he found himself facing a silenced automatic held lightly in the huge hand of a *moreno*.

Senhor Bretas was on top form, despite the hour. He was explaining about the infra-red beams that quartered the outside of the house, making it impossible for an intruder to reach the building undiscovered.

'An Olympic high-jumper,' Bretas said, 'assuming he knew where to leap and was capable of surpassing his personal best by about a metre, would stand a chance. But we don't get many of those down here.'

Kees listened impassively, waiting for the bottom line. It wasn't long in coming.

'Well,' Bretas said conversationally. 'Perhaps we'd better find out who you are and what you've come for. Then I can best decide what we're going to do with you.'

Kees had already decided that he had nothing to gain by lying. He would tell the man the truth, play for time and try to manufacture an opportunity to escape. To be handed over to the *Policia Militar* would mean weeks of interrogation and probably torture, followed by a slow lingering death in the cells – though it looked as if his host had little enough use for the authorities when it came to policing his grounds. He looked at Bretas in the eye.

'I'm here looking for something you have acquired which is rightfully mine. Listen to me and I think you'll realise what I say is true.'

Bretas laughed surprisedly. 'An intelligent thief. An intelligent foreign thief with a penchant for stories. Well, I happen to like bedtime stories, but I warn you it had better be good.' To one of the mulattoes he said, 'Fetch Suzeth. Tell her to come here immediately. And you – turn some of these lights out.'

After a short delay, the girl Kees had seen through the window came into the room. She stopped in amazement when she saw the Dutchman, and put her hand over her mouth.

64

'Ramon, what's going on? Who is this man? What's happened?'

Bretas patted the bed beside him. 'Come, my dear, sit down; this man has come far to tell us his story. The least we can do is listen.' He motioned Kees into a chair in the corner of the room furthest from the door. Two of the mulattoes stood back several paces, guns still at the ready. A third slid out through the door and closed it behind him.

Kees closed his eyes. It seemed he was committed to giving Bretas and his girlfriend small-hour entertainment. He began half-heartedly at the beginning, but after ten minutes found he had almost forgotten the silent listeners. Once more he relived the night with Noélia in the squatters' camp, the death of Nigra, the eventual ascent to the Eagle's Beak. He traced his journey from Sabaca to Campo Grande, from there to São Paulo. Spoken aloud it was possible to imagine the distances already involved in this journey. At last he concluded, and looked about him at the motionless figures in the darkened room. He was surprised to see that the girl had tears streaming down her face.

Bretas leaned forward. '*Senhor*, I often wonder about the history of diamonds before they came to my house. Thanks to you I now know that the truth can be stranger than all my little fantasies. It is unfortunate that the stones of which you speak are no longer in my possession. I found a buyer only last weekend.'

Kees knew instinctively that the time had come. Voice flat, he asked, 'Who was he?'

Bretas laughed and went to sit up. 'Naturally I cannot divulge –' It was as far as he got. In one movement Kees landed on the bed next to the girl. With the gunmen unsighted, he knocked her out of the way and got an arm round Bretas' neck. With his other hand he pushed his thumb and forefinger against the man's eyes.

'Tell them to drop the guns or I'll blind you.' Bretas croaked out the order through a flattened windpipe, and the two men let their guns fall to the floor. They made no sound on the thick pile carpet. Now get the other one in from outside.' It wasn't necessary for Bretas to repeat the command: the guards had got the message.

With the three men standing together and the girl sprawled terrified on the floor, Kees said: 'Now tell me who you sold them to.' He slightly relaxed the pressure round the man's throat, but increased it on his eyeballs. Bretas groaned but said nothing. A thumb like an iron rod was making agonizing progress towards the inside of his head.

'Cane,' he ground out. 'Jack Cane, you must know him. The film star.'

Kees absorbed the information without relaxing the pressure. It was bizarre enough to be true, he supposed. 'Where? Where's Cane?'

Bretas coughed painfully. 'He's gone to Manaus. They are making a film on the Amazon. Believe me. For God's sake, my eyes!'

Kees moved off the bed, forcing the Brazilian to his feet. 'I'm leaving now *Senhor*, and you're coming with me. Tell your *capanga* to move over there and not to attempt to follow us. How many more do you have in the house?'

Bretas shook his head. 'No more. They are all here.'

Firmly Kees pushed him past the end of the bed and over to the balcony door.

'You,' he said. 'Suzeth. Lock the other door on the inside.' The girl moved to obey and then turned, the key in her hand. 'Bring it here! Drop it into his dressing gown pocket. Now back away.'

Still with Bretas in a crippling grip Kees backed through the balcony door. Like dogs watching for their chance the *morenos'* three pairs of brown eyes followed every move. Safely on the far side of the door, Kees told Bretas to move the key to the outside and lock the balcony door. He was in the process of manoeuvring the man into a position where he could carry out these instructions when a brown blur moved down the balcony towards him at a dead run. Violently, he pushed Bretas forward and heard his head crack against the glass door. Then he turned to face his attacker. He saw the glint of a knife and felt the blade slice through the flesh of his upper arm. He dropped to one knee, raised his right forearm stiffly between the man's legs, and helped him on his way over the rail. Strangely silent, the man had time for only a gasp of pain before his head smashed into the garage wall and his body crumpled to the ground. Kees wasn't far behind him. He jumped onto the garage roof, ran along it and leapt out onto the lawn. Then he was sprinting flat out for the linden tree.

Kees was hurrying across a small *parque* when the pain in his arm forced him to stop. He tucked himself into the shade of a *canna* bed and started to take off his sweatshirt. He had it over his head when a voice said 'Don't move.' Someone grabbed the top of his shirt, and when he looked up there was an armed man he'd never seen before, backing away with the blood-soaked garment.

Wilson Alviera looked down at the half-naked and wounded man kneeling in front of him and felt his confidence soar. His exhaustion of the last few days was forgotten. It never even occured to him that the man might have failed to get the stones.

'Come on, come on,' he said, almost urinating with impatience. 'Give me the diamonds.'

Kees looked at the figure in front of him and realized he was dealing with some sort of nut. But mental or not, the man had followed him from somewhere. Carefully Kees placed his hands on his knees. The slight movement sent a cascade of water droplets from the *canna's* broad leaves straight down his back. Involuntarily he shivered.

'What diamonds?' he forced out.

Alviera was beside himself with the need to piss. He would have used the gun there and then but he wasn't sure it would work and didn't want to make any noise.

'I was there when they cut the girl up,' he said. 'I saw Lani find them. And I was there when you visited him. And now I'm here.' He was hopping from one foot to the other now and Kees realized that he didn't have a lot of time.

'The diamonds,' he said softly. 'Of course.' Slowly he reached down to the pouch hanging from his belt. It had been emptied by Bretas' men, but he made a show of removing his belt and

67

sliding the pouch to the end. When it was in his hands he reached forward and lobbed it gently past the other man just out of his reach.

Alviera's eyes only followed the pouch for a split second, but even that was too long. He fired the little gun once as the fist caught him in the throat, but the bullet buried itself in the orange soil of the lily bed, and the noise seemed less dangerous than the bark of a healthy dog. Kees hit Alviera once more, a short vicious blow with the heel of his hand that pushed his nose back into his head. The Brazilian squealed once, a slaughterhouse sound, and died instantly.

Kees looked around but there was no-one to be seen. He dragged the body in among the tall plants and left it there, then tore one sleeve from his sweatshirt and applied a rough tourniquet to his upper arm, slowing the blood flow. By using his teeth he managed to get some sort of tightness into the material, and then he tore the other sleeve from the garment so it wouldn't look too conspicuous. The arm throbbed massively with each heartbeat. Pocketing the miniature gun, he set off across the park to his lodging.

In the house on the Avenida Catarina, Bretas and Suzeth lay together in the big bed for the second time that night. Gently she traced a finger round his eyes, and then ran her hands down onto his bruised neck. The top of his head, too, had suffered, but she could testify that the ill treatment hadn't affected him adversely in any other way at all. They had just made love, and Bretas had astounded himself by his performance. And already he was feeling like some more of the same. His hand dropped between the girl's legs, and he felt them relax apart at his touch. For the first time he knew intuitively that it had been really good for her as well.

'Ramon,' The girl's voice was warm and sleepy.

'Yes, *querida*.' His fingers sought her soft spots with newly acquired expertise, found them swollen and aroused. The excitement of the night was paying dividends in the most unexpected way.

'Will you report what happened to the *Policia*?'

Bretas moved to cover her. 'No, of course not, we don't want the police around here.'

The girl opened her legs and he felt the pressure of her nails on his back. 'And Jack Cane? Will you tell him what happened?'

Bretas was engulfed by an elemental warmth. 'No,' he gasped. 'Cane can look after himself. That *gringo* haggled so damn much I nearly gave him the stones.'

Five days later Kees lay back in his hammock and watched the river glide by from the third-class deck of the government steamer *Leopoldo Peres*. To his left and right several hundred other men and women did likewise, while a cheap radio played *samba* and the air smelt of fuel oil and bananas. The trip up-river against the current was a slow business, but another seven days would see him back in Manaus; he hoped he wasn't too late, but if Bretas were to be believed in film star Cane had only just bought the stones.

He had filled out since his illness, though his face was still more than usually dominated by his china-blue eyes. So far, the Coronel's loan had taken him halfway round Brazil in the search for his stones. But it was not as if he could stop himself: from city to city he knew he was compelled to follow the trail to its unknown conclusion.

Tired, he reached stiffly towards his jacket with his bad arm and brought out a cloth eyeshade, a memento from one of those periods in his life when he could afford to fly. A small tag on one side said 'Cathay-Pacific', and a child with brown slanted eyes watched him wonderingly as he protected his eyes from the reflected glare of the sun. The world was full of them, Kees thought: half-breeds, *caboclos*, mulattoes – most of them poor from the day they were born, living fruitless lives and old at thirty, worn out by tropical heat and constant toil on a diet of *mandioca* and fish.

He let his fingers twist in the netting that hung down from the side of his hammock. Noélia had been like that, he supposed. A half-breed destined to be old at thirty. Maybe, because she had been brought up by the missionaries, she would

69

have aged more gracefully, but now no-one would ever know. He felt the net cutting into his flesh between his fingers, and the creep of slow and unaccustomed tears behind the eyeshades. 'Noélia?' he questioned, forcing himself to whisper the name. 'Noélia?' But already the word seemed strange to his tongue and it was only in the moist darkness behind his lids that her face was as brown and beautiful and full of life as it had ever been.

Chapter 6

At six in the morning the narrow streets crowding the river at Manaus were deep in shadow, but where the land ended and the jetties probed their rickety wooden fingers out into the stream the sun was already a golden glory, easing the damp from chilled bones and launching a new day towards the sea. From cargo boats, old river horses, oranges were being unloaded that had travelled three days by truck and two by boat to reach this port. Between their faded flanks, sharp and eager, nosed smaller fishing craft with their restless, shifting silver cargo glinting and slippery in the bright clean air.

Kees hefted his bag and walked away from the river and up into the town. The market was already a bedlam of activity, and he shouldered his way through the press of vendors' food-laden trays balanced precariously on their bobbing heads. Kees felt for the last few cruzeiros he owned, a thin, dirty wad of almost unrecognizable paper, and looked around him at the food for sale. On the corner was a stand selling Tee-shirts, with a sign declaring '*Camisas Mississippi Queen – aqui em Manaus – 35 cruzeiros*'.

Kees forgot the food and walked by the shirts. They all bore the same paddle-steamer motif with the name of the boat in big letters beneath. He went on down the street heading for Pieter Schlater's house, where not so long ago he had started for the Argentine. Full circle, and half the team gone. He knocked loudly on the door but there was no reply. After some minutes an old woman across the road told him Pieter was away on the river. As if on cue other doors opened, and soon the little street was full of women in black anxious to advise him of Pieter's probable location, but more anxious, it seemed, to find out what had happened and why he was alone.

Kees realized from their questions that on this street at least his comings and goings were common knowledge, and he made a mental note to mention it to Rita, Pieter's housekeeper. To deflect their queries, he said simply: 'Is there somewhere that I can stay?'

A large woman reached into her pocket and came up with a key. It was big and looked as if it might have fitted the lock on a dungeon. '*Venha.*'

Kees followed her past three houses and then she turned into a small alley. She stopped at a derelict door, ludicrously undersized for the key which opened it, and led him up to a clean but gloomy room on the top floor. It had a basin, a trucklebed and a window that appeared to be made of opaque yellow glass. He washed and changed, then before the sun was much higher in the sky walked back through the town to the state-controlled Embratur office next door to the Amazonas Hotel. An assistant, a voluble man in his late forties, was only too pleased to impart what he knew of the filming. It was, after all, the biggest thing to happen in the town in recent years. A huge riverboat had been restored and was to be used as principal set and means of transport in the making of a television series for the U.S. Many stars were involved, and the number of tourists in the town had nearly doubled in the last month. Proudly, he slid open a drawer and pulled out a Tee-shirt. Kees nodded. It was the same as those he had seen down in the market. The man smiled and put the shirt back into the drawer.

'For my son,' he explained. 'Now, is there some other way in which I can help you?'

'Yes,' Kees told him. 'Who do I see for a job on that boat?'

Most people in Brazil took Brett Alders for an American, and in that they were one hundred per cent right. Not that Alders would have thought of himself as typically American; it was just that the world, which had been brought up on re-runs of 'Bonanza' and 'The Rifleman' subconsciously thought of the wild west whenever they saw anyone remotely resembling Chuck Connors.

Alders was a big man, and it showed in the way he folded himself carefully down onto a collapsible chair that had probably been designed for someone a foot shorter. With equal care and deliberation he poured himself a cup of coffee, well past its best and left over from breakfast, and looked out over the balustrade. The tropical hotel on the Rio Negro was one of a chain that Varig Airlines had built across Brazil while land and labour were still cheap. Some were always well booked, like the one at Manaus and another overlooking the Iguassu falls; others, like the hotel at Santarém five hundred miles downstream, were huge monoliths rising out of the surrounding carpet of tin shacks and banana palms. Often completely empty, their size was a source of constant amazement to the awe-struck locals, who could never quite believe that such a giant had arisen, almost overnight, in their midst, or that there were people who would pay a month's earnings for a night's rest.

Alders relaxed and let his eyes roam up from the parrots cavorting in the frangipani across the placid uncluttered miles of the Rio Negro. Islands lay low on the skyline; one, owned by the hotel, had been converted into a sort of open-air exposition of tropicana. Boardwalks curved through the jungle revealing caymen on the one hand and rare orchids on the other. A bar under the wide shade of a palm leaf roof served drinks from old world and new – scotch and *guaraná* – while favouring the perspiring clientèle with views of a small lagoon surrounded by a reasonable cross-section of the Green Hell. This, a boat trip or two, and a short trek to see tame Indians who undressed for the occasion, was as far as most businessmen and their wives felt it right to follow in the footsteps of Pissaro or Fawcett.

A loud knock on the door broke rudely into Alders' reverie.

'Come in!' he yelled. There was no reply. He turned his head to call again and realized that someone had entered the room.

His eyes followed the newcomer as he came nearer, dressed in faded blue that matched his eyes. His hair was cut too short to grip, a flush cap of rape-seed gold above a tanned face.

'Hi,' said Brett uncertainly. 'Can I help you?'

The man moved out onto the balcony through the sliding glass doors.

'Kees Kuyter,' he said, and stuck out a hand. 'I'm looking for a job on your riverboat.'

Brett was taken off guard by the blunt approach. 'Look,' he said, shaking the man's hand. 'We have an office set up in town to deal with crewing. You're in the wrong place.'

The stranger smiled disarmingly, 'I was told that when it came right down to it you're the man who does the hiring and firing.'

'Yes, but ...'

'Then I'm in the right place.'

The two men looked at each other appraisingly. Alders could only sympathize. There had been many occasions in his own life when he bypassed the front office men. Suddenly he made a decision.

'Have some coffee.'

Kees smiled again, and his face opened up. He pulled up a chair and sat down. The coffee was now stone cold; Alders sipped distastefully and swore.

'You might prefer to forget the coffee,' he said at length. 'So tell me, what can you do?'

'I've got a seaman's ticket.'

Alders frowned. 'Thing is, you're a little late. We have our crew, and apart from a coupla jobs you don't look as if you'd fit, the list is full.'

'Try me.'

Alders stared at him. 'Why do you want to get on the boat so bad?'

His visitor shrugged faintly. 'I like boats. I like it out there,' he waved over the water. 'You have a unique craft and it sounds like you're going on a unique trip.'

Alders toyed with his spoon. 'How would you fit in as a galley slave or a waiter?'

'I'd fit in fine.'

'Pay's not up to much.'

'Neither's the beach.'

'What the hell,' Brett thought to himself. The man looked more eligible for the skipper's job than anything else.

'You know what we're up to?' he asked.

The other man shook his head.

'O.K., let me fill you in briefly. We're making an on-going TV series, but a series with a difference. We're using big names, Jack Cane and Attica Alloui heading the list. The whole thing kicks off on a Mississippi riverboat in the 1880s. There's a freak storm and the whole shebang goes through a time slip, winds up in the past on the Amazon, date unknown, leaving the writers a certain flexibility in subsequent episodes.'

He grinned wryly. 'You still want to go?'

'I can't see the plot making too much difference in the galley.'

'O.K., well, we'll be out touring the Green Hell for some time, so you may get bored enough to start reading the scripts. Now, if you go to this address and tell them I sent you they'll fix you up.'

The Dutchman took the proffered card and stood up. 'Thanks.'

As an afterthought Alders called: 'Take all your papers along with you. You American or what?'

Kees stood framed in the doorway. 'No,' he said, 'No, I'm not.'

Alders waited for him to go on, but the door closed quietly, hardly disturbing the cool conditioned air of the room.

Alone again, Brett Alders sat down and tried to concentrate. Over the past months he had become totally involved with the whole business of the paddle-steamer: it was he who had found it rusting and disused eighteen hundred miles up the Solimões; he who had arranged for it to be recommissioned; he who had followed the progress of the engineers, carpenters and painters for week after week as the impossible was achieved and the abandoned old *Leticia* became the *Mississippi Queen*. Money had flowed like river water under the boat's stern wheel, the costs spiralling with no expense spared. Alders had a fairly astute idea of the costing and profit margins involved in the making of a network TV series. And he knew that this rate of expenditure didn't add up. To confuse matters still further, it now seemed that some outside agency was taking a close interest in their progress. Quietly he reviewed the steamer's history, trying to find a clue that would explain some of the recent events that he found so worrying.

She had been built on the Upper Clyde by McEwan & Clark nearly a century previously, the largest of three steamers supplied by that company to PARC, the Pará and Amazonas Rubber Confederation. When the rubber barons had died this ship, like so many others, had been consigned to a riverside graveyard.

Alders had travelled to Iquitos, two thousand three hundred miles up the river, in his four-week search for a suitable vessel, and found the *Leticia* near the town of that name on the Columbia-Peru-Brazil border. She had been beached higher by the floods of previous years, and lay in marsh some way from the water. Several families had been using her as home for some time, and threadbare clothes fluttered gaily from the rails on the upper decks. He climbed on board and made a preliminary investigation, noting that the wheelhouse was locked and also the engine compartment. Wide-eyed pot-bellied children watched him furtively from behind doors and companionways, scattering on tiny feet when he turned towards them. That the wide sweep of the teak decks had suffered little during the years of torrential rain and baking sun was in itself a testimony to craftsmen long dead. Fittings everywhere were of heavy brass, and on the treads of the main staircase these were worn with use. His overall impression had been one of nostalgia. A fine vessel, built to incomparable standards, had served its purpose and been left to rot. Later Alders inspected the hull as best he could, and found the huge stern wheel much in need of repair.

During the night he had managed to contact her builders, still a going concern in Scotland. For them it was already the next morning, and a long talk with their managing director obtained the cooperation he required. Twenty-four hours later a forty-five year old technical adviser by the name of Stuart was on his way to South America with a briefcase full of papers and a sliderule. Simultaneously, a naval architect called Hoffman was packing his bags at his home in Palm Beach.

It had taken Hoffman and Stuart just four days to assess what needed to be done aboard the *Leticia*. During that time they both convinced Alders that they knew their way around boats and he asked Stuart if he would like to take a more prolonged interest in the refit. The Scot, who had fallen in love with the vessel and had done his last serious travelling in destroyers in 1944, said he would. It would be a shame, he said, to let all the innoculations go to waste in Glasgow. Within the week Alders had him seconded to the project.

Meanwhile, the local authorities had located the old man who was the boat's official caretaker. For some years he had been paid a small retainer to keep an eye on both the vessel and the land around it, but although he still received the money it was obvious that he took his duties anything but seriously. He did, however, furnish the name and address of the owners, and Brett took the flight from Tabatinga to Bogota. Señor Ferrada was on the board of an import-export company. He explained that the boat had been willed to him and his brother as part of his uncle's estates; now his brother was dead, and the vessel was all his. Had Señor Ferrada ever been to see the *Leticia*, Brett enquired. The Columbian shook his head. He had sent someone down to inspect the vessel and understood that it was not in working order. Not, he added quickly, that it couldn't be put right by someone who appreciated its antique value. Brett made him an offer of five thousand dollars, which was, as he pointed out, considerably more than its scrap value given its location. Ferrada caviled, and mentioned a much larger sum. Brett made a big show of taking his leave, and Ferrada had to move fast to catch him outside the elevator. Six thousand dollars cash? The company lawyer was called and a deed of sale drawn up. Brett caught the next flight south.

The whole town turned out to see the *Leticia* refloated. Hawsers tightened as three big timber tractors took the strain. Slowly the *Leticia* moved back onto the long, greasy timbers that had been laid as a slipway. When the tractors could go no further the strain was taken by the *Tigre do Eufrates,* a powerful tug from Manaus. Yard by yard the huge paddle-steamer slid on her flat bottom down into the Amazon. As the last squatter realized that this was the end of his free housing and leapt onto the muddy banks, the weight of the stern crumbled the rich alluvial deposits at the river's edge and the steamer floated gently out onto the brown flood. Three weeks later she was safely berthed at Praia Negra, eighteen hundred miles downstream where the river joined the Atlantic Ocean.

That moment had marked the start of the big spend. And the start, too, of the seemingly insignificant incidents which added up to something tangible enough to make Alder's stomach knot uneasily when he thought about them. But at least the time had arrived when he could pass the buck. Turk Bostan, founder of the Bostan Entertainment Corporation which was financing the series, would be in Manaus in the morning. And then, Brett thought, someone else could live with the headaches.

Kees knelt unsafely in a dugout canoe and watched the squat outline of Santiago's back as he paddled through the night waters of the *várzea.* Regardless of the heat, both men were dressed from head to foot in an attempt to baffle the frenetic insects that strafed them in the search for blood. Santiago mouthed Spanish curses, and Kees flashed a torch in the direction of the bank. They were crossing a *lagoinha* among the mangrove, and the yellow beam revealed the nightmare shapes of the vegetation. Just half an hour in the canoe, Santiago had said, and we'll get a couple of nice caymen – a little excitement to liven up the evening. So here they were, crossing the Styx the hard way, hunting alligators.

The *Mississippi Queen* was now moored alongside a huge floating hotel complex called the Beija Flor. The entire place had been requisitioned by the film company and towed to a group of small islands ten miles from the city. It was all but surrounded by vegetation some hundred yards away, and there was only one feasible way of reaching it. As Alders had a barge blocking ninety per cent of this channel, tourist boats operated by the agencies in the town soon gave up making the pointless sightseeing trip downriver.

The area round the hotel was gradually beginning to look like a small harbour. Besides *Mississippi Queen*, there was a powerful diesel cabin cruiser called the *Jacaré*, and the river barge she would tow. The barge had a large refrigerated hold and would carry provisions as well as a host of technical impedimenta in the way of camera spares, dollies, mounts, lights, cables, stock and props. The barqe had another asset: its roof had been strengthened to take the weight of a small helicopter which was fitted with a Tyler camera mount for aerial footage. Other floating transport consisted of a Hamilton waterjet runabout for quick runs ashore and a small flotilla of Indian canoes, which arrived with colourful cargoes of beads made from polished fish scales, and all the numberless seeds of the rain forest

Kees had soon settled into his new surroundings and quickly found out when Jack Cane would be arriving. He made his mark on Signor Annelli the chef by addressing him in mellifluous Italian and from that moment could do no wrong. For two days he explored the paddle steamer and set about trying to get access to cabin keys so that he could have one made before they left. His thoughts were dominated by the two imponderables that faced him: had Cane really bought the stones; and if he had, would he have them with him?

Kees felt the canoe lose way as Santiago stopped paddling. A Chilean jack-of-all-trades employed by the Beija Flor management to run small excursions for guests keen on fishing or birdwatching, he whispered: 'There, *amigo*, there!'

Kees pointed the torch ahead and switched it on. Instantly he saw the two red dots ahead reflecting the beam and waited for them to submerge. But they didn't and slowly the canoe drifted nearer and nearer, Santiago hissing strange Chilean imprecations through his teeth and gently correcting their drift. The red dots grew brighter still, held unerringly in the light. Santiago swung the paddle inboard and picked up a short thrusting spear. Kneeling right in the prow he held in at arm's length, pointing vertically downwards. Slowly the red eyes slid from sight beneath the water. Not a ripple showed where they had been. The dugout drifted imperceptibly forward. Violently, Santiago jagged the spear down through the water. In an instant the surface of the creek boiled into activity and, still holding the spear, he leapt out of the canoe. Kees steadied the wildly rocking boat, aiming the light rigidly at the struggle not six feet away. Out of the turbulent water rose Santiago, his arm round the throat of a five-foot cayman. Its tail jerked viciously, and the spear sticking out of its back protruded under the Chilean's arm, making it look as if man and beast were both impaled on the same instrument of death. Then a knife caught the light and the cayman jerked convulsively once, knocking Santiago on his back in the shallows.

Dripping water, beaming, and hugging the dead reptile, Santiago extended a hand towards Kees and together they loaded the carcass into the bottom of the dugout. Santiago squelched as he sat and picked up the paddle. Kees looked down at the ugly reptilian head taking up most of the free space and sat on it. Then he switched off the torch. The Chilean was in good spirits as he paddled for home, and called out for the *pinga* bottle.

'Sometimes,' Santiago sang, 'I catch them alive for a *hombre* in the city. Then you see some action, *amigo*, I tellin' you.'

Kees grunted, and thought that Santiago, though perhaps completely nuts, at least had his balls in the right place.

'You cheated,' he reproached the figure in front of him. 'Used a knife.'

Santiago's peals of laughter cut through the night hard enough to frighten the mosquitos. '*Madre de Diós,*' he choked. 'I been so long with *gringos* I even understand their jokes! *Puta!* What you think, Dutch, I should stab him with my old man, *si?*'

Kees half smiled in the darkness. As they paddled back towards the Beija Flor, he thought that if selling the odd skin to hotel guests was Santiago's sideline, then he was welcome to it. Whichever way you looked at it, there were easier ways around to pocket a buck.

★

The next morning there was little to do and Kees sat out by the pool on the floating hotel. The pool was just a big hole some one had left in the superstructure when they were building the Beija Flor. Steps at its edge led straight down into the Rio Negro. It had the advantage, though, of being enclosed under the surface by strong wire mesh to keep out some of the river's more unpleasant denizens. Kees was just thinking about what might happen if a school of very young piranha fish swam through the mesh and grew till they couldn't get out again, when an extremely attractive girl came out into the sunlight. With an almost naïve friendliness she sat at the next table and smiled at him.

'Hello,' she said. 'I'm Ginny.'

'Kees,' the Dutchman told her. 'I think we must work on different sides of the camera.'

The girl laughed happily. 'Well, I was going to say something similar to you. I suppose that means we're both behind the camera.'

Kees warmed to her voice. It was modulated and English through and through. 'There's behind the camera and behind the camera,' he said. 'The next time we meet I may well be wearing white and serving sautéd potatoes,'

He stopped as a youngish man sat down next to the girl. 'Darling,' she said. 'Meet Kees. Did I pronounce it properly?' The man got up again and leant across.

'Roderick Ross,' he said, and the two men shook hands. 'Have you been here long?'

'No,' Kees told him. 'A couple of days. May I ask where you fit into all this?'

Ross coughed and Ginny cut in: 'He writes the scripts.'

Kees nodded politely. 'Brett Alders gave me a very rough idea of what it's all about. Sounds interesting.'

Ross chuckled. 'There is a certain amount of scope,' he said. 'It's like writing the history of the world from your imagination.' He took off his sunglasses and relaxed in his chair. 'We came up the river as far as Santarem on the maiden voyage with Brett. He's quite a character.' He glanced out over the water. 'And the *Mississippi Queen*'s a pretty remarkable boat.'

'Who was on board besides you?' Kees asked.

'Well,' Ginny said. 'There were nineteen, but most of them were designers and people working under Ian Stuart and Bill Hoffman. Those are the men who worked with Brett to get the boat back together. Then there was Miguel Tabox the captain, but he's left now. And Signor Annelli, the chef. You must have met him.'

'Yes,' Kees told her. 'My boss. He found out I spoke some Italian, so I'm pretty well placed.'

'He's a darling,' Ginny said. 'You know he almost gets seasick drinking a glass of water. We had to keep reminding him that the river is a flat calm.'

Never having seen a bigger river than the Thames, Ginny was staggered by the dimensions of the Amazon. When she and Ross had flown into Manaus they saw the Rio Negro and the Amazon jockeying for position, side by side, mile after mile, until the black waters were absorbed by the brown and disappeared. Every year when the Amazon was in flood the Rio Negro was denied passage into the main stream, and its waters built up and up covering vast tracts of swamp and mangrove with the glassy blackness of a lake the size of Poland.

The floating dock at Manaus would rise with the waters, in some years up to forty feet, and still the Negro, some ten miles wide, controlling billions of tons of water pressure, had to bide its time till the greater waters of the Amazon fell at the end of the rains.

She had read that the Amazon had one thousand tributaries bigger than the Rhine, and knew that the Negro was the biggest of these, but seeing was believing and the real thing took her breath away. As far as the eye could see stretched water, islands, crescent-shaped peninsulas and the winding course of the *igarapés*, reaching uneasily from river to river through the jungle between them. Ginny had felt the stirrings of real excitement. This was the basin that was said to contain two-thirds of the world's river water at any one time; the vegetation which produced half the earth's oxygen. When their plane sank towards the ground she barely noticed. The big Boeing had swept down over Educanos creek, a *favela*, tier upon tier of poor houses built on stilts in the mud at the river's edge. Its shadow flickered briefly on the beautiful roof of the opera house and the sun-bleached canvas awnings of the stallholders in the fish market. She felt an illogical and unearned sense of achievement. She had arrived in Manaus, an oasis of civilization in the middle of the world's greatest rain forest. Manaus, Amazonas, Brazil.

Ross's voice brought her down to earth. 'Assistant chef had a *barrogudo* monkey on board,' he was saying, 'and Hoffman got pissed and bought a parrot from some street vendor in Belem, so it was quite a party.'

'Must have been brought up in a Catholic mission,' Ginny said. 'All we could get out of it was "Ave Maria, Lauro". Hour after hour.'

'Tell me,' Kees asked. 'I know Brett Alders, and that's about all I do know. Have you any idea who's financing the whole thing?'

'Yes,' Ross said. 'The bills are being paid by the Bostan Entertainment Corporation, the B.E.C.'

'The record company,' Ginny said.

Ross grunted. 'That's probably one of their sidelines,' he said. 'They're a multinational company with a wide range of interests in the entertainment field. The company was founded by Turk Bostan: you've probably heard of him.'

Kees shook his head. 'No. I was thinking of Boston, Massachusetts.'

'Well, you should meet Turk Bostan, he's arriving today. He's a pretty fantastic man. His father owned a small garage in West L.A.. and somehow he built up this empire. I suppose that's the great American dream. The funny thing about America is that it comes true for so many people.'

Kees looked over to where the *Mississippi Queen* lay serenely at anchor. It was a dream, he told himself. The whole episode from start to finish. There he sat, having travelled halfway round Brazil, naïvely waiting for an actor to show up with a small fortune in uncut stones so that he could steal them back and live happily ever after.

While he looked, the smooth roar of a powerful motor pulsed

in off the river, and the jet propelled runabout swung past the blockade barge at forty or fifty knots. Whoever was at the wheel knew what he was doing, because the sleek hull seemed to spin in its own length, and the stern sank to its gunwales in water. Then the enormous power of the big Crusader motor dragged it up and forward again, until it settled in a welter of foam by the riverboat's boarding platform.

A crew member took the line, and two men climbed out of the boat and began to ascend the steps. Even from a distance one of them was striking, with powerful shoulders and a thick mane of black hair.

'Jesse Cochran the director,' Ross said. 'And the chap driving the boat who looks like Zapata – that's Turk Bostan.'

Later the same day Brett Alders sat on the promenade deck of the *Mississippi Queen* and carefully pulled an insect out of his Coke with thumb and forefinger.

'Hey, you guys,' he muttered gloomily. 'How many times I have to tell you to keep out of my fuckin' drink?'

He looked up to see Turk Bostan sliding into the seat opposite. He seemed quite pleased and was wearing half a dozen necklaces in a variety of colours.

Alders grinned. 'They got you.'

'Sure did,' Bostan told him. 'Worse than Hawaii.' He gestured to the man behind the poolside bar. 'What's it to be, Brett?'

Alders stared sadly into his Coke. A small flying beetle was skating precariously on the surface; as he watched, it collided with a bubble, panicked and started for the bottom.

'Fresh Coke would be just fine.'

'One Coke, and a Cuba libre. Bacardi,' Bostan told the waiter. He looked at Alders' tepid drink. 'Ross said you were really into those *vitaminas* things.'

'Yeah, well,' Alders swirled the liquid and insects in his half-empty glass, 'Nothing worse than warm Coke.' He was silent for a moment, then came straight to the point. 'There's something funny going on here, but when I look at the facts they don't really add up to much.'

'Shoot,' Bostan told him, and leant back in his chair. 'Just because I look as if I'm sleeping doesn't mean I can't hear you.'

'O.K. First, Belém. When we were rebuilding the boat a guy in a Volkswagen followed me all over the damn town. Used to watch us at work with binoculars and take a lot of pictures.'

'Maybe he worked for a news agency.'

Alders grunted. 'Funny you should say that, because Stuart and I got him cornered one day down by the water, and that's what he told us. I asked to see his press card but he said he didn't have any I.D. on him. We let him go, told him not to show around there any more.'

'And?'

'I wasn't quite so paranoid then; he dropped out of sight and I forgot about him. But Stuart saw him the next week coming out of a building in the town. Some big property outfit.'

Bostan sat forward as the waiter arrived with their drinks. 'Did you get the name?'

'Sure – I, uh, made a sort of file. I have it right here in the hotel.' He sipped his fresh Coke and went on. 'Next thing that made me uneasy was an airplane, while we were heading through the narrows. Darned thing wouldn't leave us alone. The others just thought he was some sort of rich nut with nothing better to look at and time on his hands, but I had a squint at him through the glasses to check out the number and there's some dude with a camera up there snapping away. Another news agency? Not on your sweet life. In a case like this there'd be no reason for them not to make normal contact. Anyhow, the next thing that happens is quite a few of the crew quit, and that's the most illogical thing of all.'

Bostan finished his drink and licked his lips. 'How so?'

'We're paying them pretty well for this neck of the woods. And Miguel Tabox, he really loved this old tub. I'd swear to it. I mean, he was nearly in tears when he left. Olviera, too, his first officer.'

'Tabox, the skipper, what was he like?'

Alders spread his hands. 'He was a pretty straight sort of

guy. Knew the river like his hand. I mean, all the crap they gave me about personal problems was just so much horseshit. But don't ask me why: it's just a feeling. Someone somewhere is keeping an eye on us. Maybe the government. I don't know.'

Bostan looked at Alders shrewdly. 'You kept all this pretty much to yourself, Brett?'

Alders smiled ruefully. 'To tell the truth, I was scared they'd all laugh the place down. Stuart knows what happened in Belém.'

'And Ross?'

'Shit, no. He'd make a joke out of anything.'

'Right.' Bostan sat up and put his elbows on the table. 'Let's keep it that way. I'll pass the information on and maybe make a few enquiries myself. The plane registration for a start. And that phony reporter. By the way, do we have a full ship's crew?'

Alders nodded, relieved to have said his piece. 'Pretty well, yes. They're still interviewing for a third engineer.' Unconsciously he lowered his voice. 'What do you make of it all? Figment of an overactive imagination?'

Bostan sat looking out over their own little part of the Negro. The sun was going fast, and herons jostled for position in the branches of a single mango.

Slowly he turned to face Alders.

'Imagination?' he said quietly. 'Not at all. I pay Ross to have one of those, not you.'

With Alders and the sun both gone for the night, Bostan sat in the twilight watching the colours changing across the river like a great celestial light show. Turk Bostan was five foot eleven, and as strong as his backers hoped. His thick black hair grew out over his collar like a mane, and a black moustache covered his top lip and descended over enough of his jaw line to make him look saturnine when the occasion demanded. Despite the nickname Tudor Bostan was not from Turkey; he was by birth a Rumanian from the Black Sea town of Constanta.

86

Methodically, he thought about what Alders had said and married it to his own information. The ensuing picture was far from clear. Getting nowhere, he allowed his mind to reach back down the years to the point when fate had taken a hand in his own destiny.

The Bostan family had emigrated to America in 1937 when Tudor, their only son, was two. By many years of working all God's hours they had managed to build up a thriving family business, and had sent Tudor to one of the best Catholic schools in West Los Angeles. But the biggest break of all had happened one weekend right on the station forecourt, when a runaway truck had come careering down the hill from the direction of Bundy Avenue, heading straight for the garage. Parked on the forecourt was a gleaming Rolls belonging to Viktor Totm, one of the Bostan family's best customers. Totm had made a healthy fortune out of film distribution while still on the bright side of forty, and that morning he'd been standing by the car, totally unaware of death rushing down the hill towards him. Tudor had charged Totm and their bodies crashed onto a pile of old tyres with seconds to spare. The truck spun the Rolls bodily into one of the garage pumps, and ploughed on into the lube bay, killing the driver. Totm suffered a sprained ankle and from then on took a direct interest in the boy's education and career. And Tudor had proved to be an extraordinary protégé.

Viktor Totm, Bostan freely admitted, had put him where he was today. And Totm himself, once often in the news, had retired into obscurity while his corporations continued to amass for him the almost legendary wealth of a Hughes or a Ludwig.

Bostan's heavy fist closed tightly round the empty glass, threatening to shatter it. Although he was one of the few people who ever saw or talked to Viktor, he knew little of Totm's real reasons for insisting that this production, already well over budget, should be shot almost entirely on location. It was illogical, and the only link was the fact of Totm's tremendous investments in Brazil. It was true, for example, that all the renovations to the riverboat had been paid locally from a variety of sources. Perhaps Viktor was trying to export capital illegally, and this was a convenient way of doing it.

Bostan fingered some of the necklaces that had been thrust upon him that afternoon. One was made of the scales of the *pirarucú*, an Amazon monster growing to four hundred pounds. They were so tough the Indians used them to file their nails, while the tongue of the same fish was a grater in Amazonian kitchens. Bostan let the necklace drop, and started to his feet. He hoped there was nothing important of which he was unaware. This was a big country, and they were going a long way from civilization. If Viktor had made enemies, fifteen hundred miles up an isolated waterway in the heart of Amazonas would not be the place to find out about it.

The Fazenda Sabaca, where Kees had so recently recovered from his fever, lay quiet at the heart of a continent of darkness. Down by the creek untold numbers of mosquitos spiralled among the bamboos, and in the corral cattle shuffled and coughed under a torrid moon. Far-reaching, the dirt road ran north into the night on its ramp above the *pantanal*.

On the long verandah an armed man swung gently to and fro on the edge of a hammock, and, inaudible behind the fine insect-mesh and heavy roller-blinds of the big study, a meeting was in progress.

Coronel Castro Silveiro Falco listened to the speaker, and looked around the room through half closed eyes at the four men he had brought together. By far the most impressive in stature was Karel Machado, a strong Paulista of mixed Germano-Spanish blood and one of the biggest land speculators south of the Equator. Next to him sat Spartaco Barros, wiry owner of a ranch so big he had thousands of hectares yet to clear. To Falco's right his business adviser, Herr Gustav Kieler, looked dispassionately out on the room through rimless glasses.

Many years ago Falco and other big ranchers in the Mato Grosso had formed a cartel to control the land and mineral wealth of that vast state. In the last twenty years only one thing had stood in their way: an American who with uncanny foresight had bought worthless tracts of land that were later revealed to be areas of high mineral concentration. Falco and the others had been waging a war of sorts against him for the past decade, and gradually the weapons in that war had got dirtier. Three years previously they had organized a standing watch on his business activities, through the auspices of a company called Overseas Land Development and their contact Amerigo Lind.

Now Lind had arrived from New York, and was amply filling a leather armchair, making points in the air with his brandy glass. He found little difficulty in holding everyone's attention.

'Six years ago, Viktor Totm and his Brazilian partners acquired one of the last stretches of land they were to buy in this country, sectors K171 to 177 on the state survey. It brought their holdings in the Mato Grosso up to two hundred square kilometres. That, to some, would be no great cause for excitement. But it only represents nine per cent of their traceable holdings in Brazil, and in South America as a whole,' he shrugged, 'I couldn't even hazard an informed guess.'

There was a grunt from Barros; the others waited for Lind to go on.

'As you know, things came to a head after the last government geological survey. The findings were restricted, but our host of tonight' – Falco remained motionless – 'was able to obtain information that confirmed the discovery of valuable deposits in the north. We quickly made moves to buy the land before the survey's findings were correlated and delivered to Brasilia.' He paused, then: 'You may remember that the land was readily available for development at a bargain price; all, that is, except the area we wanted. Subsequent investigation showed that it had been bought three years before – three years! This astounded me until I learnt that in 1968 a U.S. government agency had photographed Brazil in detail from a high altitude using a then advanced multi-spectral technique for accurately locating areas of high mineral content in the earth's crust. These findings, besides being illegally obtained, were top secret.'

Lind stopped and shifted in his armchair while Kieler took

the opportunity to rise unobtrusively and replenish the drinks. Lind sipped cognac, and watched the liquid swirl gently in the bottom of his glass.

'We tried to buy, but Totm wasn't interested. We threatened, and he laughed. We arranged for his partners to emigrate, die prematurely, be arrested for fraud. He got others. But piece by piece we have slowed him down, and over the last few years he has been withdrawing from Brazil, selling here and there, moving capital illegally in one way or another. He has sold assets which we didn't even know about direct to American interests. Then there was the *Isla Verde*, eight thousand tons, re-registered and sold: we didn't find out about that until too late. At Leticia he backs an extensive smuggling operation supplying narcotics to the U.S., and –'

Barros interrupted. 'You say Totm runs a drug ring?'

Lind smiled expansively. 'There's no doubt. Columbian cocaine. The best sniff in the world. So I'm told.' His face became serious again. 'It is imperative for our future monopoly of the northern and southern states that we control K173 and 4. And Totm won't sell.'

His voice stopped, and with an effort sat forward on the edge of his chair.

'Some time ago a highly paid informant employed by an entertainment corporation in the U.S. provided us with information of Totm's latest scheme for converting his holdings into U.S. dollars. He has sponsored a network TV series to be shot in Amazonas. No expense is too great, I am told. Big names like Jack Cane, and scripts to be shot on location. Not in their jungle, *senhores*, but ours. Brasilia is basking in the publicity, but metaphorically speaking each of those little silver film cans will carry its own small part of Totm's gains safely out of Brazil to Los Angeles.'

There was silence. Kieler made a note. Machado said, 'Well?'

'The details have not been finalised,' Lind told them. 'Naturally we had to consult you first. But we have infiltrated this enterprise. They converted an old riverboat which is now manned with our own people. We feel that in the wilder reaches of some river it won't be too difficult to arrange a disaster. Totm has one of his only friends organizing this venture for him, a guy called Bostan. Perhaps if Totm's few friends start to disappear he might learn to co-operate. *Quem sabe?* All may yet work out to our advantage.'

It was two in the morning when Barros and Machado left the Fazenda Sabaca. The Coronel sat hunched forward in the lamplight opposite Lind, and for some minutes neither of the two men spoke.

'I didn't know that,' Falco said suddenly. 'Cocaine. When did you find out?'

Lind laughed. 'That was a little something – how shall we say? – *pour encourager les autres.* Now they have morality on their side. Whatever we do will be excusable.'

The Coronel shook his head. 'Karel never needed morality as an excuse for anything.'

'No,' Lind conceded. 'Perhaps not.'

Falco breathed deeply. 'When we do what has been discussed here tonight, it will finally spell out for Totm that anything he attempts here in the future will be sabotaged. He must logically instruct his agents to liquidate.'

Amerigo Lind clasped his hands on his stomach and looked at Falco's face. For the first time he realized that the Coronel was looking his age. Perhaps he had faced up to the fact that an organization the size of Totm's could never be seriously hurt by a local attack. But it was not Lind's function to point out things like that. On the shadowy perimeters of controversy where he contrived to make a handsome living riches were not showered on those who advocated peace.

Falco broke in on his thoughts by saying, 'A close friend of mine was killed recently. Perhaps you met him. The doctor from Campo Grande. Lani.'

'Oh?' Lind expressed concern. 'No, I don't think I did. How did he die?'

Falco hesitated slightly. 'He was murdered. By a madman, I should imagine. With a knife.'

'You're not saying ... ?'

'No, no.' The Coronel shook his head. 'Nothing like that.

No, a doctor is bound to make enemies. Perhaps he was killed by the relative of a deceased patient. Such things have happened.'

Chapter 7

The *Mississippi Queen* had left Manaus a couple of weeks behind schedule – a cavalier delay considering that the rainy season was approaching – setting off unobtrusively up the main stream of the Rio Negro. Flanked by the *Jacaré*, with the barge and runabout in tow, the big white sternwheeler was a major spectacle and despite the early hour the river was soon thick with hordes of sightseeing boats. By ten o'clock the number of attendant craft had almost doubled, and the sight was so impressive that director Jesse Cochran sent off Peter Horitz, the pilot of the Alouette, with one of the camera operators and a wild Arri to get some aerial footage.

Actors, electricians, kitchen staff, technicians, crew – everyone aboard the *Mississippi Queen* lined the railings on the broad scrubbed decks and watched as the motley flotilla circled round them, the air full of thrown bottles and the sound of hooters and whistles. Above them the little helicopter hovered like a curious insect under Horitz's deft touch.

Turk Bostan laughed heartily and sipped a Cuba libre. Some of the B.E.C. management were aboard, but after a forty-eight hour visit they would be flown back to Manaus from the landing strip at Santa Maria.

'Reminds me of '65 in Bangkok,' Turk said to Ann Harper, his head of publicity. 'They'd re-started the Royal Barge procession, and I got my boat right in there opposite the Wat Arun. Soon as the barges had passed the action really began.

Amazing sight. Bottles flying, boats weaving, people bailing like crazy. And the water over there's not clean enough to drink like here.'

'You're kidding?' Ann Harper exhaled a pale jet of smoke through pursed lips. 'This black stuff's drinkable?'

She looked around the gathering and was pleased to note that photostats of her press releases were providing most of the conversation fodder.

'Seems that way,' Turk was saying. 'According to the experts the black water rivers are free from just about everything you'd expect to find in a South American river. No sediments, fewer insects, and because the upstream population is almost nil, no crap floating around either.'

Ann wrinkled her nose and looked past Turk to see if Attica Alloui was on deck. 'Sounds too good to be true.'

Bostan moved away and glanced out over the watery landscape. The attendant craft were thinning now, and the helicopter coming in to land. The day that had seemed unlikely to arrive was here, and would soon be history. Everything had gone smoothly, but Turk looked down at the black water sliding beneath the steamer and Ann Harper's phrase rang in his ears. 'Too good to be true,' he muttered, and then with a shake of his heavy head, he tore his eyes away and prepared to mix once more with the deck full of celebrating people.

Jack Cane had quit the impromptu party on the promenade deck and retired to the shady interior of his cabin to nurse his headache. Once inside he locked the door, stripped, and took a leisurely shower. Then he dried himself off, wrapped the towel round his waist, and opened the twin locks of a small attaché case. Inside were various documents and contracts, a small Texas Instruments calculator, a Minox C, a tiny Mitsubishi message recorder, two Patek Phillippe watches, a small leather pouch fastened with a drawstring, and a thirty-two callibre revolver.

Cane spent a couple of minutes looking in the mirror at one of the best known faces in the world, appreciating with a completely reflexive vanity the thick hair, dark eyes and slightly cruel lips that had made him one of the world's favourite *vaqueiros*; then he passed fifteen minutes regarding his contract, and pondering the fates of the many people he had known who one minute had been household names in their own TV show, and whose next appearance had been in the question, 'Hey, whatever happened to that guy who used to play the private eye in that series we used to watch?'

Actors would, if given a choice, rather work in films. Cinema was prestige, professionalism, where a scene would be played and replayed until it was right. Television, dubbed the 'maw' in the industry, was a voracious animal, insatiable in its demands for new faces. In the early days TV chiefs hadn't realized that over-exposure would kill their stars as surely as the plague. Big names had been lured away from movies with offers of twenty-year contracts. Doubtless those same contracts, securely vaulted, were still bringing smiles to the faces of actors who had not graced a TV screen for a decade and a half. The public liked to see their favourite stars in their own familiar shows. But when the shows palled or lost appeal they didn't want to see that star in a new show. By and large they expected – and got – a whole new package.

Jack Cane thought that his agent had negotiated a good deal. For a start these shows, twenty-two hour slots the first year, were far from run of the mill. They had nothing to do with the New York Police Department, the Ponderosa, or Chicago in the Twenties. Cane paused for a moment. Whatever happened to Eliot Ness? and the Virginian?

Then he considered the money, which boiled down to eighty thousand dollars per episode with a ten per cent increase per annum if the show made the grade. He was well aware that a successful show could expect five or six years of syndication, and as a big name he would come in contractually for about an extra hundred thousand dollars a year on top of earnings. All in all about two and a half million, give or take the pennies.

It seemed to make the chances of being chewed up in the maw a little more worthwhile, and he slipped the contract back into the case and idly loosened the drawstring on the leather pouch. The little stones cascaded into his palm and he chuckled, glad he'd decided to take the risk and keep them with him. It was always a little disappointing when you possessed something which spent its time hidden from sight at the back of a safe deposit box. He hadn't frittered his money away during his time on top. He could be over-exposed tomorrow and still have enough to live a life of luxury for the rest of his days. Telly Savalas had once been asked what he would like to do when his series folded. Never at a loss, Savalas had quipped: 'Play Cyrano de Bergerac.'

'That's it, baby,' Cane thought, reaching for a sheaf of recent press cuttings. 'We got to hang in there while it lasts.'

Attica Alloui stood by the latticed window of her cabin and watched the spectator boats thin and then disappear altogether. Distances on the Negro were so deceptive: one minute the boats had been right there, and the next they were corks sliding away across the glassy surface. She restrained a sudden crazy impulse to try and call them back and urge them to stay. It was strange; she lived her life in hedonistic isolation on the edge of the world's greatest desert, and called it home; but the proximity of the world's greatest river system and rain forest made her feel hemmed in and uneasy.

She had rightly been called one of the most beautiful women in the world. Her hair was a glossy black, her eyes bold and dark brown; she had a small nose, and alway there was the indefinable legacy of Berber blood which had given her mystery, allure, and success in one of the world's toughest professions.

She had been launched onto the screen eight years before at the age of twenty-one, and had won instant acclaim in Europe for her part in Lafay's award-winning film 'Bidonville'. The same year she had played the female lead in 'Pharaoh', one of the last great biblical epics, and success had followed success until suddenly, four years previously, she had slung it all in for an Algerian husband and a few million acres of desert, dates and mineral rights on the fringes of the Sahara. The marriage hadn't lasted and the breakup was the last publicity she'd received.

Someone appeared at the cabin door, and Attica beckoned in the slight figure of Fátima, her personal maid and the one link with home she had insisted on bringing. No Hollywood matron for her, she emphasised, and B.E.C. had raised no objections. Now it was hard to believe that the girl was the same person who had left Algeria. In beige slacks and crisp cotton blouse Fátima was considerably more exposed than she had ever been at home, and she had been quick to make her number with the makeup girls. Ah well, Attica thought. She was over fifteen and would just have to take her chances like all the other girls on the boat.

In the kitchens Signior Annelli issued rapid instructions in a mixture of Brazilian *gíria* and Neapolitan Italian, alternately berating and encouraging his staff. Without a pause in his verbal stride, he stopped an immensely strong young Negro called Dominó who was crossing the kitchen with a mountain of plates.

'Dominó, Dominó, how many times I have to tell you, eh? Make two trips, O.K.; carry half as many. Same thing in the end.'

As Dominó's face was obscured by the plates, Annelli was unaware of the effect he was having. But suppressed laughter from the other side of the column of crockery suggested that Dominó might well be pulling some faces at his expense. Annelli slapped the man on the rump, at which the Negro pretended to stagger and fall. The Italian threw up his hands in despair and moved away to where a man was tenderising steaks. Annelli stopped him.

'What you trying to do? Kill it again? Like this, see, easy, you going to break your arm.'

'The meat is tough, *chefe*,' the man told him.

Annelli glowered at the steaks, 'Tough? Of course it's tough! Meat from the ranches of the Mato Grosso goes two ways: southeast and northwest. The good meat goes southeast to the coast. And where are we?'

The question seemed to be rhetorical, so the assistant said nothing. '*Si, si*, quite right,' said Annelli, taking his silence for

97

affirmation, 'Northwest. But still, you won't make it better nailing it to the floor.'

He mopped his brow. Dinner tonight was a special occasion, and *Senhor* Brett had explained that important people would be on board for the first two days. After that, as Brett had tactfully put it, less exquisite food would be perfectly acceptable.

Annelli walked down the short passageway to the kitchen washrooms and on the way nearly collided with Kees on his way to his cabin. The man was a cut above average, the chef thought, and wondered for the tenth time why he was working as a waiter.

'*Buona sera*, Kees,' Annelli greeted him as they passed each other. 'Are you nearly ready?'

'*Buona sera*, Signior,' the man replied. 'Everything is fine upstairs, no problem. Tonight will be a great success.'

Annelli beamed, for when this man said something, it was with such authority that one could almost believe it would happen just as he said. With renewed optimism he disappeared into the kitchen.

Kees studied his reflection in the small mirror of his cabin. Well groomed, fit, better fed than he had been in months, the face that looked back at him now was a far cry from that of recent weeks. They said he looked like a younger George Peppard, and Kees smiled to himself, because in the strange world of these movie people it seemed that everyone had to look like someone, remind one of somebody; it was as if the only means by which they could remember a new face was to tag their likenesses to someone well known enough never to be forgotten. But who had George Peppard looked like before he looked like himself?

He straightened his tie and turned away from the mirror. One of his few possessions was a battered cassette-recorder and one cassette. Recorded on the sixty minute tape were the dozen or so numbers that had caught his imagination in the countries of South America. Nearly all of them were Indian or Andean music, featuring the natural instruments of mountain and jungle and poorly recorded. He listened now to 'El Condor Pasa', a haunting melody that originated in Peru at the beginning of the century, some fifty years before it was commercialized by Simon and Garfunkel. Hearing for the thousandth time this sad, powerful refrain, he felt he could see the broad wings of the great bird, carrying it high above dwarf forest and puna.

With music filling the cabin Kees sat on the bunk and reached under its frame. He had befriended one of the cabin maids, and it had been easy to get an impression of the master key and a copy made. His fingers told him that the key was still taped securely where he'd left it. For the moment he'd done all he could. He knew the riverboat blindfolded, and had established himself in the kitchens. Now he had to wait for an opportunity to search Cane's cabin. Beyond that he hadn't cared to think. Only two things bothered him, and they were nothing to do with Jack Cane. One was the almost tangible feeling of mistrust he felt for several of the crew members. They were of a type he had seen often; hard, ruthless men who would sell their sisters for a square meal, not at all the easy-going people one usually associated with the river. He wondered if anyone else had picked it up: probably not. There was, for most people, a language barrier. And in any case the new skipper and several of the other officers were last-minute replacements, and you never got the best at the last minute.

Kees punched his finger downwards and the cassette ejected noisily. The other thing that bothered him was something he had heard the captain, a man called Pereira, discussing with the mate. It was the name of a river that had caught his ear, the Japura. Kees had seen the sailing schedule, and knew the waterways they would be travelling. And the Rio Japura was not among them.

The first twelve days had passed quickly, life on the boat falling into a routine. Even more than usual, the day-to-day shooting schedules had to be arranged precisely. The fact that the barge carried the bulk of the spare equipment and accommodated various of the staff made good liaison and planning between the different departments crucial. The weather was another consideration. In principal the Amazon winter was just beginning and would last until October, but here astride the Equator the temperature hovered in the eighties all the year round. Advisers to the B.E.C. had suggested that the first filming trip should be wrapped up by June, and as the height of the rainy season varied from May in the north of the basin to January in the south, the best idea would be to commence sailing upriver in mid-April. The advantages were several: slightly lower temperatures, the bulk of the rain already under the keel, and wide easily navigable waters on the smaller tributaries until September. As things had turned out, they weren't far off schedule.

The rains were the only natural factor to be considered, for in the jungle the names of the four seasons meant less than nothing. Some trees shed their leaves, while their neighbours flowered or bore fruit. The forest rhythms were haphazard and random.

Mile after changeless mile the river unfurled its banks. Armies of trees lined the water's edge, linked together with crazy skeins of vine and liana, and beneath the crowns of forest giants smaller trees waited patiently for a monster to weaken and fall. The jungle itself was a dark gloomy place where no light shone, and so the forest floor was free from the wild confusion of the canopy. But the river's banks were so overgrown and dense that it was sometimes difficult to see where water stopped and land began. *O rio mar*, the river sea, was just that: a huge basin which flooded seasonally from north to south like the slow-motion pulsing of a giant heart. The rivers were the highways through this unknown land. With a boat, fuel, provisions and a chart a man could expect to survive. But take away the aids, return man to the trees: then the jungle would reveal itself as an unhealthy place for the human bacterium. Whether from hunger, fatigue, disease or simply desperation, the chances were that man would die.

The bridge of the *Mississippi Queen* contained navigation equipment that would have frightened a superstitious skipper in the nineteenth century, but Captain Jorge Pereira was not unduly impressed. He studied a chart of the Japura River area and listened to the noise his fingernail made as it scratched the stubble high on his jawline. Pereira was a man of indeterminate age, with shoulders that had once possessed the power of a young bull's but which were now losing their shape. His legs were short, so that from the back he looked like an old-fashioned kite, broad at the top and tapering almost to a point. His knowledge of certain riverine areas was second to none, a fact directly attributable to the activities of his youth. Smuggling, in one form or another, had existed in the upper Amazon since the advent of authorities to police the frontiers. Even today the profession was still pursued enthusiastically, and the *zona franca* of Manaus often unknowingly exported large amounts of merchandise which ended up in other cities in the same country.

Jorge Pereira was a bitter introverted man who had made no friends in the last twenty years of his life. And yet he was an enigma often discussed in the waterfront bars of the river towns, where there were those who could remember him as a young man, carefree and gregarious. Something had happened to change him, all agreed, but no-one had ever found out what.

Pereira looked up from the chart as the mate walked in, a man called Cancian Scaffa. Pereira gestured to him to close the door.

'How much longer?' Scaffa asked.

'If we keep sailing, two and a half days,' Pereira told him. 'Tomorrow we can start preparations.' The previous night he had received a coded radio message from the unknown organization which was making him rich to do this thing. It would be the last contact there would be before the job was done, and like all previous contacts it left Pereira none the wiser as to who was footing the bill. The only clue he had was the southerly accent of the man who had initially found him in a Santaren bar; the unmistakable accent of the Mato Grosso. For just a moment Pereira wondered how he could have sunk so far that he was now the bought executioner of scores of people who trusted him, and whom he hardly knew. But then the old bitterness came back, and he realized that the men behind him knew him better than he knew himself.

Scaffa looked out over the dark face of the river and the endless line of trees that seemed, as always, to be monitoring their progress. 'You know your way around the rivers, Jorge,' he said grudgingly. 'Have you been to this place before?'

Pereira looked blankly ahead and wondered if this trip would in some unknown way vindicate him from the years of inadequacy. 'Yes,' he said softly. 'I have been on this river a thousand times.'

Chapter 8

As the sun broke cover at dawn on the sixteenth day, Cancian Scaffa and a man named Luiz stepped unnoticed into the throbbing engineroom of the *Mississippi Queen*.

Chief Engineer Andy Gregg was wiping his hands on an oily rag, an act which often left the rag cleaner than before. But he barely noticed, gazing in satisfaction at the mass of pipes and gauges that insinuated themselves into every corner of the engineroom, unified in their common purpose of serving a big diesel mounted in their midst. Gregg was a Newfie, though originally from Halifax, Nova Scotia, and in his time a lot of engines had responded to his ministrations. He'd spent endless hours coaxing the best out of the worst in the way of motors, from tired old Greys in fishing boats off the Grand Banks to the larger problems found in rusty freighters on the South China Sea. He was, as Scaffa knew, alone, and thinking about a girl he'd met in Frobisher Bay when the wrench held easily in Luiz's right hand crushed the thought forever into a pulp of splintered bone and tissue.

Gregg fell forward, his face coming into contact with the scalding surface of an unlagged pipe, and his nerves performed their last service by jack-knifing him away from the heat. Face up, he lay twitching on the metal deck, his eyes grotesque with just the whites showing.

Scaffa and Luiz hauled the dead engineer towards the door. A third man gave the all clear, and they bundled Gregg's body into a walk-in cupboard used by the cleaners. Scaffa wiped his hands on a roll of towelling and looked at the body. 'You want to take it easy,' he said scornfully. 'We've only got one wrench.'

Luiz grunted. 'Don't see it makes a lot of odds,' he said. 'A few hours more or less, what's the difference?'

Later that morning, at six thirty, Jesse Cochran decided to change his plans for the day's shooting and rang the unit manager to explain what he wanted. Then he got in touch with Brett Alders, whose job it was to liaise with the captain.

'We've been passing little estuaries, Brett, with clear ground to either side. If you check your script I think we could do shots 930 to 933, which'll save us a lot of time. You and I can check out the location in the runabout.'

'O.K.,' Brett's voice came over strongly on the phone, 'but I thought you wanted to head on to this rubber baron's place as soon as possible?'

'Sure,' Cochran told him. 'But we were due to arrive at night anyway. You square it with the skipper, and tell the kitchen what's required. I want to have everyone involved ashore by ten at the latest, before the sun gets too high.'

He rang off, aware that all over the boat things would be happening fast. First the barge would come alongside, so that after a quick breakfast Jack Cane and Attica Alloui could go down for wardrobe and makeup. Jack Bertram would be getting the camera crew together, and young Keith Mayall, the clapper loader, would be hurrying to ready the mags and sort out filters and batteries. Script girls would be duplicating the relevant sections of the script, and down in the kitchens Annelli would, in his chaotic way, be organizing a hamper containing enough sustenance for a dozen or so people on a run ashore. Cochran stretched. Dozens of technicians, overpaid stars, a riverboat, a jungle estuary and three precious hours. And the result? Just seventy seconds of cut film.

At six fifty Turk Bostan answered the bedside telephone in his cabin. He had been up for some time preparing radio messages and planned to leave the boat by helicopter as soon as they arrived at the derelict mansion of Carlos Tinto. A private jet would be at his disposal in Santa Maria to take him the thirteen hundred miles to Salvador for a meeting with Viktor Totm.

'Brett here,' said the voice on the phone. 'I don't know if you aim to be there, but Jesse's arranged some impromptu shooting this morning because he likes the terrain. Shots 930 through 933. He wants to be away by ten.'

Bostan picked up a copy of the script, wedged the phone between ear and shoulder, and thumbed it open. The idea of a run ashore was suddenly appealing, but he had a lot to do on board. 'O.K.,' he told Brett. 'Count me in. I'll make it if I can.'

In the kitchen, Brett put the phone down and walked through the communicating door into the restaurant. On the way he passed Kees just turning up for duty. 'Just in time,' he said. 'There's a panic on for packed lunches. Twelve for a shore trip. They'll be leaving in the Hamilton as soon as possible.'

Kees headed straight through into the kitchen. 'Coffee?' he called over his shoulder.

'No time!' Alders yelled back. 'Maybe later!'

In the kitchens people were already at work getting the breakfast together. Kees moved to a vacant table and started to arrange things, but his mind was elsewhere. It seemed a golden opportunity, if Cane were going ashore, to have a look at the inside of his cabin. Now that the moment had arrived he felt tense in anticipation of disappointment. It now seemed a long shot that had brought him here, and he could think of a dozen things Cane might have done with the stones, supposing he'd ever had them.

Kees reached for a knife and steel. It was no good thinking about it: there was only one way to settle the matter and put his mind at rest.

Cancian Scaffa walked into Pereira's cabin left of the bridge at seven ten. Pereira looked up quickly. 'Well?'

Scaffa nodded. 'Things are all set. We just have a little less time than planned.' He added: 'We had to take Gregg out.'

Pereira nodded out of the cabin window. 'It means some of them will be ashore,' he muttered, 'But it's still too good an opportunity. The river is deep here.' Almost to himself he whispered: 'And where can they go?'

Scaffa coughed to break the silence. 'They'll have that jet runabout,' he ventured. 'There's nothing we can do about that.'

Pereira shrugged. 'Fuel for thirty kilometres only, and after that ...'

'They could row, Jorge, even go with the current.'

The captain got to his feet and walked over to a general map of the upper Amazon basin. 'You still don't quite understand,' he said. 'First, they don't know where they are and have no means of finding out. And it's been raining heavily further south, so the main streams will be full, which means –' he swept his hand over an area of one million square miles of jungle – 'the waters will rise and back. Have you looked over the side recently? There is no current. And in the next week or two this water will actually start to flow back towards its source, and then the rains will start here too. This is the mother and father of all rivers, *O rio mar*; its ways are sometimes beyond comprehension.'

Abruptly he turned his back on the map. 'Now, you know how we planned it. You, I and Luiz in the helicopter. Suarez, Roho and Jeroba in the *Jacaré*. They cast off at ten fifteen. We'll get airborne at the same time. As for the speedboat, I'll request it to inspect the hull, then it will be alongside. They will be left completely to their own resources. It will just take them longer to die, that's all. No-one escapes from the jungle.'

By eight a.m. the *Mississippi Queen* was lying still as an island on the mirror-dark waters of the river. The peace was disrupted for the second time in half an hour by the sound of the runabout, as Alders expertly brought it alongside the steamer. Both he and Cochran climbed up the boarding stage onto the deck and headed down to the restaurant.

Jack Bertram buttonholed Cochran just inside the door. 'It's O.K.?'

'Sure,' Cochran told him. 'Light's fine and the water looks great. First boat leaves at nine. With the gear.' He moved on and sat down opposite Attica Alloui.

106

'Looking forward to *terra firma*?'

Attica smiled. She got on well with Cochran and he knew it. 'I don't get *mal de mer* on rivers,' she said. 'At least, not yet.'

The restaurant door opened, and Jack Cane came in raising a wan hand in general greeting. He had found distraction the previous night with one of the girls from the wardrobe department, and was still feeling fragile.

'Jack,' Cochran called out. 'Over here.'

A pretty production assistant passed the table and gave him a bright smile, but Cochran was checking the shots against the shooting schedule. When he looked up, Cane had joined them. 'O.K.,' he said. 'We shouldn't be too long over this. Let me tell you what I had in mind.'

Kees walked quietly along the promenade deck, his soft-soled shoes making no noise on the wooden planking. The two cabins at the forward end of the deck had been allocated to Jack Cane and Attica Alloui, and they were half as large again as most of the others. Isolated from the rest of the top deck accommodation by a narrow gangway spanning the ship, they had the advantage of a panoramic view forward as well as to port and starboard.

Kees was now near enough to Cane's cabin to see that the door was already open. As Cane had gone ashore, it stood to reason that the cabin girl was cleaning up inside. He passed the gangway leading to the other side of the boat and saw a flash of green as someone hurried by. He recognized Fátima, the Algerian girl. Another half a dozen paces and he came to the door of Cane's cabin. It stood ajar, and as he looked in the bathroom door opened and a girl came out into the main cabin carrying a pile of damp towels. He watched her as she walked towards the bed, and then crossed the deck to the other side of the boat. He glanced towards the shore; it was still early, and there was time enough. Kees slipped quickly into the cabin and locked the door behind him. He knew the key would work because he'd already tried it in Manaus. Without preamble he began a systematic search of the cabin, looking quickly and efficiently in the obvious places, and drew an expected blank.

Next, he felt carefully through the pockets and linings of Cane's extensive personal wardrobe. In one of the jackets there was a hide wallet, but it only held a few new cruzeiro bills. He sifted papers from a drawer in the dressing table, trying to establish a connection between Cane and Bretas, but there was nothing. At ten fifteen he cocked his head and heard the helicopter take off, and by then there was nowhere left to search. He'd checked the carpets, curtains, fittings, bed and bathroom, all without success. The long chase across Brazil seemed suddenly irrational, prompted by emotion and lacking in simple common sense. The same old questions rose up to taunt him: had Cane been the buyer? Had he been forewarned? Was he, in any case, paranoiac enough to risk carrying a fortune in uncut gems up the Amazon on a film location?

Kees sat on the cabin bed in deep thought. He felt so drained and irresolute that he was unable even to feel anxiety that he might be found in someone else's cabin. The only move left to him was a direct confrontation with Cane, and that meant waiting till the time was right, and the time was never likely to be right in the confines of the boat. After some minutes he resignedly got up and went to the door. His delay in Cane's cabin probably saved his life, for at ten thirty two simultaneous explosions ripped the *Mississippi Queen* from stem to stern, and thirty seconds later she was on her way to the bottom.

Ashore, the crew had run into a synchronization problem with the sound gear, and at ten o'clock a frustrated Jesse Cochran got on the radio to Brett Alders aboard the paddle steamer. Moments later Brett appeared climbing down the steps to the runabout, and within minutes had picked up two technicians and was on his way back to the workshop in the *Mississippi Queen*. The three men had barely climbed aboard when the unmistakeable sound of the helicopter beat its way in waves across the placid waters of the river.

Bostan leapt to his feet and brought his radio to his lips. No-one started the chopper except Pete Horitz, and he knew better than to dicker with the motor when the crew were filming. Alder's voice came on the air.

'Brett,' Bostan barked. 'What the hell's going on? Get up there and see what's happening.'

Alders needed no prompting. He sprinted up the steps to the top deck and across to the starboard side where the *Jacaré* and its barge were moored out of sight of the cameras on the shore. As he arrived at the gangplank that led across to the barge's roof the noise rose to a crescendo and the chopper lifted into the air. Alders had a quick glimpse of a face, and then the machine slid over the steamer's superstructure and out of sight; it had been impossible to see who was flying it. Eddies of torpid air veined with exhaust fumes washed around him, and he turned away from the noise, cradling the small transceiver in the lee of his body. He never saw the rifle aimed at him from the after deck of the *Jacaré*, and would have had no time to take evasive action anyway. Standing up there against the sky he made an easy target, but the marksman still managed to foul it up and the bullet hit Alders in the navel and went on to sever his spine. His legs collapsed under him and the radio dropped to the ground and slid away. Horrified, he tried to move to retrieve it, but the lower half of his body was just dead meat. Seconds later he saw the blood flowing out of his shirt onto the teak decking, and in the background the *Jacaré*, blurred now and indistinct, sweeping in a broad arc away from the steamer's side. Alders heard the radio calling his name. But he was much too tired to answer.

Turk Bostan stood impotently on the river bank and watched as the chopper circled like a lazy bird high above them. Beside him the rest of the cast and crew watched the machine's slow spirals with various degrees of interest; Bostan repeatedly thumbed the transmit button on the transceiver but there was no reply.

Suddenly, travelling quite fast, the *Jacaré* came into view, heading downriver and out into midstream.

'Jesus Christ!' Cochran muttered. 'What the hell's up?'

Bostan shook his head grimly and trained field glasses on the helicopter and then the launch, but both were too distant to see who was in them.

On the riverbank there was almost complete silence. Bostan panned the glasses along the side of the paddle-steamer. The *Jacaré* was hightailing it, the helicopter watching. He was suddenly certain that something quite terrible was about to happen, and an impotent fury gripped him which turned quite suddenly to a cold nauseating dread. They were helpless. He moved over to Attica, took her hand in his. There was no-one among them who had not been visited by the same premonition of horror. Jack Bertram swung the big camera round on its head and framed up the paddle-steamer. When the explosions came, and the beautiful entity that had been the *Mississippi Queen* fell apart as if in slow motion, the camera was already turning.

The kitchen on the paddle-steamer was situated above and slightly forward of the engineroom. The explosive charges were more than adequate, and most people were killed outright where they might otherwise have been able to survive and swim ashore. Signior Annelli had no chance. The floor lifted where he was standing and a column of flame roared through, carrying with it a core of shrapnel in the form of sections of shattered piping and fractured steel. Annelli's body simply ceased to exist, plucked from its bones by the blast, cooked to carbon by the heat. He had time for neither surprise nor regret, and in that he was lucky.

On the barge Paula Wainwright, an attractive and friendly make-up girl, was less fortunate. After the morning's fittings a big Negro called Joe had come in looking for an outsize pair of sneakers. Paula helped him look through a wicker basket full of paired shoes, tied by their laces, that had not yet been unpacked and sorted. As Joe bent over the basket and reached for a pair he thought might fit, he made an interesting discovery; his hand pushed hard against the girl's breast, thinly encased in a lawn blouse, and his ready apology died at birth as he felt the instant reaction. As he watched, her knuckles whitened on the basket's rim and she leant forward, staring fixedly at the shoes.

'Hey, did I hurt you?' Joe asked her, half-joking. Tentatively, with a sudden intuition, he put his hand back on her breast. 'Here, let me rub it better.'

The flesh was firm beneath his hand, and in amazement he felt a vibration start to thrill through her body as he touched her. Still she leant forward in the same position. Sure now, he quickly slid a hand under her skirt and between her bare legs. Scarcely had he registered her evident arousal when she turned and moved against him, her pelvis pressed close against his front.

While not fully understanding what he had done for Paula to present herself to him in this way, Joe was nevertheless not the man to turn her down. None too gently, he half-dragged half-lifted her behind the stacked basket and laid her on the floor. He got out of his shorts in record time, pulled her panties off and fell between her spread legs. Her cries started immediately he entered her, and he kissed her hard on the lips, pulling her blouse open with one hand to free her breasts. She seemed to climax from first to last and the incident was so sudden and gratifying that Joe finished in under three minutes.

He lay there feeling awkward while the girl's cries died away, and then suddenly she opened big, hazel eyes and gave him a wide smile, totally lacking in embarrassment.

'You've discovered my little secret,' she told him, and sighed contentedly. 'God, I needed that.'

Joe tried to leave then, but she clung to him, and soon he was proving once again to be all, if not more, that she had hoped for. When the *Mississippi Queen* started to go down Paula thought for a moment that the roaring noise and the sudden violent rocking were just concomitant to the prowess being shown by the big stud sweating his heart out on top of her. She felt his rhythm start to falter at the noise and dug her nails into his backside. 'Don't stop,' she forced out. 'Please, not now!'

It was the last reasonably coherent thing she ever said. Scaffa and Luiz had done as good a job on the barge as they had on the steamer, but the timer on the barge was running fifteen seconds slow. When the charges detonated in the props room, only a thin partition separated the blast from the wardrobe department just along the corridor. As intended, most of the force of the explosion blew a massive hole in the vessel's side and bottom. But part of the blast lashed sideways, picking up half a dozen empty scuba tanks and a selection of lead weights and projected them through the bulkhead. The noise was so great that Paula and her lover heard nothing: they were both instantly deafened. But a hot wind scorched the air, and as she opened her eyes Joe's head and face were carried away by one of the flying air tanks. Paula screamed silently, but her mouth and eyes were immediately flooded with his blood. She struggled to breathe, miraculously unhurt, and tried to get out from under his weight. But he was still deep inside her, and she had to claw her way backwards on the makeshift bed, pushing with her hands against rubbery wet tissue, his blood still pouring out over her shoulders and breasts. She was still blinded and deafened when the river swept in through the bulkhead and submerged her. Suddenly she could see again in a tiderace of deep red water, and her body floated easily away from his. She tried to reach the door, but already the water was filling the room. She felt herself weakening, and the acid river-water was burning her eyes. Now it had reached the ceiling and she was left with no air. An excruciating pain built up in her forehead, forcing her to scream. Pressure: the barge was going down. The air that had carried her scream mushroomed its way upwards and slid away out of sight. She didn't want to die, not here, not now, not like this, naked and trapped. Bravely, she stood the pain that built up in her chest until she could stand it no more: she inhaled water, choked, convulsed, tried to breathe again. Her mind slipped away, gave up. Her lovely body stiffened, then relaxed, only to stiffen again. The ruby water turned to umber then to black. Lips to the ceiling, she kissed for the last time.

Roderick Ross was asleep when the boat blew up. The explosion tipped him out of his bunk, and then the world turned upside down and he found himself falling towards the door. He held himself steady with one hand on either side of the door frame and tried not to panic. For a moment the boat seemed to steady. Ross looked around him. There was no way he could get to the other side of the cabin, and if the bloody tub turned over he'd be feeding the fishes. The sound of another explosion helped him on his way. Squatting down, he moved through the door and over to the rail. Beneath him, a long way beneath him it seemed, the river bubbled and boiled around the new water-line. The boat lurched again, and that clinched matters. With an expression of extreme distaste Ross leant out over the rail. Then, one hand over his nose and the other clasping his balls, he jumped.

Fátima was leaning on the rail on the top deck and wishing she were back in Algeria when the noise came and the ship canted suddenly towards the shore. Had she not had one leg hooked through the railings she probably would have been hurled overboard. As it was, her leg snapped cleanly against the metal bars and she was left hanging forward, unable to move. Biting her lip, she stared down into the water: she couldn't swim. Slowly she sat down and tried to extricate her twisted limb, while the noise beat at her back and receded. Seconds later she risked a look round, just in time to see the funnel leaning forward at a crazy angle. Even as she watched it leaned further and fell towards the forward cabins. Frozen with fear, she stayed where she was, now almost sitting on the rail, and watched terror-stricken as the water rushed to meet her.

Kees was on his way out of Cane's cabin when the sudden change of deck angle caused him to stagger. Quick as a cat he regained his balance and worked his way back to the other door, forced it open and climbed up through it. The angle at which the boat was leaning was now so pronounced that he was able to stand with one foot on the cabin wall, the other on the deck. What he saw was astonishing. The *Jacaré* was gone, and the chopper airborne. The barge appeared intact, but the paddle steamer herself was obviously sinking fast and debris and smoke were clinging to the surface of the river. Even as he watched there was another peak of sound, and the side of the barge disintegrated. Kees was on the point of going up and over the partially exposed bottom of the boat, when he saw the pathetic figure of Fátima clinging to the rail on the shoreward side of the ship. It was then that the funnel crashed down on the forward deck. Smoke poured out into the sunlight, but Kees didn't hesitate and in a crouching slide he descended the deck space between them.

'Come on!' he said, gesturing over his shoulder. 'You'll get sucked under if you jump there? Back this way!'

The girl was clearly in a state of terrified shock. *'Je ne peux!'* she managed. *'Ma jambe!'*

Kess looked down at her leg, twisted and obviously not fit for use. Behind them the deck angle steepened. There was no time to lose.

'Sautons!' he urged her. *'Ensemble!'*

He got an arm round her waist, but she wouldn't let go with her hands. He broke her grip by brute force and hefted her under one arm. She screamed as her leg dragged over the rail, and then they were falling through space towards the river.

As the water closed above their heads Kees felt the girl begin to struggle. Grimly, he found his way to the surface. 'Kick your good leg,' he told the girl mercilessly. 'I'll support you! Kick, damn you, or we'll both be dead!'

Getting a hand under one of her arms and beneath her breasts, he pulled her up towards his chest and started to kick out. She trailed limply in the water behind him, but he found that she was light and buoyant as a feather and soon they were making good progress away from the boat. As he swam, Kees wondered dazedly what the hell had happened, and looked regretfully at the half-upturned hull of the riverboat, now settling visibly in the water. At least, he thought, he still had his life, though many must have lost theirs. It seemed an almost inadequate compensation. The trail that had led him here was a long one, and now he supposed it was finally ended. The diamonds had been found in a nameless river. Perhaps it was fitting that in such a manner to a nameless river they should return.

Unconsciously, as if already aware of their vulnerability, the little group on shore moved closer together. The *Jacaré* had disappeared round a bend in the river and the helicopter was gone. No-one even noticed: the six pairs of eyes were fixed unwaveringly on the scene three hundred years away across the water. Bostan stared white-faced through the field-glasses.

Immediately after the explosions everything was very quiet. The riverboat tilted drunkenly towards the shore, loose chairs falling like toys into the river. The big stern wheel, so painstak-

114

ingly reconstructed, lifted and revolved slowly, half a turn.

'Come on!' Boston ground out. 'Where the hell is everyone? Attica, that's your girl by the rail. Why in God's name doesn't she jump. Christ, the bloody thing's going to turn over!'

Roderick Ross and the Dutchman came into view, separated from each other by one deck. Ross hesitated, moved to the rail, hesitated again, jumped. Bostan followed his fall, saw the head reappear, the feet start to kick him away from the steamer. 'That was Ross,' he said quietly. 'He's afloat.'

'Fátima!' Attica cried. 'Look, someone's going to help her!' It was true. A tiny man's figure made its way to her side.

'It's that Dutch guy,' Bostan said. 'She won't jump.'

His fingers tightened on the glasses. 'Let go, you stupid cow!' He watched the two figures fall awkwardly over the side, saw their heads emerge above the water. The almost inaudible hum of the camera seemed insect-like in its monotony. About ninety seconds had passed since the first explosion.

Reluctantly, Bostan handed his field-glasses to Attica and started stripping off. 'Seems there aren't going to be too many survivors,' he said bitterly. 'Those there are may be hurt. Who's coming for a swim?'

The young clapper loader, Keith Mayall, had been standing in a trance. Now he came to life. 'I'll come.'

Jesse Cochran didn't even seem to hear. He stood at the water's edge, his fists clenched, and his brain had already discarded the possibility of an accident. 'Bastards,' he whispered, 'fucking, murdering bastards.'

'I'll come out if you like, Turk,' Jack Cane said. 'Though heaven knows I'm not too hot a swimmer.'

Bostan waved the offer aside; he was stripped down to his underpants and on his way into the river. 'Two's O.K., Jack. If something happens to us, you and Jesse'd better do your best to get the others out of here.' He looked at Keith. 'You ready?'

Mayall had stripped too, and Ginny was holding his clothes distractedly, shading her eyes with her free hand and desperately trying to follow Ross' progress towards the shore.

With a bravado he didn't feel, Mayall asked: 'What's the

best thing to do if you're surrounded by piranhas?'

Bostan shrugged. 'They say if you keep on the move, the fish'll leave you alone. Provided there's no blood around.' He realized what he'd said and tried to cover it up. 'Anyway, we'll soon see if it works that way.'

The two men plunged into the river and started to swim, Boston with a jerky but powerful breaststroke, the younger man using an easy crawl that marked him out immediately as a fine swimmer. They made good progress in the still water and were about halfway when the *Mississippi Queen* went under. A wave reached out towards the shore, throwing Ross and Kees forward, and then hiding them from sight. No-one had really known what would be left when the steamer sank from view. The answer was – nothing. The barge had sunk seconds before, and the runabout had gone down with the *Mississippi Queen*. Flotsam bobbed and swirled, and then Attica's expression became horrified as she looked out over the river through the binoculars.

'Some people! They're ... drowning!' she cried. 'I can't look.'

Cane took the glasses, swung them up. Immediately he saw what she'd been looking at: four people hanging onto a large baulk of timber. They seemed to be splashing frantically and trying to get out of the water. The timber kept turning over. Now there were only three heads, and their cries were coming to shore uninterrupted. Suddenly Cane realized what he was watching and yet he couldn't turn away. Now he even recognized one of the figures: a girl. His hands were sweating on the glasses. Out in the river the water boiled and the cries turned to screams. The timber rolled again. 'My God,' Cane muttered. He watched the girl. Just the girl. She seemed to be trying to walk up out of the water, her arms flailing the surface. Her front was scarlet and she sank from view. They all sank and were gone. Eaten alive.

Cane found he was shaking. He turned away and caught Bertram's eye. The cameraman was white as well, unclipping the magazine mechanically, wiping the front of the big zoom lens. 'Worst thing I ever saw,' he mumbled to himself. 'Worst thing I ever saw.'

Before too long Ross arrived ashore, closely followed by Bostan. Thirty yards behind them came Kees and Fátima, hanging on to a hefty piece of wood, with Keith Mayall swimming easily alongside. Ginny rushed into the water to meet Ross and burst into tears.

'Did you hear them?' she sobbed into his ear. 'The screams while they were dying? Oh, Rod, Rod!' She clung to him, and he smoothed her hair, speechless, watching Attica helping Bostan carry the limp form of Fátima up onto the bank. No-one trusted themselves to say anything. The needs of the injured girl were at that moment a blessing in disguise, acting as a much-needed buffer between the events of the past few minutes and the grim reality of their situation.

Kees unbuttoned his shirt and looked out over the river. A stray current was taking a line of debris slowly towards a backwater a quarter of a mile downstream. It would be worth checking later. Then he looked at the group of people clustered round the girl on the ground. Ten, including himself. Mentally he catalogued them, sorted them into teams. Ross, the writer, and his girl. Bostan, the logical leader, and Attica Alloui. And her pretty little assistant with the busted leg. Jack Bertram and Keith Mayall, the top and bottom of a very competent camera crew, the middle links now gone Jesse Cochran, young swinging film director. And Jack Cane, a not so young but still swinging film star. Kees sighed inaudibly and looked downriver along the bank where battalions of trees crowded the sunlight. The jungle was a big place, unfriendly and unforgiving. Wherever they were, it was north of the Solimões, the main Amazon, southwest of the Rio Negro, and the rains were on the way. They would be lucky to beat the house : the odds were stacked in all the wrong places.

Chapter 9

In the helicopter there was very little room to move. Scaffa was piloting the machine, one of the talents he had acquired in the Brazilian Air Force before he had been cashiered for running a private passenger service across neighbouring borders. Pereira occupied the filming position, and Luiz had somehow crammed his bulk in behind. Below them the riverboat was sinking fast, and Pereira scanned the upper decks for signs of life. There was surprisingly little. He slipped his headset over his ears. 'Where are they all?'

Scaffa circled the sinking craft. 'I suppose many of them were in the dining room. Not the best of places.'

Pereira turned his attention to the barge: it had virtually disappeared. The *Jacaré* had already rounded a bend in the river. 'O.K.,' he told Scaffa, 'let's go see our friends on the launch.'

Luiz's voice came over the phones. 'They'd better slow down if they want to make it to Santa Maria.' The other two said nothing. Now they could see the *Jacaré* under them, and two figures on the deck giving them the thumbs up. Pereira glanced at his watch. Luiz was waving madly.

Without warning, the *Jacaré* disintegrated amidships. The bow seemed to shoot forward like a skimmed pebble, and the tiny figures were engulfed in a core of blood-red flame which flowered out and up like a momentary crown. 'Move, for Christ's sake!' Pereira yelped into the headset. 'I don't want to be burned out of the sky!'

Obligingly, Scaffa sideslipped towards the bank. A column of black smoke tunnelled upwards as full fuel tanks ignited and burned fiercely aboard the wrecked launch. Luiz was a hired killer with an atrophied conscience, but somewhere along the line, perhaps as a boy in the *favelas* of Belém, he had come to believe in sides, choosing them and sticking by them. 'There was no need for it,' he said. It was a statement of fact.

'Loose ends,' Pereira informed him. 'Imagine them running into the first one-horse town on the river in a boat like that. Questions. Police. Half the government will be in a panic by tonight when the radio stays silent, half the world interested by tomorrow. So ... no loose ends.'

The noise of the fresh explosion had beaten its way through the tepid air and into the trees on either side of the river. The thick riverine undergrowth absorbed and stopped the sound, but in one place a small, almost dry creek pierced the mantle of wood and the sound rolled uninterrupted along it. A bare two hundred yards from the river the creek widened into an *igapo*, a comma of water left over and isolated from the last floods. To thousands of birds the lake was a feeding and breeding ground, and among those thousands was a large colony of egrets and another of scarlet ibis. They rose as one when the thunder rolled in from the river, and Scaffa's sideslip took him right in among them.

The chopper turned into a flock machine, shredding the birds feather from flesh. Violent thumps shook the craft as it clawed for height, and clouds of pink and white feathers spiralled downwards. Pereira gripped the sides of his seat, but Scaffa remained cool. 'We're out of it,' he said at last. 'Must have been the bang put them up.'

Pereira relaxed a little. 'Let's see if we can get to the rendezvous point without any more disasters.' His heart was beating overfast inside his rib cage. 'My heart,' he half-joked to Scaffa. 'It doesn't like near misses.'

Scaffa grinned across at him. It was at that moment that the motor cut out completely and the helicopter sycamored down towards the waiting trees.

There was no time to do anything, still less to feel scared.

Scaffa cursed briefly as they fell, and then they were all bracing themselves for the impact. The craft, its air intakes completely blocked by dead birds, crashed heavily into the top branches of a huge jacaranda tree where its purple flowers made a colourful bubble on the green surface of the forest canopy. Foliage fled upwards past the windows, scraping and tearing till it slowed, stopped. Terrified monkeys leapt out of the trees in panic, some of them crashing the one hundred and thirty-five feet to the gloom of the forest floor. Birds, snakes, butterflies, hornets – a host of creatures fled together across the jungle rooftop. Soon their various alarm calls faded away, and there was silence so absolute that it rang loudly in the three men's ears with the clarity of a tuning fork. Enmeshed in the high branches, the helicopter looked like the skeleton of a creature long since dead.

Pereira, Scaffa and Luiz exchanged glances. Luiz crossed himself for the first time in twenty-five years. Gingerly, Pereira opened the door on his side of the cabin and scented air flooded in. Scaffa opened his door as well, forcing it out against the cracking resistance of smaller branches. The craft lurched.

'Mother of God,' Scaffa hissed. 'I can't take much of this. What the hell's keeping us up?' It was a good question. At the front, back or sides there was no evidence of a branch of any substance.

'The rope,' Pereira told Luiz. 'You're sitting on it.' Gently Luiz probed under his body for the heavy polythene bag containing the slim line.

'Here,' he said. 'Will it bear the weight of a man?'

Pereira grunted. 'We'll soon find out.'

Scaffa said. 'That's nylon. Strong enough to take the weight of an elephant.'

Luiz wasn't convinced. 'How the hell are we going to hold on to it? And is it long enough?'

Pereira had tied a wrench to one end of the rope. Cautiously he shifted position slightly and started lowering it out of the door, feeding the rope through his fingers.

'Fifty metres,' he said. 'We have fifty metres. No tree's as tall as that.'

'Ours is taller than the rest –' Luiz started, but fell silent under a withering glance from Scaffa.

The rope went limp and Pereira jerked at it a couple of times. The spanner fell and took up the slack. As it went down, Pereira talked. 'If there's anything aboard that you think might come in useful, try to lay your hands on it without moving too much. There's a lightweight supply cover in the back; we'll take that, it's waterproof. We've got a pistol, a rifle, no food, no medicine – Luiz, do you have your knife?'

The other nodded.

'Look in the tool kit, there must be a file to sharpen it – and electrical wire, for fixing traps. What else?' To Scaffa: 'Bring all the maps and pencils. And Luiz, give him a screwdriver. Get that compass off!'

With nearly all the line paid out, the spanner got immovably wedged. 'May that be Mother Earth,' Pereira prayed. He zipped up his jacket and turned slowly to face the others. 'We could have knotted the rope,' he said. 'But I'd prefer it was as long as possible.' He shivered. 'I'll go first. What worries me is pulling this bloody machine out of the tree after me. Cristo, it's black down there, black as the Negro.' He leant forward and stripped the white tropical seat cover off the back of the seat. 'Protect your hands when it's your turn.'

'How will you signal?' Scaffa asked.

'Fire your gun,' Luiz suggested.

Pereira looked at him scathingly. 'It's only forty metres: I'll just try shouting. Otherwise come down when the rope no longer bears my weight.'

Pereira fastened the end of the rope round the door frame with a bowline.

'Wish me luck,' he said. Now that the time had come he could feel his own reluctance; it was like descending into the black depths of a river, and Pereira hated the thought. But that was something between him and his past, and he slid quickly out of the cabin. The branches dragged at him, slowed his progress. Carefully he let himself down, trying hard not to move jerkily. Above him the outline of the helicopter gradually broke up until it was just another shape in the endless skein of branches.

Quite suddenly, Pereira found himself below the crown of the tree and able to look down. The sight sickened him. It was akin to looking down from the inner apex of a cathedral roof while hanging above the altar on a piece of quivering cotton thread. Pereira trod hard and felt the rope catch reassuringly between his feet. Then he moved out slightly and down over a branch. Six feet further down his eyes levelled with the piece of rope where it was chafing against the tree; already whiskers of nylon filament were apparent at the point of abrasion. Pereira blanched, and started on down in earnest. Within seconds he was hanging in a gloomy void, while in the near-darkness below, around and even above him reared the die-straight trunks of the forest giants, branchless and huge, like piles driven in prehistory to support an unbuilt city.

A spider on his web, he slipped towards the forest floor. Fifty feet. Thirty. Pereira gasped with the tension on his arms. Like a stranger from another planet his feet reached out for earth, scraped it, rested, stood secure. He looked up, staggered and stepped on something hard. The spanner. He wanted to laugh. Great booming cries of laughter echoed in the vaulted forest, rebounded mockingly from buttressed trunks, died to a whimper in an eternity of trees. Pereira sobered, looking about. He was alive, it was true, but for how long?

During the time that Jack Bertram and Attica were improvising with a mike boom to splint Fátima's leg Turk Bostan was trying hard to assess the situation. So much had happened in such a short time that he was, like the others, in a state of shock. He didn't dare think about the carnage that must have taken place aboard the boat, the sheer bloody destruction of scores of unsuspecting people. For the first time in his life he found himself being deeply critical of Viktor: how much had Totm known that he hadn't passed on? Viktor had misjudged his enemies, who had, through their hired agents, proved capable of efficient sabotage and indiscriminate killing. A pawn in the game, he, Bostan had sailed his team into the jaws of the Green Hell that would probably cause their deaths as surely as a bomb, but in its own slow way.

He realized that the solution to any problem as fundamental as survival must have tentative beginnings. They could start by pooling their resources, trying to rationalize the imminent future. Or perhaps the best course would be simply to wait until the inevitable air search got under way. Viktor would comb the whole of Brazil for them if it proved necessary.

Bostan watched the Dutchman get up and move into the group around the girl. She looked up at Kuyter through half-closed eyes and said simply, '*Merci. Je serais morte ...*' He smiled, but his eyes were on her leg. Jack Bertram had straightened it as best he could, but it still looked wrong. Kees touched it gently and could actually feel the edges of the fracture under the bruised brown skin. As a break it was clean enough.

'Hold her,' he told Attica. He pointed past Bertram. 'That black bag.'

'The changing bag?' Bertram was surprised.

'Fold it and let her bite on a corner. Listen,' he told Fátima. 'Your leg will be perfectly all right, but it must start out straight. You understand? Otherwise ...'

He was still talking as he gripped the leg above and below the break, pulled and twisted slightly, and felt the muscles pull the bones together. The girl arched her back and gasped, but by that time it was over. Bertram took the corner of the thick changing bag out of the girl's mouth.

'Call these Wren's drawers in the business,' he said. 'Never thought I'd see them used for anything like that. Thanks,' he told Kees, 'I hadn't the nerve to do it.'

Kuyter splinted the leg and wrapped a shirt round it. Then he bound the whole thing in a broad cocoon of camera tape.

Attica touched him on the arm. '*Tu parles français?*'

'*Oui.*'

'*Alors, if faut que je dise la même chose.* Thank you. From the bottom of my heart. You have acted so bravely, there in the river. I –.' She was unable to finish as Bostan cleared his throat and began to address them.

'We are ten,' he started. 'Looks like that's all the survivors there are.' Abruptly he stopped talking as emotion welled up in his chest and made speech impossible. His own words rang in his ears. How could it be that the incredible sentence he had just uttered was the truth? How could he face them, knowing what he knew? What had Viktor done in this God-forsaken country that had earned an act of retribution like this?

He felt a hand on his arm and saw Attica gripping his wrist. Her delicate fingers seemed to possess at that moment an exquisite strength, and the bite of her nails on his skin allowed him to shift the focus of his mind. Recrimination wouldn't get them out of here. He realized with shame that he had been near to breaking. With an immense effort he cleared his throat and turned to face them again.

'I'm sorry. Look, we are the survivors, and whatever the odds we must go on trying to be just that. Our means of transport, communication and food may be all gone, but we still have our lives and our ability to think and act.' He hesitated. 'Obviously there can be no-one here who thinks that this thing was an accident. It was too carefully planned and executed.' His voice strengthened as anger surged into it. 'I'm forced to conclude that it was the work of Pereira and his goddamned crew. I can't see any alternative. The question in your minds must be – why? You may think I have some private knowledge of this awful thing: believe me, I don't. But I have to tell you that before we sailed, Brett Alders told me that in his opinion the craft had been under observation since the time she was being refitted. There were little incidents in Belém and on the river. And he reckoned that the original skipper, Tabox, and some of the officers quit for reasons other than the ones they gave.'

He stopped and looked round at them all. Should he mention Viktor, his huge parcels of Brazilian land, the thousand and one ways he could have made powerful enemies? He decided against it, and pressed on.

'You'll see that there was really no reason to suspect anything, let alone a cold-blooded massacre.' He looked down for a moment. 'Before we get around to seeing what we have and what we don't, I don't know if there are any among you who are at all religious, but I guess the least we can do is to observe a two minute silence and think about our friends and colleagues who are now at the bottom of this river.' He turned and faced the calm clear surface of the river, and the others followed suit.

This water, Attica thought, has taken the hopes, worries, possessions, illnesses, debts and laughter of sixty people. She appreciated Bostan's attempt to force them to think, to tie up the incident in their minds so that having come to grips with it they could cope better with their own predicament. She realized, too, that he had felt awkward, like an actor with corny lines. He was assuming responsibility, which was predictable, just as it had been almost predictable that he would swim out to help the others ashore. Thank God for Bostan, she thought. Whatever his faults, he was a man.

The pile of film equipment was stacked in a heap, an imposing pile of silver and matt black boxes, and Bertram looked at it sadly. Some of the best gear in the world, sophisticated, expensive, a specialised product of the twentieth century, and in the final analysis totally useless. It couldn't be eaten, used to provide food or ridden, so it was out, junked, just like that. And only an hour ago a small host of people had been complying with its every whim. Under his instruction, Keith Mayall had stacked it neatly. Bertram just had the feeling that if he got out alive he'd have to come back for it: he couldn't bear the thought of fine machinery left slowly rotting over the years.

He had, however, sorted out those items which he thought might come in handy – an expensive fixed-focus 90 mm lens which, apart from its photographic applications, would serve to start a fire of two. And two tripods were in pieces; a small Miller had seemed just right for the girl to use later as crutches, and the legs of the big cine mount would serve as struts for a litter in case they needed to move her before that.

But Kees had shaken his head and said that the binoculars would do just fine for lighting fires, if they ever got to see the sun, and as for crutches, they were out of the question; not only were they impossible to use over the sort of soft ground they could expect to find, they could cause the girl agony both in her leg and under the arms. She must be carried, at least for a few days. Jack Bertram didn't argue as he seemed to know what he was talking about, and to have already assumed that they would be going on a trek.

The only other items that were finally considered useful from among the camera gear had all been in the accessories box: rolls of strong cloth tape, a packet of chalk, tape measure, ball of twine and the changing bag, because material of any sort was at a premium.

'O.K.,' Bostan said at last. 'Let's see what else we have. Firstly medicines. Did anyone bring any ashore?'

Jack Cane, Bertram and Ginny all had, the most comprehensive collection being Bertram's, who carried a small private medical bag with his personal camera gear. Altogether there was a bottle of paracetamol, another of aspirin and a tube of insect repellent; some Band-aids and aureomycin, cherry-flavoured lip salve, Nivaquin, salt tablets, Milk of Magnesia, Sylvasun and Sennacot.

'Jack,' Bostan went on. 'Food, Any offers?'

There was a collective shaking of heads. Jesse Cochran produced two candy bars, but besides that there was just the hamper lying in the shade full of Annelli's lunches.

Bostan grimaced. 'Well, that's that. There should be a bottle of cognac in there somewhere, legacy from Brett.' There was a silence which Bostan hurried to fill: everyone had liked Alders. 'Clothes – Jack, you and Attica aren't really dressed for the new parts. There's been a re-write.' Cane and Attica were wear- the respectable fashions worn by visitors to New Orleans at the end of the nineteenth century.

'Thing to remember is,' Bostan continued, 'that it gets cold in these parts at night. I don't know that for a fact myself, but –'

'It seems cold,' Kees interrupted quietly. 'And when the rains come, colder still. We must take all the clothes we can find.'

Boston gave him an uneasy look, but went on: 'Weapons. Do we have any guns?'

Jack Cane was on the point of declaring the .32 he was carrying in his attaché case, but then decided against it. Instead he shook his head with the others.

Kees watched Cane's eyes. 'Some of us have knives,' he suggested, palming his hunting knife. Several of the others had pocket knives with a variety of attachments, and Brett had brought a machête ashore on his first run for clearing a space.

'I suppose we'll be using that a good deal,' Keith Mayall said.

Kees shook his head. They could all do with a little encouragement. 'When we get away from the river into the forest there's little undergrowth,' he said. 'It's like a well-kept park.'

Bostan stopped sorting equipment. 'Hey, Dutch, hold your fire. That's next in the agenda, our course of action, not a foregone conclusion. Let's get this right – we may never have to walk anywhere. When our radio stays silent, they're going to put up an air search. As long as we have the means of attracting attention, a fire, say, they'll spot us. But in any case, surely the first rule is to stay by a river? Try to make a raft, maybe, float downstream?'

Kees shook his head.

Bostan appealed to the others. 'Look, all our lives are at stake. I'm the first to admit I know very little about the jungle. If you know things I don't, don't be coy. Let's hear them.' He paused briefly. 'Well, do you?'

Kees was silent for a moment, then he squatted down in front of them on the ground and picked up a stick. Now was as good a time as any to relay the bad news. But his first remark was harsh in tone and ambiguous in meaning, and was poorly received.

'I'll tell you what I think and what I'm going to do. You don't have to do the same.' He ignored the exclamation from Cochran, and gouged two lines in the earth. They made a lopsided Y, and in between the forks he scored an X. Now he had their attention.

'Our captain, Pereira, whatever else he was, knew the rivers. To take a large boat off the main waterways in any season one must have special knowledge.' He toyed with the stick. 'I say "off the waterways" because these people would have been stupid to take us within twelve hours of our destination and sink us. And we know they weren't stupid. If this is the Amazon, this the Negro, then we must be somewhere here, because for days now we've been travelling just a little north of west. It's early April –' he glanced at his watch, '– the sun should be almost overhead at midday on the Equator. We can check that. With luck, we're still a degree or two south of it. If we sit down and work out the time we've been sailing and for stoppages, and try to assess our average speed and direction it should give us a good idea of where we really are. But as for air searches, forget them. Have you all seen the jungle from the air?' He glanced up and round at their faces. 'Could you see a speck of dirt on the ground from where you're standing? Because that's what we are down here. Nothing.'

'Then what must we do?' It was Attica, her eyes fixed on his face.

'First, we must see what's come ashore from the wreckage. It's scattered along the bank down there. You see the river? It's stopped moving completely. Maybe tomorrow it'll start to flow backwards.' He stopped, and could almost feel their frustration and incomprehension. 'Look,' he started, 'it's always raining in the Amazon basin. Now it's finishing in the south, the big rivers are all full; in the north, even the Negro is slowed and blocked, so the waters rise everywhere. What will happen here, I can't say. But look how deep the water must be even now to swallow a huge boat. Look at the shore, the trees here. You can see it floods. Maybe twenty, thirty, forty feet. And here the rains are imminent and conditions will be impossible.'

Jack Cane spoke, his usually well-modulated voice harsh. 'If what you're saying is true, what the hell can we do? If we stay here we're doomed. To build a raft and float the wrong way for six months isn't my idea of salvation. We can't walk downstream, it's impassable.' He laughed a little wildly. 'Maybe we should just give up and shoot each other now?'

Kees looked at him. 'With no gun?' His voice toughened. 'There may be a way out, but we must move fast. South. We must try to walk a little west of south until we reach a river that is flowing – perhaps the Solimões, and perhaps we can then contrive a way of floating downstream.'

'How will we know,' Attica asked, 'if it's the right river?'

Kees held the stick easily in his right hand, and snapped it in two between thumb and forefinger. 'When we come to water that is brown and muddy, plagued with pium flies and mosquitoes, flowing slowly from right to left, when we realize it's a clear day but you still can't see the other bank, then,' he stood up slowly, 'we will have found the river sea.'

Chapter 10

The ketch was beautiful, sleek and fine, and along the side of the bow was inscribed in gold *Quadalquivir*. It was the name given by the Moors to a Spanish river, and derived from the language they had brought with them across the sea: *wadi kebir*, Arabic for 'big water'.

Viktor Totm was a thickset man of medium height. In spite of his wealth he had refused to succumb to the soft life, and his yacht, a sixty-five footer designed by Sparkman & Stevens, was no toy. In it he had sailed the oceans of the world, sometimes green faced with *mal de mer* but always enjoying the struggle against a tireless adversary, the sea.

In the after cabin Totm waited impatiently for the phone to ring. Above the tall aluminium masts rose the steep, rocky cliffs into which the yacht club had been built; and above them against the sky were a cemetery, church and several hotels lining the Ladeira da Barra, which led up into the Brazilian city of Salvador.

Totm was worried. Twenty-four hours previously the scheduled twice-daily reports from Amazonas had ceased. As the riverboat carried auxiliary radio equipment Totm awaited the second report; when it too failed to arrive the knot of unease solidified into something far more unpleasant. First he had checked with his people in Manaus: could the fault be at their end? No, they assured him, transmissions which had been clear and as regular as clockwork had stopped abruptly. Next Totm had contacted the director of one of his subsidiary holdings and told him to get a plane up to the next rendezvous immediately. It was, in fact, tomorrow that Turk Bostan was due to have left the boat and flown down to Salvador for a meeting. Totm had acted quickly on the fears relayed to him by Bostan: investigation of a company called Overseas Land Development had revealed a disturbing skeleton of facts; and early that morning he had learned that the Xeruini River, a tributary of the lower Negro scheduled as the location for the next week's filming, was empty; moreover the ruins of deceased rubber king Carlos Tinto's estate were deserted. The pilot had flown the length of the river upstream and down, as far as it was navigable, and seen no sign of life. Reluctantly Totm got through to the ministry in Brasilia to request a priority air search of the entire region. Then he placed a call to New York.

At his elbow the phone, wired into the city's network as part of the club facilities, beeped softly. A voice told him: 'New York for you, *Senhor.*' Totm spoke in Hungarian.

'Stefan, Viktor. Something is very wrong at this end.' He listened briefly, and broke in: 'No, I feel it is too late for that. The best thing you can do is send me Cěrvak. Yes, now. Send him down on the plane. And give him the files to read.' Again a pause. Totm's fingers drummed impatiently on the glass-topped table. 'Don't blind me with technicalities, Stefan, I neither know nor care what a spoiler jack is. Ring Eastern, then; get a 707. And Cěrvak. Here.'

Andrej Cěrvak was five feet ten inches tall with a shaven head. His face was broad, with its planes chiselled away at angles round the slanting Slavic eyes usually hidden behind amber sunglasses. From the neck down he looked, and was, a difficult man to stop.

The chartered jet touched down lightly, and two stewardesses saw him smilingly off the aircraft, still curious about their only passenger, who had devoured four steaks and little else. From the airport building a white Mercedes with tinted windows took him to the yacht club.

Viktor Totm watched Cěrvak's muscular body, immaculately

suited, walking towards the yacht. It seemed that everyone in business these days had to have a man like this, and the better your position, the more sophisticated your help. Steps tapped along the deck, directions from the crew: Totm stood up.

'Andrej,' he said. 'What took you so long?'

Cĕrvak widened his mouth to show white teeth, square-cut like the rest of him. 'Chief,' he said.

It took Totm two hours to outline what he wanted and give the details to Cĕrvak. The chain of events had started with the disloyalty of one of the B.E.C. management, John Mayfield. His actions had been induced by Amerigo Lind from a company called Overseas Land Development. And Lind himself operated under the instructions of Coronel Silveiro Falco, the biggest land-owner in the Mato Grosso and owner of the Fazenda Sabaca. When Cĕrvak left, his instructions were clear and his budget unlimited. As calmly as a salesman with an order for furniture he accepted unquestioningly this order for retribution.

Totm watched him go, implacable, efficient and, to the best of his knowledge, incorruptible. He blamed himself for never using Cĕrvak until it was too late. Sweet as honey, blind as a bullet, what real use was revenge?

The noise started without warning, a groaning growl that broke suddenly into a series of reverberating booms. It seemed to feed on itself and multiply until the air was heavy with sound, and echoes and answers came from far away as troops of howler monkeys moved through valleys in the leaf-green canopy.

Attica opened her eyes very suddenly and sat up. Around her the others were doing the same. High above a vague indistinct light filtered through the network of branches and leaves. She scratched at a bite on her cheek, but imediately it started to itch even more, so she smeared it with saliva and concentrated on leaving it alone. To her left and right the twelve foot high buttressed roots of a huge tree formed a sort of nest in which she had made her bed. Beside her lay Fátima, and further round the tree, Ross. The others had all found little niches in close proximity. She looked into the forest, out between the trees, and saw Ginny and the Dutchman tending the beginnings of a small fire.

The English girl had been a big surprise, pointing out things of interest until she realized that the others were just too depressed to respond. It turned out that she had been brought up in Malaya with a jungle like this as her childhood playground. Attica watched Kees crouch by the fire talking quietly to the girl and felt a slow stirring in her mind, a feeling almost forgotten in recent years. She looked down at Fátima and envied her extreme youth. It took her back to her schooldays in Algiers, and suddenly she remembered an old *clochard*, a tramp who had come every Friday one winter to gaze at the girls on their balcony at the lycée. The balcony had been along the corridor from the dormitories and was forbidden territory; but the elder girls used to stand there in their nightdresses, whispering and looking down into the darkness of the Alleé du Marché Couvert. Some of the girls had started teasing him, inching their nightdresses above their ankles and giggling. Attica remembered the night the old tramp reached under his *djellaba* and started to masturbate, his hand working fast on himself as he stared slack-mouthed at the young schoolgirls above him. One of the girls pulled her garment slowly up her legs until her cleft was easily visible from below. The tramp seemed to lean forward at the sight, as if he was about to fall, and the movement of his hand stopped. He grunted loudly, and the girls ran shrieking to their beds. From then on Friday night was a special occasion; the young girls, at the beginning of their lives, and the tramp near the end of his, were in a bizarre symbiosis that in some way served them both.

Attica realized that Fátima was touching her arm. The girl spoke in Arabic. 'Mistress, can you help me?'

Attica got an arm round the girl's shoulders and helped her up. Slowly, they moved round the tree and into one of the empty alcoves between the roots. Fátima held onto the wood, her body tense with expectancy of pain from her leg. Attica unzipped her trousers and pulled them halfway down, smiling at the girl understandingly.

'If you will go and break your bones, of course some things are not so easy. Come, move your good leg forward and lean back against the trunk. No-one can see. I'll get you a tissue from my bag – I think it's the last – after that we'll have to use the bark from the trees.'

Fátima smiled at that, and Attica left her and walked back around the tree.

The previous day had been a nightmare, their first full day in the jungle. On the afternoon of their shipwreck Kees had thought it better to camp by the river for the night. He had sent Jack Bertram and Keith along the bank armed with the machête to see if anything had been washed ashore. They returned two hours later looking shaken and ill. Attica had overheard only a small part of their whispered conversation, but picked out the name of Alders. She hadn't asked them what they'd found because she had no desire to know. They distributed some of the packed lunches, and found a tin of salt as well as Alder's bottle of cognac. Kees had put both salt and cognac aside. Then he went through the camera gear again, this time extracting two silvery lens boxes measuring about ten inches square, explaining that they would serve as cooking vessels. The mid-afternoon had been taken up with a general conversation about their various duties. Fresh in her mind was Kees's face, bleached-out hair, brown skin and eyes that belied his years. She hung on to his every word, because he alone seemed to know, to promise salvation. He gave them things to do, objectives to aim for, spoke to them like children. 'Keep clean,' he'd said, looking at her. 'Everywhere. Particularly your feet. Dry them whenever you can or they'll rot. Wash your socks every night, dry them by the fire or next to your skin. We're lucky: three gas lighters and some spare gas, a little salt and most important of all – this.' He tapped his wrist where watch and compass lay side by side on the same strap. 'Without it, in the jungle . . .' he let the words hang. 'We're also lucky that there's no lack of water. But food is the problem. We must get some fish quickly and dry it. If it starts to rain we may never get another chance.'

So they made their first attempt at living off the land, or at least the water. Ginny had curved two lengths of vine into a circle and taped their ends together. Then she put the back of one of Bertram's shirts loosely across it and lashed it there with string. The result was a little like a fine shallow sieve. She made holes in the material with Kurt's knife and held the finished item up for inspection. She was beautiful, Attica had suddenly realized: long thick hair and a lovely body. Kees took the sieve and smiled down at her. 'Not bad,' he said. 'Now let's see if we can catch something.'

Turk had cut some hefty bamboo poles, and all the men disappeared upstream where a quiet creek led off the main river. The water was covered in patches by floating grass, and jewel-bright birds buzzed its surface. They walked barefoot into the water and surrounded a small area of weed. Kees stood ready with the sieve. On the word, the men disturbed the water with the poles and, like magic, glints of silver appeared near the surface. He slid the sieve sideways into the creek and lifted it out. Two fish flapped in the wet cloth. They all laughed, and Jack Cane said, 'Hell, it doesn't look like we have much of a food problem here.' Within an hour they were back with the others talking excitedly about their success. As their first evening came on, Kees told them about sleeping off the ground on ferns or bamboo, and they set about collecting material. He also explained about the four species of piranha that are reputedly dangerous to man and are attracted to movement in the water. He told them to avoid rotten logs, the home of all manner of ticks and parasites. And above all, that there was in the jungle a very real danger of starving to death. But by that time they had a fire going, with its smoke driving away the insects and fish skewered over the embers; they felt lucky to be alive, and things didn't seem too bad. And how could you ever starve in a land transected by rivers, each one teeming with fish?

The first night had been noisy with unknown sounds, splashes in the river from fish or strange fruit falling into the water. Once an insane scream bubbled out of the darkness and fell awkwardly away to nothing. Frogs called to each other, voices deep from throats as big as a boxer pup's, and when dawn came after a sleepless eternity the silence was shattered once again by howlers, their strident choruses heralding the new day. The confidence of the previous evening gone, the survivors got ready for the first day's trek. As the sun came up over the river behind them and they set off among the trees, hordes of insects surrounded them in private clouds of misery. What little repellent there had been was soon gone and they progressed slowly, Jack Bertram and Keith doing the first stint of carrying Fátima on a makeshift litter. Soon even the few possessions they had weighed unbearably, and unsuspected muscles started to ache. Footwear which had been fine for day-to-day living soon revealed its inadequacy for a march through this sort of terrain. Before long they were strung out through the trees, each lost in his own thoughts, watching feet sink into the thick humus of the forest floor, watching hands, pale against the dark wood of fallen trunks as they clambered wearily over obstacles. Worst of all was the knowledge that it was all just beginning: if they were so soft that the trek was unbearable on the first day, what would it be like in a week's time, when they might be exhausted and undernourished? Though with few exceptions they all had these private thoughts, no-one voiced them, and outwardly morale was good.

It was after they had stopped for a midday short break that the first real hindrance had been encountered. The ground started to moisten and fall away, and shortly the light ahead became brighter. Kees called a halt, and pointed in front of them.

'Swamp,' he said. 'Any track is better than no track at all, so we'll head round it. That's about thirty degrees off course, but it's unavoidable.'

Turk Bostan, strangely silent all day, and Ross took over as litter bearers. Fátima thanked all of them profusely, and the men responded with smiles. Once again the little convoy set off. Five minutes later there was a crashing of foliage and a bellow from the rear, and Cane came running desperately along the line.

'Stop, for Chrissakes, somebody come: it's Jesse, he's been hit!'

Kees broke into a run himself back down the way they'd come. It didn't take long to get to Cochran's prostrate body, face down on the leaves. Kees knelt, and turned him over. There was no need to take a pulse: the top of Cochran's skull was crushed in. He looked around: no more than three yards away a large brown fruit was half buried in the forest floor. Kees shook his head as the others gathered round.

'It was a chance in a million,' he muttered.

Attica fell on her knees beside him, hesitated, then gently closed Cochran's eyes. '*Pauvre* Jesse,' she said.

There was a long silence. Bertram looked down at the fruit, bent, half lifted it by its stalk and changed his mind.

'What the hell is it?' he asked quietly.

Kees looked up. High above their heads could be seen small clusters of yellow flowers, and among them more of the brown fruit, growing directly out of the trunk of the tree. As he looked another fruit detached itself and came plummeting to earth like a missile.

'It's a cannonball tree,' he said. 'Let's move him away.'

They prepared to bury Cochran in a shallow grave scooped out of the leaves. Kees searched the body for personal effects, and then in spite of protests from the others took the shoes: for someone they would come in useful. The watch, medallion, I.D. bracelet and wallet he put into Attica's bag to be sent to the next of kin if they got out. Hesitantly, Jack Bertram asked if they might share out Cochran's cigarettes. Kees tossed them over. Roderick Ross held Ginny's hand. It was incredible how quickly they seemed to have adapted to the presence of death. Yesterday morning it would have been a terrible thing if someone had passed away on the boat. Now a good friend had died, and no-one shed a tear. They were all just standing there, looking lost and stunned.

Kees filled in the grave, covering Cochran's body with humus. The forest people would never bury their dead, he knew, considering it savage. They hung them in the trees, with the jaw tied up so that it wouldn't drop off when insects and climate ate through muscle and ligament. Some tribes devoured the dead flesh, and many took the stripped skeleton, burned it, then crushed the bones to eat the ash with other food. Eating the bones, they believed, allowed the dead one's spirit to live its afterlife in peace.

Kees wiped his hands on his trousers, stood up and looked around. 'Ten little nigger boys,' he thought, 'then there were nine.' Ginny taped two pieces of wood together in the form of a cross and wrote Cochran's name on one of them with a Pentel. It was a futile gesture, but somehow important, and when it was done they moved off again. As they disappeared among the trees, untold thousands of insects were moving slowly through the leaves to Cochran's still-warm body. In one form or another his elements, juices, moisture, would be absorbed into the trees, would all make their tiny contribution to the foliage far above; he might even help to nourish one of the fruit that killed him.

Jack Cane sat on the assorted pile of leaves that had been his bed for the night, and watched Attica helping her girl round the tree. How he felt could only be described as grim. His calves caught fire every time he tried to use them, and he had the beginnings of big blisters on both feet. His face was swollen from the countless bites of the tiny pium flies that had stayed with them most of the previous morning, and then unaccountably left them alone. It was worse, Cane knew, for the litter bearers; they couldn't use their hands. And that was another thing: there seemed no way he could any longer avoid carrying the girl. Cane shook his head and massaged his feet. Surreptitiously he reached behind into his attaché case and brought out a full tube of insect repellent. It didn't seem to work, but psychologically it helped. And damned if he was going to share it with eight others: a tube split nine ways did nothing for no-one.

Attica came back round the tree and he watched her movements, full of natural grace. She reminded him a little of Zenilda, a girl he'd picked up in Salvador before flying to Manaus. She had taken him to the lighthouse at eleven o'clock on a Sunday night. Cane was amazed to find thousands of people there. It turned out that the kids who owned hot-rods would drive them down the coast highway at full speed, coming into the crowd-packed area in front of the lighthouse in a series of skids, broadsides and miscalculations. *Farol*, as it was called, was a regular thing in Salvador every Sunday. The police stayed away until about twelve-thirty, at which time, every week, there was a raid. Hundreds of people leapt over the sea wall and fled along the sands. Others melted into side streets. Still others were arrested. Cane had found the whole thing bizzare, but Zenilda was flushed and excited. He could picture her now, tawny sunstreaked hair, green eyes, long fingers, and a skin the colour of *café au lait*. Her mother, an old Bahiana, fried *vatapá* by the steps of Barra beach.

Cane realized he was doing himself no good at all thinking along these lines. But any escape was better than facing up to their true predicament.

Kuyter was getting fish out of an airline bag that Keith had been carrying. The thought of it made Cane gag, yet at the same time he was aware of his raging hunger. Before he could stop himself his mind ranged quickly to thoughts of cold tomato juice piquant with Worcester sauce, good, thick rashers of Danish bacon and steaming rough-glazed jugs full of coffee. He sat there, helplessly salivating, sick at heart. It was perhaps the first time in his life he had come face to face with a situation from which it was impossible to buy his way out.

It had been in Salvador, too, that the dealer Bretas had flown to see him from São Paulo with a bag of illicit diamonds for sale. He thought of the little chamois *sac* in his case, the dollars those stones represented. Like the camera and pocket calculator they were useless, trading beans from a society where survival of a sort was almost assured, but the quality of that survival was infinitely negotiable. Here, nothing was assured: even the nights seemed cold, confounding the knowledge that this was almost at sea level on the Equator. Cane felt resentful of the mischance that had placed him in this situation. Only too well, he knew his limitations; and he wondered how long it would be before the others knew them too.

Over by the fire Ginny glanced up at Kees and smiled tiredly.

'Now if I were in London,' she said, 'there'd be eggs and toast and marmalade and butter.'

'Don't torture yourself,' Kees told her, 'Here it's fish and more fish.' He held his hands over the fire. 'You know, you English were in at the start when it came to living off this land. You had a naturalist called Bates who went native out here, used to send insect specimens back to England. He wrote in his diary how he used to eat fish and mandioca for lunch, and then, to vary the diet, mandioca and fish in the evenings.'

'Well,' Ginny said, 'there are lots of things we could gather when we come to a clearing. Perhaps we ought to stop and spend a day collecting food.'

Kees shook his head slowly. 'That's the trouble,' he said. 'It takes all day to get enough to keep you alive. But today we'll try to find a clearing, as you said, and we can all look for specific things.'

'What about animals?' Ginny asked him. 'There must be some.'

'Most of them live there,' Kees said pointing upwards, 'and stay there. Of course there are pacas and tapirs and capybaras, but they hear us coming a mile away. If we were staying in one place for a day or two perhaps we could fashion traps like the Indians, find one of their paths to water; they say the animals always travel east-west in the forest, and use the sun to find their way.'

'Can't see how they know where the sun is,' Ginny said. 'Sometimes it's sad being a human being. We have all this knowledge about other species' instincts, and no instincts ourselves to be able to profit from that knowledge.'

Turk Bostan joined them, tightening the belt of his trousers. He grinned wearily at Ginny with a little of his former panache, but behind the look his eyes were haunted, and it was obvious he hadn't slept.

'Bet you wish you had never got the job,' he told her.

Ginny smiled at him warmly. Bostan, she was convinced, was a good guy having a rough time.

'Don't you worry about me,' she said. 'My father grew rubber north of Penang. If it wasn't for you lot I'd have been home by now.'

Bostan laughed a little, and she could see the thanks in his eyes.

Kees told him: 'Don't carry a cross for me either, Turk. Life puts us where it wants. If I wasn't here I'd probably be involved in some other disaster.'

Bostan half turned away, and his voice came out even deeper than usual. 'Thanks, you two.' He walked round the fire looking quizzically at Kuyter. 'You spent a lot of time in places like this?'

Kees watched the water start to boil in the aluminium lens box. 'Some,' he said. 'Not quite like this.'

'Where did you learn English?' Ginny asked him. 'It's perfect.'

'Some of your ex-colonies,' he told her. 'When I was a kid.'

'Do you speak other languages?'

'Sure he does,' Bostan cut in. 'Should have heard him in Italian and Portuguese on the boat.'

Kees had borrowed Jack Bertram's razor and soap. Now he needed a mirror from Attica's bag. 'Excuse me,' he said, and rubbed his chin ruefully. 'Time for a shave.'

Ginny and Bostan watched him walk away towards Attica's tree. 'I wonder who he is?' Ginny mused. 'Not exactly the run-of-the-mill waiter, is he?'

Kees propped Attica's mirror on a bulge in the tree and set to soaping his face. Fátima looked up at him from the ground and said something to Attica in Arabic. Kees kept a straight face.

'That's very true,' he said.

Fátima coloured, and Attica laughed. 'You weren't meant to understand that,' she said. 'It'll go to your head.'

Kees pulled the blade across his chin and winced; it was less than sharp. In Arabic he said: 'She can't run away from me with a broken leg.'

Fátima's colour rose higher still.

'Shame!' Attica told him. 'Chasing young girls when there are grown women around.'

Kees moved his head and saw her face in the little mirror, framed by trees. She became aware of his look, and their eyes met and held in the small piece of silvered glass wedged like a tiny window on the huge treetrunk. The razor stopped its motion momentarily, and the scratching noise was replaced immediately by the distant creaking and groaning of the cipós high above them as a breath of wind swayed the jungle vines. Kees kept his voice light.

'As if we don't have enough problems.'

Her face disappeared from the mirror and he felt her hand alight on his arm.

'You will help us overcome them.'

Turk Bostan watched Kees shaving with Attica's mirror. He felt a twinge of envy for the man, but it was quickly replaced by relief that there was someone the others could look up to and lean on besides him. In his own setting he knew he was as good as any, but this wasn't it. No ratings here, he thought; no stars, costs or product – just trees and water, insects, and a group of frightened, bewildered individuals.

Only a short time ago he had flown down into the Sahara with a briefcase full of promises designed to coax Attica out of her hideaway and back into the public eye. He had landed at a private strip near the Algerian town of Ngoussa, expecting rolling dunes. But the country was like a moonscape, reddish-brown rocks and rubble stretching out bleakly to either side. A Citroën-Maserati had met him and carried him towards a dark green phalanx of palms that seemed to have their roots in a shimmering carpet of air an indeterminate distance above the ground. Sooner than seemed possible, this distant object was right in front of them and they swept into the cool among the huge boles of the trees. Flashes of white and green coalesced slowly into pillars, arches, courtyards, and then the car was stopping, big tyres crunching gravel, the windscreen framing the beauty of the oasis called the 'Wells of Hope'. Later he had flown her to Piccolo Romazzino on Sardinia's Costa Smeralda to meet Viktor Totm, and the Hungarian's personality had clinched what money could not.

The enormity of what had happened suddenly threatened to overwhelm Bostan. His brain filled with scenes from the past few days so quickly that he felt as if his head was about to burst. Unseeing, he backed away out of sight of the others and stumbled blindly among the trees. That they would all die, he no longer doubted. The jungle seemed to stretch forever in every direction, and they were more helpless than ants on the forest floor.

142

Beneath her bright exterior Ginny was extremely worried: Ross's legs had swollen overnight, and now the swelling seemed to be spreading upwards to his trunk.

She loved Ross and had know him for years. He had been her first lover, when she was just seventeen; a young hopeful determined to leave her home in the country and stake her independence in a tiny bedsit off the Earls Court Road. There had been other men since, but she had always returned to him, sometimes for solace after an affair had turned sour, sometimes just because he was there. That Ross had loved her for a long time, she knew; but he had been clever, reeling in the line slowly and never trying to curtail her freedom. Eventually, emotionally exhausted and confused, she had sat down and counted up the men in her life that she could depend on absolutely, whatever the circumstances. That count had only used up one finger on her left hand, and the next week she had suggested to Ross that they might live together.

Since then his career had blossomed, and he had been able to buy a flat in Knightsbridge overlooking the park. Looking back, Ginny realized how impossible she must have been when she was younger, and she loved him all the more for his patience.

It was funny that in some ways they were so different. Ross was such a cautious person. He even mistrusted the principles of powered flight, and it was really very amusing to watch him in the air caught in a blue funk. On the way to Brazil she had teased him mercilessly.

'Poor old thing,' she told him, and watched him cringe at both adjectives and noun. 'All these years I've been thinking of you having a marvellous time with all the hosties, pinching bottoms and joining the Mile High Club when in reality you're scared potty.'

Ross had reached forward to sip his plastic coffee. 'Stuff's a bloody insult,' he ground out. 'Think of the cost of these South American flights, I mean, think of the *cost* while just down there is the original land of the coffee bean, with millions of the little buggers all lying around in steaming brown heaps – and the best the airlines can come up with is this, this revolting bilge-water.'

'It's no good getting angry Rod, just because you're terrified. Flying is safer than –'

'Crossing the M1 in thick fog on a pogo stick. Yes, I know all that rubbish. Anyway, it's not the flying, it's the takeoffs and landings.'

She had leant over then and smoothed his hair. 'Darling, the plane's only half full. And there's only another twenty minutes before we land.'

Ross had brightened slightly at the thought of *terra firma*, but refused to be mollified.

'Might only be half full, but the men are bloody enormous and most of the women pregnant. It's an absolute miracle that we've managed to claw our way into the air at all!'

Ginny had burst out laughing. 'My *God* you can exaggerate! One bird halfway gone and you make it sound like the postwar bulge!'

The thought of this exchange, so recent, had brought a smile to her lips which slowly disappeared as she forced herself to face reality. Tomorrow, she reasoned, the swellings could be gone. Illnesses in the tropics sometimes only lasted forty-eight hours, and often you never knew what you'd had. Determined to look on the bright side, she turned her attentions to serving the fish on plates of stiff green leaves. The *pescadas* they caught had been cut into strips and rubbed sparingly with salt. There had been no time to dry it. As she distributed the boiled fish, Ginny felt curiously amused at their rapid deterioration into roles, with the men out hunting and she automatically taking on the cooking.

Cane ate with a grimace of distaste. Kees looked up at him; as always the actor's small attaché case wasn't far way, and Kees found himself more and more anxious to look inside it. He smiled wryly to himself; he felt nothing for Cane. Perhaps he could walk the man to death over the next week or two.

'Jack,' he said quietly. 'It's you and me to carry the girl.'

Cane nodded without enthusiasm. 'I'll go behind if that's O.K.,' he said. 'You lead the way.'

It was a lot easier behind the stretcher than in front of it, as

Cane had reasoned, but Kees said nothing. He fingered his chin, where a razor cut had just stopped bleeding.

From nowhere, a cloud of pium flies found the group, and immediately everyone was hurrying to cover their exposed skin. There was no point in staying longer. Shouldering their burdens, they moved off through the forest.

Chapter 11

Though the sky was still dark blue, a black shape quested at high speed over the river, well content with the inadequate light. Before the sun's tentative fingers reached out over the land, the bulldog bat dropped, rose to skim the surface, dropped again. When it lifted and sped away over the trees to its daytime hideaway, a fat fish was securely taloned by one back claw. Unimpressed by the efficient display, a *jaburú* walked deliberately through the shallows on stilt-like legs, looking for breakfast, ignoring the floating yellow flowers from the high crown of an *ipê* tree, while like falling blooms themselves bright green and yellow *anacás* parroted raucously against the sky.

Pereira stirred, and turned his back on the river. Ungraciously, he stuck a boot in the direction of Luiz' arse and told him:

'Up, *puteiro*, no good lying there with your *saco cheio* dreaming of some *biscaia* with big breasts.'

Luiz groaned, and Pereira turned his back on him disgustedly, and walked towards the fire where Scaffa was grilling fish.

'See the bat?'

Scaffa nodded. 'Easy for that *bastardo*. Ten seconds; two days' food.'

Pereira squatted. 'We didn't do so bad.'

They had been lucky. The rope from the helicopter had frayed through when Luzi was still fifteen feet from the ground. He landed heavily on his backside, but the forest floor at that point was even softer than usual, and he'd got away with a mild

146

bruise. More to the point, in Pereira's opinion, was the fact that they'd got most of the rope back.

The previous evening he'd split the cord down a bit, and then set off looking for a fishhook. After half an hour's diligent search he found what he was looking for, the trailing switches of the *jacitara*. A climbing plant, it relied on the murderous spikes lining its tendrils to grip and cling like grappling irons to other jungle plants, and its extremities were lined with particularly hard, curved hooks. Carefully, Pereira cut himself some sections of creeper, and moved down the river bank till he spotted an area of mud pockmarked with blowholes. Squatting he dug down with his hand and came up with a short, fat worm. He repeated the process and then rejoined the others.

While Luiz and Scaffa made beds for the night and organized a fire, Pereira set about the first stage of catching a big fish. A hundred yards along the bank, some ten minutes from the others, he found a slight current flowing out of the mainstream into an *igarapé*; already the river was rising. Here the water was cloudy, and along the creek Pereira noticed a tree full of herons gathering to roost for the night, a good sign.

Pereira had been fishing these rivers all his life, and he didn't bother to weight the barbed end of the *jacitara*. He threw the line out and pulled it back across the surface in a series of little jerks, each hook sheathed with a length of worm. On the second cast a thin, shovel-nosed fish about a foot long appeared from nowhere, took the barbs and disappeared. It was a formality to pull it in. Next, Pereira took out his clasp knife and cut the fish into sections; he also cut a long and a short bamboo. With a wedge of wood jamming the knife open at about thirty degrees, he used the cord to bind the blade rigidly in that position, converting the whole knife into one large hook. He hollowed out the sections of the smaller fish, and slipped them over both blade and handle, using the partly unplaited rope end to bind bait, metal and wood into one indigestible bundle.

Gently, with the pole, he tested the depth of the water where the current stopped. At full reach it sank about five feet to the bottom. Pereira nodded to himself, and tied the smaller bamboo onto the line about five feet from the knife; then he looked around for a suitable anchor tree, but there wasn't one. In the end, he passed the rope round the base of several large bamboos and a couple of palms. Rubbing his hands together, he walked back to the water's edge.

Bamboo and baited knife hit the water together, about fifteen feet from the bank, and the knife went down. Pereira sat on his haunches, the rope slack in his fingers, watching the thick length of cane. He didn't have long to wait. In one flurry of movement, the bamboo disappeared and stayed under. The rope in Pereira's fingers hardly moved, but he knew he had to strike before the fish regurgitated. Even then the knife could defeat its own purpose and cut its way out under tension.

Pereira heaved, and it felt like striking an *aroeira* log. Keeping the rope taut, he dug his heels in and leant backwards till his backside was nearly on the bank. Remorselessly, the fish took it all back, and the bamboos started to shake. Salt coursed into Pereira's eyes and he closed them, inching his way backwards up the bank with the rope wrapped round his hands and biting into his flesh. Suddenly he could see the outline of the fish below the surface. *Piraibá*, the giant catfish of the Amazon! He remembered one in his father's day that had been three metres long and weighed two hundred kilos. Slowly he brought the fish in, its mouth gaping hugely and the line disappearing down its throat. Man and fish surveyed each other while Pereira tried to work out how he was going to kill it. The problem was solved by Luiz, who stumbled out of the bushes to find himself witness to an uneven tug of war: with the fish half out of the water, Pereira was giving away seventy pounds.

'*Cristo!*' Luiz managed to say.

Pereira half-opened one eye and closed it again as sweat flowed in.

'Quick!' he hissed, arms nearly out of their sockets. 'Help me!'

Between the two of them it was the work of seconds to drag the five-foot monster onto the bank. It flipped once, exposing a light belly, and then lay still, balefully watching its captors. Pereira rushed to the river to scoop up water and wash his face. Luiz walked round the fish mistrustfully with his hand on his gun.

'No!' Pereira told him. 'Here.'

With Luiz's hunting knife he approached the monster, and drove the point downwards through one eye. The fish quivered in its death agony, and then lay still.

'*Piraibá!*' said Luiz.

Pereira grunted. 'Help me cut it up.'

All that night they had taken turns at keeping the smoke going, feeding the flames with deadwood, then damping them down with leaf and greenery. And by morning some forty pounds of the best flesh lay partially smoked and stacked under the trees. In the absence of salt to cure and time to dry, smoke was the only preservative.

With the sun well up, they set about looking for mandioca, the staple diet of the Amazons. It was Luiz who found a clump of the plant, eight feet tall with its distinctive seven-pointed leaves. The three men set to digging up the tubers, and Scaffa cut the end off one and touched it with the tip of his tongue. Pereira looked at him questioningly.

'*Doce*,' Scaffa told him surprised.

Pereira nodded. There was two varieties, sweet and bitter. Nine times out of ten one found the latter; that these were sweet and could be cooked and eaten directly would save them time and trouble.

They fashioned a backpack out of the helicopter's supply cover, and loaded it with fish and manioc. Then they cut into the jungle and set off parallel to the river bank, Pereira leading the way with the rifle. Mosquitos, deterred all through the night by the smoking fire, took their opportunity to make up for lost time, but it was largely Luiz and Scaffa they attacked. Perhaps, as Pereira had said the previous day, he had been too long on the rivers, and his blood had turned to salty water.

By midday, they were approaching the place where the *Mississippi Queen* had gone down, and Pereira led them back to the thickets at the river's edge. They stopped, and stacked everything in the undergrowth except their weapons. Pereira gestured along the bank.

'Follow me and keep quiet. I don't know how many there are,

but certainly seven or eight. They may have things we can use; food and medicines.'

'Why don't we shoot them,' Scaffa said, 'and be done with it?'

Pereira shrugged noncommittally. 'They're already dead. It's just a question of time.'

'Georges,' Luiz said, 'what about the women?'

Pereira's big fist caught the front of Luiz's shirt.

'*Ai, puteiro*, can you think of nothing else? Our very lives are threatened and all you can imagine is the spread arse of some overpaid Arab tart.'

Wearily, he dropped his hand to his side and turned, holding the rifle in an easy grip. Moving as quietly as possible, the three men set off along the river. Clouds of yellow butterflies floated like chaff before them, and the call of the *serengueiro* cracked like a gunshot between the trees and vibrated to an uneasy silence. Pereira dropped into an *igarapé* that cut through the forest in the right direction. Calf-deep in the reddish water the three men moved slowly forward, working themselves into position. After an hour Pereira stopped. They were standing among the sodden roots of a group of palms, and he gestured them to stay where they were. Parting the foliage with difficulty, he climbed out of the water and disappeared.

Time hung heavy for Luiz and Scaffa as they waited for his return. Drifting clouds of insects found and plagued them and moved on. It was twenty minutes before Pereira slid back out of the greenery.

'They've all gone,' he said. 'Don't ask me where.'

The three of them climbed the bank and reached the survivors' first camp. They searched the equipment that had been left behind but found nothing of use. Pereira looked at the dismantled tripod, and the one leg that remained.

'Crutches,' he murmured. 'So maybe one of them is hurt.' Suddenly he chuckled, an unaccustomed sound evoked by the thought of someone on crutches hobbling slowly among the trees.

Scaffa moved towards the bank, and clouds of insects rose into the air.

'*Pescadas*,' he said. 'They caught some fish.'

Pereira shrugged. 'A child could catch fish in a river like this.' he said. 'But why did they go? And so quickly?'

No-one answered, and Pereira sat, pondering the question in his mind. He knew most people had all sorts of misconceptions about the jungle, and would do anything to keep out of it. Why hadn't they opted to make a raft and head back the way they'd come? They weren't to know the movements of the river would make it impossible. At least he'd have expected them to sit around for a day or two, talking it over and eating fish. It seemed that some of them realized the need for prompt action. So, which way had they gone? It required no great tracking ability to discover the trail of cut bamboo and trampled undergrowth which marked the route plainly. Pereira remarked that they had set off roughly south. That, too, was the right decision. But soon the trail petered out as the heavy foliage near the river bank died away to nothing in the forest gloom.

'Come,' he told the others. 'There's nothing we can do here. Let's get our stuff from back there and start walking. It's over one hundred and thirty kilometres to the big river. We'll never see them again.'

The daytime silence of the forest, the strange and sudden outbursts of noise at night, the perpetual half-light: all served to undermine the most important factor of all for humans in an alien world – the will to live. Strung out between the feet of monstrous trees, the survivors could not avoid feelings of impotence and claustrophobia. Sometimes, discernible as dots against the sky, a troupe of spider monkeys would be seen nose to tail, walking through the branches. Up there, somewhere, the sun was shining, macaws were squabbling in the branches of guava trees, and silky anteaters were curled in hideaways waiting for the night. *Homo sapiens*, used to lording it over other orders and genera, was reduced to marching with the ants, slugs and centipedes of the forest floor.

And about as fast, Kees thought to himself. Try as he would, there was no means of speeding up their progress. The main limiting factor was Fátima, and there was no way she could move as quickly as she was now, flat on her back, by being carried.

But even discounting her there was a marked lack of will among them, an absence of teamwork that was costing them time. People had to be told to do things, and they performed their duties lethargically, as if there was all the time in the world. This was the fourth day, and Kees dared not answer truthfully the question they kept putting to him: how far have we come, and how far is there left to go? Privately, he estimated that the main trunk of the Amazon as it swung north to pass Tefé was at least a hundred kilometres away, maybe twice that. Without maps it was difficult to say. He believed the Amazon reached up to within three degrees of the Equator, and by observation on the first day he was sure they were just in the southern hemisphere. But an error of one degree represented nearly seventy miles, and that distance through the forest could take a fortnight or more. For the tenth time, he tried to calculate their progress. Day one, zero. Day two, the day Jesse died, two or maybe three miles if one discounted the detours. Day three, yesterday, they had stopped early in the afternoon to make a real attempt at food gathering.

They'd camped in a clearing with a fair-sized stream leading away into an area of mangrove. Kees had wasted no time in allocating duties: to Bertram and Mayall he gave the machête and pointed out the various edible palms in the area, all of which would have buds that were edible. Some of the palms were sixty or seventy feet tall.

'Chop them down,' he told them. 'Start the cut on the side where you want it to fall.'

Ginny volunteered to collect fern tips and shoots.

'O.K.,' Kees told her. 'And young bamboo shoots up to a foot high. And water lillies. Take Attica with you.'

Within minutes Ginny had come running back across the clearing clutching a leaf.

'Kees! It's tapioca, isn't it?'

He looked at the leaf in her hand. 'They call it mandioca here,' he said. 'But yes, you're right. Clever girl, you'd better dig them up. But don't eat them raw, most are full of prussic acid. We'll have to grate and rinse them.'

Next in line, Rod said, 'Has she done me out of a job again?'

Kees looked at Ross. He'd hardly said a word since they started walking, but unlike Bostan it wasn't because of what was on his mind: this man was sick.

'How do you feel, Rod?'

The other shrugged. His eyes seemed smaller, because the flesh surrounding them was all puffed up, and his hands were also swollen. There was no question of the swellings disappearing; sometimes it seemed to Kees that the enlargement was almost visible. And the effect on Ross was severe. It was obvious he had great difficulty in keeping up, and his face was pale and distorted. He tried bravely to make a joke of the whole thing. 'For a chap on a starvation diet, I seem to be putting on a lot of weight.'

Bostan and Cane looked at him properly for the first time. 'Hey, I hope it's not contagious,' Cane said. 'These tropical diseases ...'

Kees turned his back on him. 'Rod, I'd like you to look after the fire. Start it small. Turk will supply you with fuel.'

Ross smiled, and gave a Boy Scout salute. 'O.K., skipper.'

That had left Jack Cane. 'If you'd care to come with me, Jack,' Kees said, 'we'll try to get something we all need badly.'

The gathering had turned out well, and in two hours they collected quite a pile of usable vegetables. Kees advised them on their preparation, and although all the food was only greenstuff their morale rose slightly at the knowledge that they could, to a certain extent, live off the land. Attica and Ginny between them shredded the mandioca with a knife, and broke it up still further with some water in the bottom of one of the containers. Then they looked around for a likely sieve; the easiest way of washing out the vegetable's lethal bitterness seemed to be to stuff it into one of Turk's nylon socks, washed first; though Bostan suggested it should be left as it was to impart a real jungle flavour. With a sockful of potential food, the girls found they could squeeze it repeatedly in the stream to rinse it through. Sure enough, after a few minutes, the starch tasted neutral, and they made it into little pie-shaped bôlos for cooking in the ashes at the fire's edge.

Kees showed Bertram and Mayall how to extract the *palmito*, the heart of the different palm buds, and warned them to be careful with the bamboo shoots: along the edge of the young leaves were rows of tiny black hairs. Indigestable irritants, they had to be removed.

The most time-consuming thing of all had been trying to build up the fire enough to burn the roots of the floating water hyacinth that Kuyter and Cane had collected from a small lake further downstream. One of the things that Kees knew only too well was that every pace they walked, they sweated. Salt loss and heat exhaustion caused lethargy and tiredness, and later on muscle cramps and urinary problems. During his time in the tropics he had several times found himself feeling weak and drained, his urine thick, yellow, and passed with difficulty. Salt was an almost magical cure, but the salt tablets they'd had with them were now gone. By getting a really hot bamboo fire going, they were able to burn a large quantity of hyacinth. Afterwards, Kees scraped up the ashes and mixed them thoroughly with water. He then filtered the thin ashy gruel twice through Bostan's well-tried sock. The ensuing liquid was boiled away, and sure enough they were left with some dirty brown crystals of bitter salt.

'Potassium chloride,' Kees told them. 'It may taste bad, but we must take turns all night to make it.'

And so they had. This morning they'd set off with a small quantity of the precious salt in a polythene bag, and those vegetables they had left uncooked the previous evening. But in fact this food was not only unpalatable, it contained no protein and was time-costly to gather. Already the fish they'd caught were gone, and early this morning they had spent two hours catching more. Fish were prolific and could be stampeded into the shallows and speared with sharpened bamboo, but many of the species were bony and fleshless; if the rains started it would be difficult to catch any at all.

Kees pressed on, feeling the frustration of their slow progress, and travelling far in his mind to make up for it. It required no great stretch of imagination to cast his thoughts back to another jungle in Borneo; that was where he'd met Chinese Billy, and experienced the strangest meal of his life.

Billy had no hair on his face, but a growth about three fingers wide that joined his ears via his neck like a chin strap. For weeks Kees found it difficult to look Billy in the eyes, his gaze being drawn repeatedly to this squirrel's tail of hair convulsively bobbing up and down on his Adam's apple.

It was Billy who had taken him to Kapitan China's place. Everyone pronounced it 'Cheena', like the Brazilian way of saying Tina. He lived in a ramshackle house near the wharf, distinguished by smelly monsoon drains and broken plastic toys all over the path. At the back, built on stilts and almost integrated into the trees, there was a timber eating-room with big rattan blinds and a long bench table. It had been a cool place, dimly lit by a lamp that somehow percolated light past the spiralling legions of moths into the rest of the room. Fluttering overhead, insect shadows boxed a lightshow on the ceiling. There had been six of them, all men, and the meal started off well. At one end of the table there was a hole, about the size of a fist. Kees hadn't known what it was for, and was a little slow to catch on even when they brought the monkey in. The Kapitan watched him closely, talking vociferously the while in Cantonese. Everyone laughed. The monkey was the odd one out; he just looked miserable and sleepy. A woman pulled back the end section of the table and pushed the monkey so that it was standing with its neck in the hole. Then she slid the table back together, so the animal was securely held by the neck. Billy filled the glasses. The room started to recede into the distance, except for the disembodied head of the monkey, the reason for whose presence at the feast he still hadn't been able to divine.

'Don't worry, Dutch,' Billy told him. 'It's drugged.'

He remembered thinking: what's drugged? The drink? Kapitan Cheena picked up a heavy looking parang and stroked the edge with his thumb. Satisfied, he nodded to the man opposite him, who leant forward and held the monkey's face and the back of its head between huge hands. Cheena squared up to the top of the monkey's head as seriously as a golfer who's got to get a birdie on the eighteenth. A sentence from a guidebook had leapt into Kees' mind. 'Red leaf monkeys are a popular food among the Chinese population'. But cooked, surely? How ... ?

Cheena's hand moved with a blur of speed. There was a wet crunch and a grunt of approval from the diners. When Kees looked up the table, the big man was wiping his hands and Cheena was cleaning the knife. The monkey, now trepanned and minus the top of its head, lethargically blinked on as if nothing had happened. Bowls of sauce were put in front of them, and Cheena picked up a long kris and a fork, and leant towards the open cranium.

'You like monkey blains, Dutchman?' he'd asked.

Borneo, the land below the wind, had been good to him, he thought, and he'd stayed in Semporno awhile, working with Billy for a man called Fatt. Fatt was a trader, after a fashion, and every night they loaded his boats full of contraband for the Philippines: gin, cigarettes and people. He could almost feel the sinking sun on his face as it drowned in the low green mantle of the mangrove, hear the crackle of the outboards as he fed them power, see the oily surface of the water churning yellow. Then the bow would lift and settle on a course across the Sulu Sea and Billy would catch his eye, sitting on a million Rothman's but smoking the pungent leaf of the Niah palm ...

Kees was so lost in his thoughts, that he almost failed to notice a slight movement through the tangled mass of vegetation to their right. They were walking round the edge of the same inundated ground above which they'd camped, and slowly coming back onto a southerly course, when another movement riveted his attention. It took him time to register what it was he was looking at, so well did the combatants merge with their surrounding in the dappled light. The dark shape that subconsciously he'd accepted as a log was now revealed as a cayman. It was a big one, maybe nine feet, but its fearsome mouth and scaly armour were proving useless in its present predicament: the cayman was held irrevocably in the massive coils of a sucurí, the giant anaconda of the Amazons.

Kees dropped to the ground, and as the others came up one by one, he motioned them to silence and beckoned them over. Jack Bertram and Keith were first, and they placed Fátima's stretcher on the ground. Bertram was looking gaunt and old; too old, Kees thought, for a hike like this.

The girl sat up, eyes like moons. '*Qu'est que c'est?*'
'*Le prochain rèpas*,' he told her. 'If we're lucky.'
Jack Cane came up, followed by Attica and Turk.
'What is it?' he whispered.
Kees gestured through the trees towards the wet ground. A breath of wind reached down from the distant treetops and swayed the *sipós* and palm crowns in the lower canopy. Crouched together, dwarfed by the huge girth of an *arapotenga* tree, they all peered down to the mangrove's edge. Nothing moved. Blue and black *morphoes* butterflies floated through the forest on six-inch wings, and sounds of distant contention floated down from above.
Suddenly Bostan said quietly, 'I see it.'
The cayman's skin was blue-green in the gloom, matching the patches on the big snake; the rest of its slowly contracting body was a rich living gold.
Now they all saw it. 'Is it a boa constrictor?' Attica asked.
Kees shook his head. '*Sucuri*. They can grow to over eleven metres. But six or seven is a lot of snake.'
'But it kills by crushing?' Rod asked.
'In a way,' Kees told him. 'Every time you breathe in, it hugs you a little closer. Stops you breathing in the end.' He paused, and a new note crept into his voice. 'Now, who's coming with me down there?'
There was a horrified silence. Cane cleared his throat nervously.
'What for?'
The question, coming as it did from Cane, snapped something inside Kuyter's head. The frustration of shepherding them through each day, answering their questions, putting up with their moans, had driven him to the limits of his self control, and now he let go.
'What for? You stand there and ask what for?' He swung his eyes angrily across their faces. 'Christ, what's wrong with you people? We're starving to death and you can't even recognize meat when you see it.' His voice was sibilant and low. 'We won't find any caviare or waiters out here. If you want something, you've got to go out and get it.'

As suddenly as he had started, he stopped. The outburst was so uncharacteristic that the others stood rooted to the spot, mute.

'We're looking at more meat than we can carry,' Kees told them tiredly. 'And there's no time to lose.' Slowly he picked up the machête and lifted his gaze. 'Turk?'

Bostan stood up slowly, and nodded. 'What'll we do?'

'Work our way closer, and locate its head. I'll make a frontal approach. It won't be able to do anything without leaving the cayman. You have this,' he thumbed the machête's blade, 'and come in from the side. They're thin behind the neck. Hit it right, and you'll behead it. Then get the hell away.' He looked at Bostan sympathetically. 'It's a chance of a lifetime,' he said softly. 'That's protein down there; life. We could walk through the forest for years and never see a living thing that wasn't an insect or a bird.'

The others watched quietly as they disappeared among the trees towards their objective. Soon the ground grew sodden underfoot and it became difficult to move without sound, each step, squelching and sucking in the thick muddy litter at the mangrove's edge. They reached a point only ten yards from the reptiles beyond which there was little cover. The air was foetid with the released gases of rotting vegetation, and mosquitos and flies harassed them mercilessly. Kees pointed. 'Work your way round there, it's drier. The head is facing to the right, you see it?'

Cayman, snake and roots were inextricably entwined in such a way that the cayman appeared to be sitting up and begging. Its long snout and head protruded from the death grip at an angle, and the irregular line of its lower jaw, teeth settling outside and not inside the upper, gave it the appearance of grinning, as if the whole idea of being extinguished in such a manner was an esoteric source of amusement.

Kees watched Bostan's figure sliding between the trees, and then he moved noisily out into the open. The snake picked him up immediately, and he felt a lurch in his stomach as the first four feet of its body reached out from the cayman, questing forward and back to assess the new threat. Anacondas, Kees knew, found their favourite prey in caymans like this one, and the web-footed capybara, the world's largest rodent. Once they'd killed, the snakes swallowed their victims whole, which in the case of a fully-grown capybara meant a pig-shaped animal weighing seventy kilos. The absence of well documented cases of the snakes attacking man might be explained by man's upright posture, making him look bigger than he really was. Or, Kees thought, perhaps it was just that men don't do much documenting in the belly of an anaconda.

Ten feet from the weaving head he stopped, raising his arms to increase his height still further. The Indians said the sucurí had eyes as big as the full moon, and as its head drew back Kees snatched a glance at the cayman. Its eyes, too, were wide open, but it was immobile, seemingly dead. On the periphery of his vision he could see Bostan coming in from behind, the machête raised. Suddenly the big coils round the cayman loosened, and with a fluidity that belied its bulk the anaconda flowed out towards Kees. Afterwards, he was never quite sure why he didn't simply get out of its way. The animal was probably just heading for the safety of the water, its habitual home. Instead, he grabbed it behind the head as it came past and tried to cut through the neck with his knife. The snake's movement were not overtly dangerous like the ripping fangs and hind claws of an *onça*, but there was no mistaking the enormous, controlled strength of its muscular body. In a second, the weight of one coil had pulled Kees to the ground, and he felt its insidious grip tightening on his legs. The knife dropped from his grip and he got both hands round the creature's neck and tried to hold its head at arm's length; he could see Bostan moving towards him as fast as he was able through the slime.

'My knife,' he called urgently, 'get my knife! Cut it behind my hands!

Warily, Bostan crouched near the tightening coils and picked up the knife. In the same movement he reached down and drew the blade forcefully across the light skin beneath the snake's throat. The fine-honed blade reached the spinal column before the reptile exploded into action and Bostan was hurled bodily into the air. He landed unhurt on the soft ground, and saw Kees, still holding the head, its jaws agape, at arm's length. His body was covered in blood, tossed this way and that as the *sucuri*'s energy and strength left it forever in a cataclysm of undirected effort. Soon just the slow creeping of muscle under the smooth skin gave evidence of recent life.

'Kees!' Bostan called from his knees. 'Are you O.K.?'

Slowly, Kuyter let go of the snake's head and staggered to his feet. His hands made an exploratory tour of his body.

'Yes,' he said. 'I think I am.'

He became aware of the others coming through the trees, and could imagine what he looked like from their expressions. Suddenly, he laughed, and the sound rang in his ears, drowning out the other noises of the forest.

'Hey!' Bostan said. 'Where's the 'gater?'

Kees looked round, but of the cayman there was no sign.

'I would have sworn it was dead: anyone see it go?'

There was a shaking of heads and Kees started laughing again: it was a good release. Boston laughed too, and pretty soon they were all laughing, without really knowing why.

Attica moved towards the two men, their arms round each other's shoulders, her face full of admiration.

'Come,' she said. 'You look like creatures from the black lagoon.'

This caused a fresh outburst of laughter, and Bostan wiped the tear from his eyes. 'You know,' he gasped, and it was the first time anyone had ever heard him swear. 'That must be one hell of a confused fuckin' alligator.'

They cut the great snake into strips, its skinned flesh pale and crossed with thin blue veins and the red of smaller blood vessels. It was twenty-three feet long, equivalent to four Keith Mayalls at five foot nine. And Jack Cane, in a fit of enthusiasm, got a tiny camera out of his case and took a picture of Kees and Turk standing beside it. The trouble came when he asked Jack Bertram if he'd mind snapping him standing by the snake as well. Bertram started to comply, but then for some reason dropped his hand and turned away.

'Hey,' Cane appealed. 'What the hell's wrong now?'

There was a general silence; the others, who could see what Bertram was thinking, were embarrassed by Cane's apparent insensitivity. In the end it was Attica who put their thoughts into words.

'I suppose he feels it would be misleading since you didn't help kill it.'

Cane was incredulous, then an ugly flush covered his face. 'Shit, I've dropped six ton elephants,' he suddenly shouted. 'If I'd been asked, I'd have gone down there and helped with the snake.' He swung round, but everyone was suddenly busy. Grabbing Attica by the shoulder, he spun her round. 'What's wrong? You don't believe me? Bitch!' he screamed, suddenly losing control. 'Tramp! You have no right to make moral judgements on me!'

The crack of her palm on his face was like a whiplash, and his hands fell from her and rose instead to his face: red before, it was now white, with an angry mark flowering where it had been struck. Turning, he kept his eyes on the ground and stumbled away into the trees.

That night was sultry and warmer than usual. They collected wet and dry wood and set about smoking the snake, the strips hung in rows over four poles. Talk was desultory, and Cane kept to himself in the shadows of the firelight's edge. One by one the figures sitting in the flickering light keeled over on their makeshift beds and fell asleep.

Kees awoke later with a griping pain in his bowels. He stoked up the fire and put on some more damp humus, then took off his socks and shoes and put them near the warmth. Quietly, he stepped out of the firelight completely and into the forest night. Some way from the camp he scooped a hole and squatted, feeling the diarrhoea run hotly from him. But there was no griping or cramps, and he was grateful for that. It was surprising that he was passing anything at all. He would make some charcoal to take; perhaps they were all suffering in the same way. He moved down to the stream, his eyes accustomed to the near-darkness, and washed thoroughly; then headed back to the fire.

He didn't see her between the plate-thin buttresses of the big tree, just heard a voice softly call his name, and when he looked all he could see was her eyes. He moved into the wooden alcove, and her hand caught his and guided him to her.

'Attica?' His voice sounded surprised.

'*Oui, c'est moi*,' she said, 'the fully grown woman.'

He leant forward, into the scent of her, and she reached a hand up behind his neck. His lips brushed part of her face, he wasn't sure where, and he could feel the swellings of the bites that disfigured them all. He realized it had been a long time since he had even thought about Noélia. First the diamonds had preoccupied his mind, then the problems of survival. Now this. The gentleness of the moment after all they had gone through was almost intoxicating. The air trembled: she was speaking close to his ear.

'Kees, are we doing well? *Dis-moi la verité.* How far does it go, the jungle? You know –' she shivered '– I think we would all be dead without you.'

His hands pressed against her front, thumbs on her breasts, fingers feeling the dampness of her shirt beneath the arms.

'What did I tell you?' he reprimanded, but his voice seemed to slur the words. 'You should dry your shirt by the fire.'

'Kees.' She would not be put off. 'Tell me.'

He ran his finger gently round her eyelid. He felt light-headed. In her film 'Bidonville' there was a scene not dissimilar to this. She moulded against him as if she'd been there all her life.

'We've come fifteen miles,' he said, 'twenty-five kilometres maybe. We've walked more, but the rest was detours.'

'And how much left?' she persisted.

He hesitated. 'I think the very most is one and a half degrees. About one hundred and sixty kilometres. Minus what we've done. But we could reach good water flowing east long before that. Say another eighty kilometres.'

The strength seemed to flow out of her at the news, and she sagged against him.

'Will we get there? What will happen when we get to the river? Even then it could be weeks or months!'

He felt her composure cracking, and kissed her hard. Her lips parted, and his tongue explored her mouth. With one hand he undid her shirt and his own, and her breasts flattened against his chest. With a quiet desperation she responded, licking and nibbling at his lips and face. His hand dropped to her slacks, slipped her zip, and moved between her legs in one movement. Tight in his grip, she groaned and moved on his fingers.

'We'll get out,' he whispered.

He had barely spoken when a blinding light filled the forest, and for a brief instant he saw her there, lit by the flash, her breasts swelling against him, her head thrown back against the tree. Momentarily blinded, he closed his eyes and heard a rumbling which gathered in intensity until it cracked around them like whiplashes in a slave's nightmare. Bitterness and frustration welled in his throat. So even this was not to be. He breathed deeply, crushing Attica to him, aware that his strength also was on the wane, and wondering how long it would be before the growing temptation to forge ahead by himself could no longer be denied. He had always held that the instinct for self-preservation must be followed, and that there was no shame involved in looking out for yourself when things got critical. But the tenets of the anti-hero were somehow easier to think about than to put into operation. Attica, for example. Could he leave her? At what stage of the game did he simply announce that he was deserting them?

It was impossible. They were locked together by all they had been through, and each day the shackles that bound him to them got stronger.

He kissed Attica, a lingering union of flesh, and felt his splayed fingers sink naturally into the little valleys of her spine. Then he pulled up her zip and looked through the monumental trees towards the canopy. As he did so, a cool wind blew, and the first drops of rain fell like a malediction on his upturned face.

Chapter 12

The green light snapped out, a red one took its place: 'Extinguish Cigarettes'. The aircraft veered to the left, to the right, its engines easing it out onto the runway. Tinny, unmistakably Southern, the voice from the small control tower filled the pilot's ear:

'OXK Five, I repeat OXK Five, yew are cleared for takeoff.'

The pilot lined up on the runway and the motors spun to a crescendo. As an afterthought, Control keyed in:

'Good luck, yew boys. An' Milt, take it easy, y'hear?'

The plane built up speed, lifted; nose up, its lights were soon indistinguishable from the stars bright as crystal in the desert sky. In the fuselage the red light blinked and disappeared, and the green one came on. 'Smoking Permitted' read the legend, and the men relaxed.

Cĕrvak sat on the hammock seat and closed his eyes. Twelve days had passed since his meeting with Viktor, and now the last part of his commission was under way. His mind moved through the stages that had led him to a seat on this plane, in the company of these men. It all came down to the great American system of free enterprise, where a man with enough money could buy himself anything he wanted. Totm's money had hired him a private assault force, and just as privately Cĕrvak was sure that Viktor would find it cheap: fifteen men, most of them left over from Vietnam, changed so utterly by their experiences that no society in the world could hope to re-absorb them; weaponry that in his opinion exceeded the modest aims of their sortie, and one aircraft. The price: just one million dollars, with a returnable deposit to cover the plane. Cĕrvak could only hazard a guess at the overheads involved. The service was provided by a Major Henessy, the scion of a family for whom the desert had bloomed with the dollar-flavoured leaves of the Texas tea plant. Even in the great expanse of the Southern states, which Cĕrvak privately considered to be one of the most primitive areas on earth, it wasn't easy to keep an operation like Henessy's quiet, and he could only presume that large and regular party contributions kept blind eyes that might otherwise have seen.

They had a range of two thousand miles, and a flight plan had been filed to Puerto Rico where they would change course and slip south through the islands towards the Surinam coast. At low level they would enter Brazilian air space near Mount Roraima, and by then, even if anyone was interested, it would be too late to do anything: the plane would simply disappear over the jungle, landing twenty degrees south of the Equator at a private airstrip belonging to one of Totm's subsidiaries.

Cĕrvak opened his eyes as a tall Negro he'd heard addressed as Rags nudged him and slipped coffee into his hands. None of the men wore combat clothes yet as they would have all the next day to acclimatize and prepare. The only worry on Cĕrvak's mind was that he had failed to locate Amerigo Lind. But with Mayfield he'd had no trouble. He waited until he left the B.E.C. building at seven-thirty after a meeting and quickly drove out to Mayfield's home. He parked the car in the spot he'd selected the previous day, and walked up the long drive and into the shrubbery near the garage. Ten minutes later, as Mayfield's car pulled into the drive, he walked towards it as if he'd just come from the house. The illusion was made perfect by the man's wife, who appeared at that moment between the neo-Grecian pillars of the doorway. Mayfield had stopped the car and operated the window. Cĕrvak leant towards him and smiled.

'Mr John Mayfield?' he said, bringing up his gloved right hand. 'I have something for you, sir.' The silenced .32 made little noise and a neat hole: Cĕrvak laid the gun gently on the dead man's lap. As he left the car, its lights still on and the motor running, he heard the woman's voice calling 'John? John? Hurry up, darling, telephone.'

The plane banked and Cěrvak craned his neck and looked at the earth below. A minute curved necklace of lights fringed the night-black throat of the gulf. From above, the light of unnamed stars finished millenia of travel as the glitter in a man's eye.

'Andrej,' Cěrvak told himself. 'You shouldn't think so deeply about things.'

The rain fell in streams from the sky, in rivers. It dropped through the canopy, carrying away badly placed nests, drowning ants and holing the frail wings of unwary butterflies like buckshot. Bolts of lightning fell from heaven to earth, like giant tracer illuminating the gloom, and along the undersides of a billion leaves hung countless billions of insects, riding out the storm on the leaping foliage.

Along the streams and rivers the first drops of rain made the water look as if all the fish had risen at the same time, but soon their surfaces were spitting angrily, lashed into ferment. The main trunk of the Amazon, already swollen, encroached still further onto the hinterland, reaching out over the flood plains until the brown waters lost momentum, moving so slowly that the rich earth they bore sank as alluvial silt up to sixty miles from the river margins.

Pereira knew that he, Scaffa and Luiz had not done as well as they'd hoped. Nearly two weeks in this *cú do mundo*, this arsehole of the earth, and they were all suffering. He was aware too, that if anything he'd slowed them down. Years of walking the confines of a ship's deck had not prepared him for an excursion of this kind. Surprisingly, it was Luiz who had shown a knowledge of various plants to supplement their diet of fish. Scaffa was tormented by ugly swellings all down his legs. The previous evening he'd squeezed one, preferring pain to the endless itching. Eventually he had extracted a large white maggot surrounded by clusters of what looked like black eggs. After that he'd been up half the night, hissing with pain through clenched teeth and huddled under the supply cover, determined to operate on each and every lump.

All three men were now lean and pale, their faces pockmarked with the bites of *mutúca* and pium. Pereira's feet were literally rotten, the flesh splitting between the toes and stinking of putrefaction. Belatedly, he had taken to washing his feet twice a day, but in the damp all of them were now getting the same problem, and the leather of their shoes was covered in mould every morning. The constant sweating caused rashes everywhere, but particularly where skin and cloth moved constantly together. Under the arms and in the crotch, sweat and heat combined to wear the skin till it bled. Without soap or body powder it was impossible to keep really clean, just as it was impossible to keep stopping and bathing. In spite of the heat it became unbearable to strip off because of the insects, and then their bodies sweated and desalinated still further. And at night, through the leaves of the jungle floor, tiny pepper ticks and *sanguesugas* homed in on the warm, foetid smells of skin, sweat and blood which to them meant food.

They sat, huddled, miserable and hungry, against the trunk of a *jatobá*, unaware that this was the favourite tree of the woodman; felled in August, its hollow centre brimmed with a fermented liquor. Pereira held his stomach and cursed. Yesterday they had been bombarded with figs blown down by the wind from far above, and the sight of the fruit had sent them on all fours like animals, gathering voraciously, reluctant to leave any to waste. It had been impossible to refrain from eating the bitter fruit, although they knew the consequences: their stomachs, long deprived of a balanced diet, reacted violently, and their bowels, which had passed nothing for days, cramped unbearably as the laxative juices flowed through them.

By eleven the rain had eased slightly, and a suspicion of daylight lightened the shadows. Pereira held the compass and watched the disc orient slowly in the thick oil. Gingerly, he stood up and started dismantling their rough shelter, saving the pieces of wire with which the cover was supported. They still had fish, he reasoned, and must have covered sixty-five kilometres. The big drawback had been having to skirt a huge area of swamp which for three days forced them to the southeast. That, Pereira knew, had been three days virtually wasted. If anything, they had been walking parallel to the big river further south.

Once more the three men lifted their meagre belongings, felt the familiar rub of the cloth and straps on skin and leather on toes. Pereira winced as his gut heaved and sweat broke out on his forehead. *Ai, Jesus,* he thought, will it never end?

At three in the afternoon they came to water. It was a black river, thirty yards wide, sodden leaves making patterns on its mirrored surface. Out from the bank, the huge dinner-plate leaves of a Victoria lily brimmed with rain.

Pereira was just trying to fathom out the next move when beside him Luiz reacted violently; the sound of his .38 ruptured the heavy dripping silence of the forest. Pereira's eyes lit up and he and Scaffa both spun round.

'Did you get it, *homem*? What the hell was it?'

Luiz grinned hugely, 'I got him, all right,' he said. 'A *bugre*. Right there. Staring at me out of the bushes.'

Pereira couldn't believe his ears, and Scaffa dropped to his knees.

'An Indian? And you shot him?' The captain crouched, shaking with fear and anger. Luiz stared into the arum lining the forest's edge.

'Maybe I missed him,' he mumbled. 'He's not there now.'

The blank wall of greenery behind them seemed suddenly even more oppressive than ever. Its presence was full of a tangible menace, and Pereira remembered the stories of Bacurí, and the men who had been slaughtered.

'Luiz,' he said. 'Before God, I should kill you and leave you for the forest people.' He turned away, stomach churning worse than ever.

Scaffa had crawled to the river's edge, where a detritus of dead wood and vegetation had collected in the slack water. He stepped down into the river up to his waist and launched himself forwards holding fast to a dead trunk.

'I'm not waiting here to have my head taken,' he hissed across the water. 'I'll take my chances with the devil-fish.'

Pereira watched Scaffa's passage. Nothing moved in the water or on the bank. He got halfway across, three-quarters, then he was struggling through the mire on the other side. Pereira shivered at the thought of what the water could contain; trapped, his eyes flickered between the wall of greenery and the opposite bank. It seemed strange that they had come out of those trees bare minutes before, but now neither hell nor high water would drive him back among them. Luiz was already in the river with a log, the gun that had caused the trouble held high above his head.

Here was the dilemma that Pereira had dreaded: on one side the unfriendly trees, and on the other the enfolding water of a jungle creek. His mind leapt back over the years in an instant, and he felt again the searing agony he had felt then, in waters such as these.

Jorge Pereira had been a normal well-adapted smuggler until one evening some twenty years earlier. Then, far up the Moço in a *barca* called the *Leão do Mar* with an illegal cargo of pelts and live monkeys, he suffered a blow which changed his personality and undermined his manhood.

The candiru is a member of a catfish genus which numbers among its species some of the smallest fishes in South America. Often they are parasites sucking blood from the gills of larger fish, but the type encountered by Pereira on that April day had other habits.

The boat was at anchor, and after eating a meal of *pirarucú*, mandioca and coffee, Pereira went over the side for a dip. Hanging onto the anchor chain he swung idly in the water and urinated. He was just about to call to his partner, Vicente Garcia, to join him, when he was struck by such a blinding shaft of pain that his body leapt in the water and a long high-pitched shriek fled from his throat.

Vicente leapt to the rail and looked down. Once on the coast he had seen a man stand on a stonefish. His convulsions of pain had broken his spine in fifteen seconds and killed him. But Jorge looked as if he'd been hit by the six hundred volts from a large eel. Vicente hesitated for a moment, but no longer; as his friend thrashed about just below the surface he scanned the water for something dangerous, and seeing nothing, he jumped.

Pereira was almost unconscious, and had obviously taken in a lot of water. When Vicente tried to get hold of his hands he realized they were both locked into position cupping his crotch. It was then that he realized Jorge was a victim of the candiru. Quickly, he towed the other man around the side of the boat and reached up to unloop a rope end that was draped over a cleat. He slipped the rope twice round Pereira's body, high under the arms, and managed to secure him temporarily to the boat. Then he levered himself over the side and started to haul the semi-conscious man out of the water.

As his naked body came out of the river, Pereira came to life, and with another scream jack-knifed against the gunwale stunning himself on the heavy wood. Vicente laid him out in the shade, and levered his hands away from his genitals. The candiru could, and often did, home in on a stream of urine. Vicente swore; Jorge should have known better. Then he got hold of his penis and worked his way along it with thumb and forefinger pressing the urethra. Up near the base, where the shaft disappeared into the scrotum, he felt a wriggling under his fingers inside the flesh. Simultaneously the body threshed again, and the hands came back like steel springs to the crotch. The candirú would wriggle up the urethra, Vicente knew, and then extend back-slanting erectile spines from the top of its head. There was no way to get at it except with a knife, and they were a week from the nearest settlement. There was also the problem of their cargo if they went into any place with a police post.

Jorge had started moaning, and Vicente said 'candiru'. The other man nodded and started to speak, but then his eyes bulged with pain and the skin over his knuckles whitened as he fought the impulse to claw himself and rip out the cause of his agony.

White-faced, Vicente got up and went to get the gutting knife. As always it was honed to razor sharpness. In a trance, not know-if he could follow it through, he started to make preparations for cutting out the fish. He found an old shirt and tore it into strips and put water on to boil. He remembered seeing the scalpel come steaming out of hot water when, as a youngster, he had had a fish-hook removed from his forearm. Lastly he got the pinga bottle off the shelf. Besides its obvious uses, he knew that alcohol was good for cleaning wounds.

With all this done he set about tying his friend down on the deck. Before securing his right arm he gave him the pinga. Pereira drank half the bottle before a spasm gripped him, whipping his body up and down on the deck. Sweat ran from his face as though from a thousand tiny taps. But Pereira was tough. *'Pronto*, Vicente, *pronto!'* was all he said.

Vicente pulled himself together and tied off the other hand. Quickly he grabbed the knife from the hot water, and then realized he must first isolate the spot. He looped a thin piece of cloth round his right hand and located the fish. Then he tied the cloth tightly round the flesh effectively blocking the creature and getting Pereira's testicles out of the way.

The skin parted easily under the knife and before he knew it the small area was awash with blood. He muttered consolations to the stricken man and snatches of prayer, and then he thought he should have put something in Jorge's mouth to stop him biting his tongue. Illogically he glanced up to see if Pereira was bleeding there as well, but as he did so the fish must have moved again because another scream wrenched its way into the air, and his friend's loins jerked into the air. With horror, Vicente realized the movement had caused the knife to slice deeply into the penis. He felt he was going to black out, his eyes seemed to be looking down on the scene from a great height, but somehow he washed the wound and carried on. Now he was working with his fingers, desperate to finish the job. He pulled the flesh open, roughly, his eyes almost closed. Pereira whimpered, unconscious and deathly pale. After what seemed an endless nightmare, Vicente extracted the small creature that could drive a man to self-destruction with pain.

Pereira had nearly died in any case, prostrated with septicaemia and delirious with fever. Vicente had been at his wits' end during the trip downriver. In total desperation, he had tried once to stop a government vessel bound upstream to patrol against smugglers. But ironically the ship's crew had thought he was selling something, and pressed on regardless.

Even twenty years later the memory caused Pereira to break out in a cold sweat. Wiping his forehead, he stared longingly at the other bank. Scaffa and Luiz were already there. How could they know, he thought, what it was like to have a phobia like this? Breathing deeply, he slithered down through the *canarana* grass to the water's edge and followed the others.

Roderick Ross was swelling daily. It seemed impossible for the process to continue, but yet it did, on his arms and legs, and round his neck, which widened from the chin downwards till it merged into his shoulders. Ginny never left his side, and Ross's eyes showed the fear that men feel when death is threatening and help far away. He was reduced to waddling bow-legged in the wake of the others, sometimes leaning heavily on Ginny with an arm on her shoulders. Kees privately doubted that he would last much longer, and was incredulous at the speed with which the disease had developed. Why had Ross been stricken and not the others? What had he done or eaten or touched that they had not? Most of them had seen pictures of people in Africa suffering from elephantiasis, but that wasn't something which developed in a fortnight.

Kees took what advantage he could of their longer halts to build cover against the rain and replenish their food supply. Several days before they had spent forty-eight hours crossing a series of rivers; a cold dispiriting business, more so as they knew that from the air all the waterways would probably have been revealed as one, meandering in coils and whorls through tree roots and mangrove. In desperation, they at last stopped and managed to make a shelter between the root buttresses of some trees. Palm leaves kept off the rain, and a small fire was kindled from the impermeable bamboo and some balls of latex that Kees had found dribbling from a rubber tree. He also found a vine similar to the matchbox bean, which he thought might be a fish poison used by the Indians. Turk Bostan helped him crush two lengths of it, and then they waded back into the river they had just crossed. A weak eddy had formed a barrage of hyacinth, lily and fallen logs, making an *igapó* or pool, and above this they started to beat the water with the vines.

'This may be it,' Kees told Turk, and pointed.

Sure enough, even in the poor light they could see the vine's sap spreading like a blue film over the surface of the water. Just ten minutes later the first fish floated dead to the surface, and over the next half hour they collected nineteen small ones of eight different types. They had just gathered them in when a peal of thunder rolled across the jungle and the rain started again.

In spite of the snake meat and fish they were in a poor way, wet, exhausted and cold. Jack Bertram shivered uncontrollably, sometimes for an hour at a time, and his breath came thick and chesty, rattling in his throat. Even Fátima's leg seemed reluctant to mend as fast as it should in the adverse conditions; although the bone appeared to be knitting, the bruises where the leg had been caught refused to heal, and the skin was taut over ugly areas of blue and green. Cane had twice more lost control of himself, once refusing point-blank to do his full time at the stretcher.

'Jack,' Kees had told him evenly, 'No carrying, no food: and more to the point, you can find your own way home.'

Fear had calmed Cane's rage; grim-faced, he'd finished his turn.

The responsibility of trying to lead a group of people who were in almost every way alien to him continued to take its toll on Kees. Sometimes he reconsidered taking a share of the food, Cane's briefcase, and cutting out: he couldn't banish the thought that he'd stand a much better chance. But among the group were people who, he realized, were more out of their element than he could possibly conceive; who had spent their lives with money, and never known the real meaning of going without. He imagined Attica, Bostan and Cane to fall into this category, not knowing that Cane was in fact the only one. Viewed in this light, most of them were doing better than he could have expected.

They were all bloody heroes, he supposed, after their own fashion. Ginny, the young English girl, was tormented by the sight of Ross' illness; Attica, rich and with servants and a beautiful home in an oasis, reduced to rags, body covered in sores and bites, her fine hair so troublesome she had asked him to cut it off. Even Keith Mayall, the young Londoner, keeping his manhood intact in front of the others but crying to himself at night, a hand over his eyes; thinking of mother, or lover, or both. Bertram, haggard and asthmatic, and Ross, perhaps the bravest of them all, not even knowing what type of disease attacked him or how it would end. Bostan and the young Arab girl were both unable to share their private feelings of guilt; the one that he was responsible for the whole thing, the other that she should hinder them by being unable to walk.

Another day, another night. In the closeness of their shelter Kees felt Attica's hand, seeking reassurance, on his thigh. Rain ran down the tree behind him, soaked into the spongy leaves.

'One thing,' he whispered. 'The big river will be coming to meet us. Slowly, hour by hour, moving our way.'

Her hand stirred softly on his leg. 'You are a winner, Kees,' she said. 'Does it never cross your mind that we might die?'

Slowly, he shook his head. 'No, I think I can say truthfully that I don't believe we will die,' he said.

She savoured the words and sighed. 'Then, when we leave all this behind us,' she said, 'you must come and stay with me in the desert.' Her voice dropped, like a mother's starting a fairytale for her child. 'Long ago, the great-grandfather of my ex-husband, a trader of some means, was lost in the Northern Desert. He had with him two camels and a simple boy who had been backward from birth. This man and boy ran out of water when a time of storms came to the desert, and they were unable to move. Although the man knew the boy was simple, he asked him sometimes if he thought they would survive; he asked not for the answer, I suppose, but for comfort from another voice. But the boy, who normally made little sense, always answered strongly and optimistically to the one question: will we survive? In the end, though half-dead, the old man believed the boy utterly, and like a great faith it kept him alive. One morning, when the sun came up, he saw the place where my house is now. He believed it was a mirage, but the boy assured him it was real. They arrived to find dates on the trees and water at hand. The old man had drawn heavily on the boy for the courage to go on. He called the place the Wells of Hope. Sadly, the boy died young, as happens sometimes with the simple, and was buried there. When the old man died his son and family claimed the land at the time when nomads were coming in from the desert. Then later, much later, oil was found and the house was built. My husband's father

174

raised up the boy's grave and had a script carved on stone from the holy city. It is still there, on the eastern side of the house.'

Her hand stopped its movement, and she said, 'Keep telling me, Kees, that we'll be all right, and I'll believe it because I want to. Then one day come to my wells and replenish all we drew from yours.'

The captain turned to Cěrvak, sitting beside him at the briefing. 'I think that about wraps it up unless you have anything to add?'

His voice rose at the end of the sentence, giving it a professional unfinished note that could be picked up quickly by the next speaker at any kind of meeting. But Cěrvak wasn't going to be hurried, and the effort was wasted.

Slowly, he stood up in the low-ceilinged room and looked at the men in front of him. They all wore camouflage combat gear but carried no insignia; nine whites, four blacks, and one man whose mother and father had put away their prejudice for as long as it had taken. He knew none of their names and didn't want to.

'I have little to say,' he told them. 'Just remember this: the man who owns and heads the outfit we're moving against is a cold-blooded killer and everyone who works for him shares his guilt. Remember too, that discipline must be maintained after the attack. No drinking – we have to get out as fast as we can. As for women –' he nodded to the captain '– in that respect, I say, to the victors the spoils.'

There were mutters of approval around the room, and chair legs grated on tiles. They synchronised watches and moved off. Across the weedy courtyard of the disused *casa* stood two C10s converted to four-wheel drive with balloon tyres. With a ground clearance of sixteen inches, differential lock, axle hangers, chains and sand tracks in the back, and their own capstan winches on the front, they were odds-on to pull out of most kinds of bad ground. The men climbed in, eight in one, seven in the other, and the vehicles started up, a puff of smoke rising above the cabs.

They were heading for Sabaca along a track that skirted the Bolivia-Paraguay border, and their final run in would be flooded for long stretches. With the sun going down the vehicles looked sinister, tinted glass hiding men and weaponry from the outside world. But out here there was no-one to see, and if there had been it would have only been some *pobre*, used to the wheeled caprices of his overlords.

It was one hundred and forty kilometres to their objective; three hours in wagons like these. In the front seat of the second vehicle Cĕrvak pressed buttons on the radio and got Strauss from Bolivia. He knew what the next piece would be before it came on, and laughed harshly when he heard it.

In the back, six men smoked and listened to the 'Blue Danube'. And all of them wondered what the joke was.

At the Fazenda Sabaca eleven men were gathered in the big study. Back copies of *O Estado*, and some east coast newspapers, lay on the table. Headlines told bare facts about the disappearing paddle-steamer, and columnists guardedly suggested what might actually have happened. The theories were as prolific as they were unlikely, one even suggesting that it was time to mount a concentrated search for the mythical warrior women of the Amazon, who might well have captured the crew and burned the boat.

The mood, Amerigo Lind noted, was jovial, only one factor marring an otherwise perfect occasion: a message had come from the Coronel to say that he would be delayed. Oscar turned the landing lights on, and up the road on the strip seven light aircraft were dimly illumined at the airfield's edge. On a clear night like this the Coronel would have no trouble on the short hop from Aquidaduana to the ranch. Two girls were serving capariña, a mixture of lime and pinga, Brazilian cane brandy, and it was with difficulty that Lind got the room's attention.

'Gentlemen,' he began, 'I'm sure the Coronel would not wish me to keep you waiting.'

Cĕrvak's assault section arrived at Fazenda Sabaca at eight thirty and nosed down the rough grass at the strip's edge with lights extinguished, parallel to the runway. The captain told the driver to stop when they reached the planes.

'Set them to thirty,' he said. 'Leave the red one.' There were two 402s but one of them was standing apart from the others. A man quietly left the vehicle through the back door. The other C10 ticked over quietly alongside. Five minutes later he was back, and again they moved slowly forward. At the corner of the strip they stopped and turned, invisible in the *cerrados*. Briefly, the captain spoke to them, and then the men left the vehicles, split into groups, and started towards the main house.

On the verandah outside the study the guard yawned and trailed his feet from the gently moving hammock, then reached up to scratch his face. This act gave him another ten seconds of life, for the garrotte cut into the back of his wrist and pulled it hard in against his throat, breaking the joint. He gasped, and reached up to pull the wire away, falling gently backwards off the hammock onto the point of a knife. The Negro kept the pressure on the wire, and beside him the captain kneed the body to withdraw the blade. Already their attention was on other things.

In the room Barros cocked his ear. *'Escuta!'*

No sooner had he spoken than two grenades crashed through the windows, hit the blinds and rolled to the floor. Technically Barros did the right thing in trying to throw one of them out again, but they were on short fuses, and so his leaning body absorbed the explosion. The other grenade spun under a chair and the two detonations, deafening in the confined space, hurled Barros, the chair and a thousand shards of red-hot cast iron straight across the room. A huge lump of bloody bone and viscera struck Lind in the chest, turning him out of his chair onto the floor. Shrill screams filled the air, and Karel Machado grabbed a rifle from the rack and leapt for the window. Violently, he used the butt to smash the glass and frame and jumped through, lacerating himself on the jagged edges. But the streaming cuts became insignificant as a burst of fire from point-blank range stopped him dead and dropped him on the glass-strewn earth. Others came stumbling from the room, and the raking fire took away their legs and left them twitching, riddled on the raised hardwood floor of the verandah. Across the *pasto* a *vaqueirada*, twenty of thirty *vaqueiros* led by Oscar, the Coronel's son, were streaming towards their horses, but they never made it. White phosphorus lit the windows of their quarters – and lit, too, the tumbling, burning figures of the men. Women's screams pierced the darkness as they also ran from the building into the scented night and a wicked scythe of automatic fire.

Cĕrvak walked through the door of the study into the carnage. The walls were red with blood and bodies lay twisted in the grotesque attitudes of violent death. Two serving girls sat together by the little bar, one of them just alive, staring vacantly at the calf muscle draped across her foot. Cĕrvak grimaced: it was messy. He put the barrel of his .38 behind her ear and ended her suffering. Turning, a movement caught his eye; a fat man trying to make himself thin, to do the impossible and hide. Something about him was familiar, and Cĕrvak moved across the room and turned him over. Lind's face stared up at him, terror-stricken. A wide stain spread across the man's trousers, and above that his shirt was covered with blood. Cĕrvak pulled a photo out of his breast pocket and compared it. It was the same man.

'Lind!' he said. 'Lind, can you hear me?'

The man nodded, speechless.

'Lind, Viktor wants to know what happened to his boats, his film, his friends.'

Lind shook his head, an animal sound of desperation forcing its way out of his throat.

Cĕrvak lay the barrel of the .38 lightly on the man's crotch and slapped him hard with his left hand. A cloud cleared in Lind's eyes and he started to cry. Cĕrvak's voice was remorseless.

'You blew up his boats, didn't you, and the film, and the friends?'

Lind nodded, tears streaming down his face, eyes hypnotized by the man above him.

'Where are they, Lind? Where did it happen?' He reached out and gripped the man's hair. 'Tell me, or by God I'll crucify you!'

Lind's voice broke free. 'I don't know – please, please believe, me, no-one knows, only the captain.'

Cĕrvak released him. Lind would not lie now. He looked around the room. 'Where is this Coronel Falco?'

Lind's head was shaking again. 'He's not here, not here yet, later, he'll be here later – please, please, for the love of God, I beg you ...'

Červak left him, and walked to the door. The man made him sick. The firing had stopped, and he led a soldier to the room and pointed Lind out.

'The slow way,' he told him.

Lind writhed as the gun came up and tried to slide away, but there was nowhere to go. The soldier lined up the profile of Lind's obese gut, and squeezed the trigger. Half a clip of nickel-jacketted shells unzipped the results of a lifetime's gastronomic indulgence, and the soldier watched Lind's hands hopelessly trying to stop the spillage. Then he walked out of the room.

In the servants' quarters of the main house three of the soldiers cornered two girls, one barely old enough to bleed. Immobilized with fear, the girls huddled together. One of the men grabbed the elder of the two and slid his knife carefully down her back, cutting her blouse, skirt and underwear in one go, leaving a thin groove in her skin that welled with red. He pulled her arms away, and ripped the clothes from her. Bodily he lifted her, fighting desperately now, and slapped her face downwards on the table. Her chin met the heavy wood and dazed her, but she woke up suddenly as two fingers covered with saliva seared into her, moistening her flesh. Incensed by the sound of her moans, and the wriggling buttocks, the soldier opened her legs wide and pulled her onto him. The girl screamed, but he lifted her head back by the hair until she could hardly breathe, her breasts raised high off the table, back arched.

The half-caste had been raised in Puerto Rico. He undid his fly and moved quickly to the younger girl. She screamed frantically at the sight of him, a mindless continuous sound which he stopped with a heavy slap to the face. Impatiently he ripped at her clothes, revealing a slim young body with the first swellings of womanhood. Roughly, he felt for her entrance, his mouth biting at her young breasts. The first man was finished, was zipping up. He looked at the Puerto Rican.

'You'll never find it.'

'I'll find it, or make it,' the man grunted. 'They have a saying down here, "*se ela pesa trinta quilos, estos pronto*".' The small girl buckled at the knees and he dropped on her. 'Know what that means?' He gasped as he forced her flesh apart. 'If she weighs thirty kilos she's ready.'

In the main bedroom above the balcony, Dona Theresa moved quickly to the big corner wardrobe where she kept her dresses. The sounds of gunfire were everywhere and she pushed the terrified Gleide, her personal maid, before her, and settled her under some material in a corner of the closet. Then she crouched in the other corner, the sliding door open just enough so that she could see through. With trembling fingers she checked the .32 she always carried with her around the *fazenda*.

There wasn't long to wait. Heavy footsteps tramped up the stairs and the door burst open. For a moment no-one entered, then the barrel of a gun poked round the door, followed by a Negro's profile. He moved straight to the bed and tipped it up, and another man following him, his eyes quartering the room for hiding places. For a moment Dona Theresa thought they were going to get away, but then both men moved warily towards the wardrobe. A black hand reached for the handle and light flooded in. She saw the big face peering down at her, the coarse features twisted in a grin of anticipation. Then she pulled the trigger. The face snapped back onto the floor showing a black hole under the jawbone. She tried to bring the gun on the other man but was too late. A booted foot crashed it out of her hand and forced her knee against her breast. The agony from her knee as the ligament tore made her incapable of further action, and the soldier got hold of her by the hair and dragged her headlong into the room. Like a madman he slapped her head from side to side until she could do nothing but pray for it to end. For the first time in her life she was totally helpless, unable to resist in the slightest measure. She felt her clothes being ripped apart, felt the areas of her pain multiply as a calloused hand twisted her breasts. His weight pinioned her so effectively that she could scarcely move a muscle. And then there came a pain so acute that her body arched convulsively, nearly throwing the man from above her. Waves of nausea flung the contents of her stomach into her mouth and she gagged on the bitter juices. She screamed long and high, choked, and tried to move again. But it was useless. The burning spread inwards from her loins and she lost consciousness.

In the closet Gleide was paralysed with fear. Her eyes were wide open, unblinking, and beyond the corpse of the dead Negro she saw her mistress methodically beaten and stripped. Even when the soldier started to slip the knife into its fleshy sheath, she made no move. Dona Theresa's screams faded into the distance, and inside Gleide's head something died.

In the darkness three men lifted the rail fences to the big corral and drove the milling animals out with gunfire. Frantic steers crashed through the rails, over lawns and shrubs, climbed onto the verandah itself, before being allowed to run off into the night. The captain assembled his men and checked his watch. Seventeen minutes had passed since the first shot was fired. He looked around at Cěrvak, who nodded.

'Let it burn.'

Petrol from the supply drums in the garages was scattered liberally through the front rooms, and a lobbed incendiary set it going. As the men began to move away the fire got a grip on walls and furniture, lighting the hoof-mashed lawn with a warm glow, as if some great revelry were underway.

At the corner of the strip the men separated and climbed aboard the two vehicles. The landing-strip lights were out, and as they had encountered no trouble the captain sent a man to fix the last plane. As they pulled away the light aircraft went up one after another over a period of two minutes. The captain leaned forward, and tapped Cěrvak on the shoulder. The Hungarian nodded and looked back at the blazing house.

'The Coronel wasn't there,' he said.

The captain felt the driver pick up speed till they were doing forty along the marshy track.

'So much the worse for him,' he said, 'when he does come back.'

Falco arrived at Sabaca forty minutes later. He had seen the light on the horizon some time before, and now a growing dread was realized: Sabaca was in ruins. He landed by the wreckage of burning aircraft, his heart in his mouth as he looked at the remnants of his home. Doubtless the *guerrilheiros* had destroyed people as well as property; his son, his wife, his friends. He knew he had to go down there, but his legs wouldn't take him. A great rage flooded his brain and he set off, stumbling through the night, guided by the firelight. Ahead of him a horse snickered, and he stopped.

'Fogo! Fogo!'

The great stallion swung round, its ears swivelling in his direction. It snorted, hoofed the ground. And then cantered to him. The powerful body of his horse gave the Coronel strength. Clasping the mane, he stood on a rock and pulled himself awkwardly onto its back. Man and horse picked their way towards the house, the Coronel tall and imposing, the stallion jet-black in the shifting light. Together, as always, they made an impressive picture.

But there was no-one left to look.

Chapter 13

The *maloca* was high, built of split palm bound over a pole framework. It was the biggest of the four dwellings in the clearing, and between them lay an area of beaten earth, some piles of grated mandioca, and lengths of strychnos for making curare. Beyond the large dome-shaped huts the clearing itself was a confusion of felled trees and ashes, among which were small, ragged plots, like miniature allotments.

The Indians who lived here had survived thus far in the face of the European exploitation of Amazonos by following two simple rules: they avoided all contact with the invaders, and if a European strayed into their territory, for whatever reason, they killed him. They had heard, if not seen, what happened when other tribes failed to observe these rules. The coming of the white man was a fear they lived with daily. First aircraft would appear, then boats on the river. Smoke hung heavily on the horizon, and game became scarce. Often they would find wounded animals, and that marked for the Japaré Indians the time to move back yet further into the forest. Other tribes who stayed subsequently experienced three things: they received gifts from the Europeans, they met the Europeans, and they died.

They were not to know how the white men brought death; had they understood the motives and the methods they would have been incredulous. For among the gifts that had been left for uncontacted tribes were blankets infected with smallpox, sugar laced with arsenic. And even if the gifts were harmless trinkets, when they met their first white he might well have been selected for the job because he had measles or flu, both deadly to isolated groups with no immunity. Lacking in such finesse were the ranchers and property men who dynamited villages by helicopter, maiming men, women and children and making life in the district impossible.

Nor were the Indians to know that they were thirty times fewer than five centuries previously, or that the head of the government agency which was meant to protect them had gone to press saying that in his opinion a few primitives could not be allowed to stand in the path of progress. The men of the Japaré knew nothing of the outside world, but they sensed the ultimate danger and retreated from it.

Through the trees not far from the village walked three Indians. They left behind them, tied into the crotch of two branches, one of their dead. He was a youngish man with long hair and looked too healthy to have died naturally. The three men reached the village and separated, each going to his own dwelling.

At sundown the jungle became very noisy and the Japaré men gathered in the big hut, walking under the red pole above the door, stained with *urucú*, annatta dye, to keep away evil. Most of the exotic sounds of the night had for them logical and simple explanations; others they put down to *curupira*, the spirit of the forest. Neatly laid out on the floor was a bowl of purplish liquid and a pile of darts. A sixteen-foot blowpipe of hollow cane reached up towards the roof. One of the women brought them beer in a calabash, fermented from mandioca, their only real crop, and they began to talk earnestly together. Other men drifted in, listened and went out, or lay back in hammocks and fell asleep. After an hour an aromatic snuff was produced and the men blew it up each others' nostrils with a long tube. Soon the atmosphere changed as the drug caused its hallucinations; talk became sporadic, loud and fitful, punctuated by long silences. Suddenly one of the men got to his feet and made his way unsteadily to a rolled skin in the corner. He pulled it out, extracted a small dark object surrounded with hair, and brought it back to the others.

He sat heavily dropping the thing into the middle of the floor. It fell lightly and the hair parted, revealing a minute human face. Small as it was, it was unmistakably European in aspect. The men passed it, running their fingers over its contours, eyes glazed. One of them held it up by the hair, the disc distending his bottom lip nearly touching the small head. He grinned suddenly, and maybe it seemed to him that the face smiled back, because he started to laugh, a tortured sound that stopped as suddenly as it began. Soon they all lost interest in the head and left it lying disregarded, staring sightlessly up at the curving framework of the poles.

The men slept well, two where they lay, the others crawling into their hammocks. But at first light they were up, alert and ready, preparing for the trip their shaman demanded.

Lightning split the forest, throwing shadows through the trees and burning the living greens into pale, unholy white. Caught in the open near the base of a tree, a giant tarantula watched the unusual creatures coming towards it. Carefully it backed off, its body encompassed by eight legs, each covered in thick, reddish-brown hairs. Lying there on the forest floor, it covered an area as big as a soup-plate.

Scaffa's foot crushed the spider into the litter, leaving it to die. Like many other things in the jungle it was an over-rated danger, its poison being suited to kill insects and small rodents, not big mammals. Woodmen, who often worked in bare feet, frequently came across nests of tarantulas and despatched them without a second thought. For men, the real dangers of the jungle were hunger and disease; its ability to sap the strongest reserves, undermine the toughest will to live.

Behind Scaffa, Pereira limped like a man already dead. In heavy rain for two days, he had tried to fish without success; the *paraibá* they had originally caught and partly smoked had lasted until the rains came. Then, in twelve hours, it had turned rancid and green. Even cooked it smelled foul, and Pereira knew that ptomaine poisoning would kill them if they ate it more quickly than hunger would if they did not. Once they had surprised a *jacuarú*, a big lizard whose tail was more tasty than chicken, but the creature had escaped, leaving them hungrier than before. Only one thing kept them going: this was their twenty-sixth day in the forest, and Pereira was convinced that the big river was close at hand. They were walking along a slight ridge when Luiz smelled smoke. Peering among the trees, sniffing the air like dogs, they moved cautiously forward thinking of Indians. As it was, Scaffa reached the remnants of the fire before he realized it was there; warm ashes and a small pile of unused twigs set near the base of a tree, trimmed palm leaves that had been used for shelter. Hope leapt irrationally in Pereira's breast. Could it be woodmen, up here, or survey men? If he'd stopped to think he would have realized immediately that it was out of the question. But here were the signs of recent human presence, and everything far too neat for it to be Indian: the shallow drainage trenches scooped out round two of the trees, the pair of crossed sticks where a spit had been supported.

'Hey!' Scaffa called. 'Look at this!'

He reached into the shadows of a buttressed trunk, pulling out a blackened silvery box its bottom fractured from many heatings. The top still bore the words 'Rank Taylor Hobson'. Pereira looked ahead among the trees, rain dripping from the palm leaf held over his head. Although the jungle was enormous it seemed they had all been heading in the same direction, funnelled together by the natural contours of the land.

'Now maybe there'll be a use for your gun,' he told Luiz.

Ginny was the first to see Pereira, and she stood there irresolute, hardly able to believe her eyes. Rod saw him too, then the others. On Bostan, Pereira's entrance from the forest had a galvanic effect. He rose and faced the man, walked slowly towards him. Pereira raised the gun, but fear flickered in his eyes.

'Get back,' he said, 'or you'll die *já*.'

But Bostan kept right on, a look of madness on his face. Suddenly a shot rang out from the other side of the clearing, and all their eyes swung round as Luiz and Scaffa walked soaking through the trees. It was obvious to them all that these three men were in a very bad way – somehow, impossibly, in an even worse state than themselves. Ginny ran to Bostan, pulled him away.

'They're all here!' Luiz called out. 'Seven of them.'

Ginny looked round the clearing. Kees had gone ahead to reconnoitre the ridge, leaving the others resting. Now she noticed that Attica, too, was missing. She said nothing, waiting to see what it was that the men wanted. Resistance, when it came, was from an unexpected quarter.

Jack Cane had been telling himself for weeks that he couldn't stand another day of the continual misery, and yet there was no alternative but stick it out as long as he could. His fear of the unknown, and of being left behind, and his hatred for the others, particularly Bostan and Kuyter who seemed intent on humiliating him at every turn, kept his limbs moving when he was ready to lie down and quit. The sight of Pereira made him momentarily brave. This was the man who had caused him weeks of physical and mental anguish, revealed him as something rather less than a hero to the others, who before had looked up to him. Furtively, he reached into his case and snatched the .32. Lifting it just the way he had been taught when he first played the part of a hired gun, he screamed 'You murdering bastards!' and pulled the trigger. The shot went to the right and low as he moved his shoulder forward, and in any case his voice had given Luiz a second to react. The .38 barked once, and Cane, though unhit, dropped the gun and fell to his knees. Luiz, whose shot had been wild, looked incredulously at the figure on the ground. Needlessly, he put another shot into the leaves near Cane's hand and watched him cringe and shake.

'Que homen!' Luiz said savagely.

His eyes dropped to the attaché case. 'Open it!' he spat out. Cane reached for the case slowly and opened it with unsteady hands. As his fingers fumbled at the catches Luiz snatched it from him and the contents fell out onto the forest floor. He kicked the papers aside with his foot and revealed the little camera, some pens, the calculator. Then the small chamois sack caught his eye. Moving his pistol to his other hand he bent and scooped it up, nipping one side of the neck in his teeth and loosening the drawstring. There was silence in the clearing and then Luiz pulled the string tight and lobbed the bag to Pereira. The leather curved in flight and Pereira's hand snatched it out of the air. He tipped the contents out into his palm and showed them to Scaffa.

'Diamonds?' Scaffa said unbelievingly.

Pereira didn't reply. Slowly he pulled the drawstring and made to put the bag into his pocket.

Luiz's voice stopped him. 'I'll keep them,' he said. 'Seeing as I found them.' His pistol was pointing casually at the ground close to Pereira's feet. 'Later we can share them out.'

Pereira glanced at Scaffa. The man nodded fractionally. Pereira left the rifle pointing at the ground and once more the leather bag arced across the clearing. Luiz pocketed the stones and relaxed. Without warning he kicked Cane's case away into the leaves.

'All right,' he said. 'Now who else has a gun?'

They all shook their heads, and Luiz stormed over to Fátima on the stretcher at the group's edge. Keith looked as if he was going to get in his way, but Bertram pulled him back. Luiz bent over the girl.

'So, my pretty *galinha*, are you hiding a gun?' He reached down and pulled up her skirt. Bostan moved again, and Pereira hit him, a short, vicious blow in the small of the back with the rifle. Boston dropped to his knees and Luiz grasped the fur between the girl's rigid legs.

'A broken wing, my little chicken, but everything else seems to work.' He grinned up at the others. 'Not *cara limpa, bunda suja* like Clara at the Anjo Azul.'

Ginny appealed to Pereira and Scaffa. 'You call yourselves men? Will you just stand there and let that filth touch a defenceless girl with a broken leg?'

Pereira ignored her; Scaffa looked her body slowly up and down. Ginny coloured and moved back to where Bostan sat white-faced on the ground. Rain splashed through the trees, spattering on their pathetic shelters. Tears coursed down her face. Christ, was there to be no end to their suffering?

Without warning an eerie booming filled the forest. Like mad, uncoordinated drumming the sound reverberated through the clearing, froze each of them to immobility. In the instant that the drumming stopped a thin hissing cut the air. Ginny registered the sound only a bare moment before the pain in her arm. She looked down, screamed, and reflexively tore a slender dart from her flesh. She felt a tightness in her chest and her heartbeat accelerated, sounding in her ears like the booming which was already just a memory. As she fell to her knees, she saw Luiz' body tumble away from the stretcher, revealing Fátima's naked thighs, and a frail dart rooted in her stomach.

Jack Bertram's hands tried hopelessly to reach the dart that quivered from his back, but he couldn't. Unhinged with fear, he fell to the ground, trying to break it free, and it was there, five thousand miles from home, writhing like a spaded worm on the floor of the Amazon jungle, that his heart finally gave out. Keith Mayall was unhit, and when he saw Bostan go down he lost his head. Desperate for a weapon with which to defend himself, he rushed Pereira from behind and knocked him over. But as he grappled on the ground for possession of the gun, Scaffa jammed his pistol against Mayall's ear and pulled the trigger. Pereira extricated himself, but kept flat on the ground. Around them nothing moved. Apart from Scaffa and himself only three others were unhit. Cane, on his knees was in much the same position as before, Bostan, now moving painfully over the ground holding his back, and someone grossly fat whom he couldn't place kneeling beside the English girl. Pereira's heart slowed fractionally, still beating much faster than normal. Luiz was nowhere to be seen. Now it was over, he broke into a cold sweat thinking what might still be out there waiting to pick them off one by one.

'Did you see them?' Scaffa hissed.

Pereira shook his head. 'You never see the *bugres*,' he whispered, 'when they don't want to be seen.'

Out on the ridge, Kees heard her call his name, and turned. A lump formed in his throat when he looked at her walking wearily up the incline, her hands pushing down on her knees to help her legs. She had what it took, he thought, and his heart went out to her. They embraced, and moved into the lee of a tree. She licked her lips nervously, and kissed him quickly. He started to speak, but she held a finger across his mouth.

'I think I may be falling in love, following you round the forest like this.'

He pulled her head down onto his chest.

'Jungle fever,' he joked, but his voice had a hoarse quality. 'Perhaps among all the others you've been bitten by the much-feared passion bug.'

Her voice was quiet and anxious. 'What do you think will happen to Ross? He's dying, isn't he?'

Kees spoke into her hair. 'I think he knows that. He's a very courageous individual.'

'And so is she.'

'Ginny? Yes. I expect part of her is dying too.'

He felt her start to stiffen in his arms, and a wracking sob tore its way between her lips.

'I'm sorry, truly, I've been hopeless these last few days. I came up here to try and cheer you up, and now look ...' She stared up at him and ran her hand along his arm. *'Faisons l'amour. While we still can.'*

He drew back from her, and turned his face angrily on hers. In the same breath she had talked of Ross dying. But when he looked at her, the anger died. Her thoughts were transparent; all you had to do was substitute the characters.

'Attica.' His tone admonished her gently. 'We aren't all going to die. Even Ross may pull through.'

'It's no good saying that!' she whispered. 'There's no need to protect me. Have you looked at us lately?' She pulled away from him violently and gestured in the air with her hands. 'We're the walking dead, we just don't know it yet.' Her voice rose hysterically. 'I'm just like the others, a chain round your ankles, aren't I? Without us you could get out easily. Well, why don't you? Why don't you just slip away when no-one's looking, and forget us?'

She was crying uncontrollably now, and Kees reached out and gripped her cheeks between fingers and thumb. He squeezed hard, distorting her mouth, and her dark eyes lifted to his, the tears dropping gently from her long lashes. She quietened as his other hand undid the buttons of her shirt and eased it back over her shoulders. Her breasts appeared, seeming tanned in the poor light, covered with gooseflesh, their nipples rigid and quivering noticeably to the beating of her heart. He transferred a hand to the back of her neck and with the other unzipped her now loose-fitting slacks. They slid halfway down her legs, and stopped. Her pants followed. The material was damp as always, like all their clothes, and her skin damp beneath it.

'Are you sure?' he muttered and she nodded eagerly, reaching for him. She stepped out of her garments, hands loosening his belt and pulling at his zip. When she touched him, her hands were cool and comforting, a nurse's touch on a fevered brow. He tugged his shirt off, laid her quickly down on the bed of sweat-soaked clothing. Her nails burnt his shoulder blades as the bones moved under his skin, and slowly, easily, she let her legs fall open, and drew her knees up on either side of his trunk. High in the sky, clouds rolled over the jungle rooftops, and she watched them as he entered her, slowly, in and in and up, like a long breath that has to last for minutes. Close together like that he didn't move, feeling her surrounding him in mutual comfort. Passion in the sense he'd always known it drifted away, commuted to something less transitory. It had been that way with Noélia. Tenderly he stroked her hair, watched her upturned eyes looking at the trees.

'Attica.'

'Oui, chéri.'

'It was nothing.'

He started to move in her, slowly at first, then faster as she responded to him like an uncaged cat, her hands pounding on his buttocks as she urged him deeper, her legs crossed tight and hard behind the small of his back, her voice a goad in his ear as he forced her to the brink.

She arched her back, gasping, as they rolled onto their sides. Tied together in a knot of thrusting muscle, they gave themselves entirely to the moment's need. His hands gripped her shoulders, pulling her down as if to impale and break her, and the small trickle of sensation that had started at the base of his spine built quickly to a gusting roar that flooded through his head and forced out his seed in a wild surge. His whole being became a giant heartbeat and the sweat stung his eyes as he felt her hanging on for the big wave, his voice calling broken meaningless words into the litter. She felt his fingers slide between them and press her roughly, too hard, but it didn't matter because the wave had caught them both and her body convulsed on his as he swelled to meet her, and the culmination of hardship, hunger, fear and loneliness locked them together, unlocked them with its spasms of release.

She moaned once, a vibrant sound, and lay back, drained, and he looked down into her blurred eyes, their noses touching, their bodies sliding with sweat and relief. And in that moment of peace, wild and eerie through the forest came the booming – distorted, frightening, sometimes distant, sometimes near – so that it was impossible to say from which direction it came.

Kees and Attica half ran into the clearing where they had left the others, before they even noticed the presence of Pereira and Scaffa. All around them lay bodies. Attica ran to Fátima and knelt beside her. Her hands fluttered uncertaintly over the dart, and then, in a fit of revulsion, she pulled it out and used the girl's shirt to wipe the blood.

Kees looked at Pereira, gaunt, cradling the rifle, and caught Bostan's eye. The man appeared to be in some pain, and was struggling upright.

'Are you hit?'

Bostan shook his head. 'Not by a dart.'

Ross pulled at Kees's sleeve, spinning him round.

'You've got to do something,' he said. 'For the love of God! Antidote, there must be an antidote.'

Kees scanned the clearing. Four people were down; Fátima, Ginny, Bertram and Mayall, and Mayall was stone cold dead. That left three.

'Listen,' he told Ross. 'Get that dart out of Bertram and feel for his pulse. 'Attica,' he called. 'You copy what I do. Christ, I'm no doctor, it's just something I read. Ross, you too, copy me.'

Quickly, he knelt over Ginny and looked into her eyes. They were wide open and clear. They followed his face minutely as he sank to the ground. Moving urgently, he scooped a hole in the damp litter and bolstered the area under her shoulders. 'Can you hear me, Ginny?' he said. Her forehead wrinkled in concentration and the eyes half closed, only to fly open again. Her head fell limply back, and he positioned himself at her side. With a forefinger he hooked into her mouth and straightened her tongue. Then he held her nose with his left hand and covered her mouth with his, breathing out till the thin stuff of her shirt swelled under his right hand.

'Kees! Ross called out. His voice was close to panic. 'Kees, I think Jack is finished. There's no pulse.'

Kees nodded, barely hearing, and pushed down on Ginny's sternum with the heel of his hand. Her eyes, open and aware, held his in a fixed regard, and her forehead writhed as she tried to blink. With his other hand he pulled her lids down and held them for a second. But when he let go, they opened again and her eyes went on watching.

'Attica,' Kees called. 'Are her eyes open?'

But it was Ross who answered him, blundering to his knees on the other side of Ginny's body.

'Yes, they are,' he said. 'But there's no movement at all.'

Suddenly Kees became aware of feet standing within his limited sphere of vision. He looked up, pushing down with his right hand. Out came the breath; he leant again.

'*Gringo*,' Pereira told him: '*Gringo*, you are *louco*. They are dead. Do you know what is on these darts?' He held one up gingerly. 'Curare, burrego, or something worse. Save your breath.'

Kees looked up at him, but said nothing. He wondered what Pereira had done to the Indians that they should attack in this way. The forest people were not normally inclined to premeditated aggression. Once again he covered the girl's mouth with his own. Pereira swore, broke the dart in two, and dropped it onto her legs.

Scaffa had ventured as far as the clearing's edge. Peering mistrustfully into the forest, gun at the ready, he looked down and recoiled. Luiz's body was right there, barely out of sight; but the corpse was headless, and the head was nowhere to be seen. Scaffa muttered to himself, and in a new wave of caution, crouched down on the ground. Pereira passed him, saw what he had seen, and squatted by him, white-faced.

Out in the clearing, Kees worked on without a break in his rhythm, and Attica did the same.

Pereira motioned to the headless corpse. 'Get the stones.'

Scaffa crawled to Luiz's body and felt in the pocket of his trousers, trying to ignore the roughly severed neck. There was nothing there. Quickly he rolled the body, and searched all the pockets one by one.

'Jorge!' he hissed. 'They're not here!'

Pereira joined him at the corpse, and he rummaged through the dead man's clothes while his eyes watched what was happening in the clearing. Suspicion flamed up in his mind and he confronted Scaffa, the rifle barrel inches from the man's chest.

'You're the only one, Cancian,' he said. 'You found him.'

Fear showed in Scaffa's eyes. 'Jorge, for the love of God, I don't have them. Are you crazy? Here,' he cried, pulling at his pockets. 'Search me if you don't believe it.'

Pereira pulled the gun up. 'The *bugres* took his head, but they have no use for diamonds,' he said. 'That means ...'

'You're wrong,' Scaffa interrupted. They would take anything that glitters, like a *gralha* bird.'

'Yet they left this?' Pereira said. His fingers extricated a crucifix from beneath the stump of Luiz's neck. He gestured to the clearing. 'Surely none of them had time to do it?' He fell silent, thinking of the Dutchman and the woman who had entered the clearing after the attack. But it was impossible. There had been no time.

Scaffa spoke softly: 'We can't stay here, let's finish them and be done with it.' He hesitated, and went on: 'Georges, have you thought that there is meat enough here to keep us alive for weeks?'

Pereira turned to look at him. His eyes registered neither shock nor disgust. He was beyond both.

'Yes,' he said. 'Yes, I have thought.'

'They did it in the Andes,' Scaffa said, 'and lived.'

Suddenly, Pereira felt more tired than ever before. 'Listen, my friend, what you do is your affair. For my part. I say let us see

194

what they have to eat over there. They haven't been living on fresh air, that's a certainty. We'll take the ones that are left with us. We can use them to build us a raft. There will be time enough to think about food after we search their bodies.'

When Ginny had pulled the dart from her flesh panic overtook her, and she dropped to all fours in an effort to hide. Lifting her arm, she sucked hard at the purple-rimmed hole where the dart had entered and tasted bitterness, then the warm salt of her blood. Totally preoccupied, she tried to get to her feet, but her legs gave out on her and she fell, rolling onto her back. Angry and terrified, she concentrated every fibre of her mind on the simple task of moving her legs, but they were beyond her control. She took a deep breath, but there was a tightness in her chest and somehow her lungs too felt dead, and her voice when she called out for Ross was a withered croak. Within a minute she was completely immobilized, only her staring eyes and the slight pulse of her heart giving any indication of life. The panic multiplied and ran in wild surges round her brain. Her thoughts and all her higher functions remained unimpaired. But she couldn't move. Couldn't breathe. God, she was going to die, and she was going to be aware of it every step of the way till at last the lack of oxygen starved her mind into submission and brought merciful oblivion.

Her body screamed for air, and Ross was by her, she could see him: oh God, she prayed, make him give me air. Suddenly, Ross was gone, and she saw the lean face of Kees bending over her. A red mist began to float across her eyes, and she tried to close them but halfway through the effort she gave up. Sweat ran into her eyes, burning salt, and she saw his face coming down, and felt his lips drop on hers. And then there came an incredible sensation, she could feel herself being pumped up, her chest was swelling involuntarily, and with it clarity cleansed her mind. She watched him, her eyes dry and on fire. His hands moved to her lids, and the fire stopped. She felt a rising tide of overwhelming emotion, and for the first time in her life was unable to express it physically in the slightest degree.

Kees breathed once more into Ginny's flaccid paralysed body.

195

He knew that curare, like other vegetable neuro-toxins, worked by stopping the chemical action that takes place in nerves, totally immobilizing the victim. Sometimes the Indians used frog skin, and some viper bites worked the same way. In theory, at least, mouth-to-mouth resuscitation could save a victim if given quickly enough to avoid stoppage of oxygen to the brain. After fifteen minutes he was still beside her, impossibly exhausted. Bostan and Rod watched him closely, while Pereira and Scaffa pil'aged their meagre supplies of food.

'Let me take over,' Ross pleaded. Kees looked at Attica. She shook her head minutely, and carried on. Jack Cane sat immobile, as if unaware of the events taking place around him.

The Dutchman put his lips on Ginny once more, and as his breath went into her, she coughed and gagged. Quickly, he took his mouth away and let her get over it. The breath came out of her without his help, and she started to inhale, but the movement faltered and died. He leant and helped her. A slight rythmn trembled in her fingertips. Amazingly, she blinked her eyes.

'Kees,' she whimpered, and then tears were streaming from her eyes, and Ross knelt beside her, crying openly. 'I'm cold,' she said. 'I'm so cold.'

Kees crouched beside Fátima, and took her wrist. Within the slender limpness there was no sign of life. He looked at Attica. 'Shall I take over?'

She shook her head, pressing down on the girls chest, so young she had never known the weight of a man.

'Do you think it can do anything now?'

He couldn't look at her easily. 'I think she's dead,' he said. 'The dart must have hit a blood vessel.'

Attica's hand hesitated as if she didn't know whether to go on or stop. Her mouth sank towards the girl's, but halfway she collapsed sobbing over the body.

'It's my fault!' she gasped. 'I brought her here!'

Bostan, who had been watching, turned away, unable to conceal his emotions. Kees comforted her as best he could. 'You did all there was to be done.'

She turned to him in a fresh outburst of tears. 'And it wasn't enough! If you had done the breathing instead of me, maybe she would be –' She stopped, her eyes widening as she looked towards Ginny and realized what she'd said. 'I didn't mean – you know I didn't mean that.'

Pereira's voice cut across all their thoughts as he tried to exercise some authority. It wasn't easy: privately, he was overcome at the sight of someone being brought back from the dead.

'We're going,' he said gruffly. 'All of us. So gather up your belongings and let's get ready.'

'Why don't we stay here tonight?' Bostan said. 'We could bury the dead decently, at least.'

'Move!' Pereira shouted. 'You think we're going to sit around here burying people with the *bugres* out there waiting to pick us off?'

Kees cut in: 'They can pick us off any time they like.'

Pereira was shaking with anger.

'You heard him,' Scaffa said. 'We're all going. Now!' He had found some more smoked snake-meat, and was chewing a piece as he spoke, the juice running down his chin.

Attica was beside herself with grief. 'Shoot me, then, you *merde*,' she screamed. '*Va te faire enculer, salaud, moi je ne vais pas bouger d'ici.*'

Kees laid Fátima on the ground and covered her with leaves. He closed Bertram's eyes, and took the roll of film from his bag which might one day show the end of the *Mississippi Queen*. Mayall he regretfully left where he was. Then he lifted the stretcher and gave it to Turk and Ross. 'Better carry her.'

Ginny protested weakly, but allowed herself to be lifted onto the stretcher. Kees was surprised there was no comment from Pereira, but the man was looking at her with a kind of awe. They filed out of the clearing, first Kees and Attica, then the stretcher, and last the beaten figure of Cane, moving like a sleepwalker. Scaffa and Pereira followed, both chewing on pieces of *sucuri*.

'I can smell the water,' Pereira said. 'It's not far away.'

The jungle was a clean place where nothing was wasted. In the clearing by the bodies a swarm of insects crawled, hopped and slithered over the humus. Yet surprisingly they did not stop by the dead, but kept moving, as if anxious to be gone. For a while there was silence, and then an anteater with its young came through the clearing, heading for water. A new wave of ground-dwelling insects appeared, and a group of tarantulas travelling the same way. This time ant-birds and tanagers swooped down on them from the trees, and ate their fill of the fugitives. A distant hissing filled the air, like the whispering of an army on the march, and the ant-birds moved on, a preying vanguard at the forward extremities of the sound. Soon the source of the noise became visible among the trees, a writhing, moving army of ants. They seemed to travel as an entity, a long, infinitely involved mesh sliding like a carpet over the jungle floor. They flowed like a slow tide, a black crystalline treacle that parted for trees and rejoined, having absorbed every living thing over which it passed.

The hissing faded slightly as the leaders tasted the air, mandibles waving gently, chitin armour glinting dully in the dim light. Then they set off again, and the hissing of their passage renewed itself. The first body they reached was that of Luiz. The army separated and flowed on, so that it looked as if the headless trunk was actually being pulled among the insects. Then the creatures climbed, and the man-shape dwindled like a sandbar before a swelling tide. The army moved on into the clearing and found Fátima, absorbed her; a million tiny jaws cutting through skin and vein, driven by the smell of clotted, jelly-like blood. They walked the breathless tunnels of her nostrils, ate pink canyon floors between her teeth, bored through the lifeless boulders of her eyes, and poured through into the darkness. The ants ate everything there was to eat – the leather of shoes, the remnants of starch in clothes. Then, as if at a given signal, they moved on, leaving the skeletons to mildew in the gloom and termites to nest in the empty skulls.

They marched for four hours, down one ridge and up another. The rain eased, the air turned cool, and although evening was drawing close it became lighter in the forest. At last Pereira called a halt. The vegetation was beginning to thicken and they found themselves struggling, plants and creepers pulling at their legs. They stopped in a small, steep-sided valley, and once again the only logical resting places were the alcoves provided by giant trees' roots. Ahead of them a big one had fallen recently; its foliage was still green. Its roots were small in relation to its size, with no big taproot; it showed how insecure most of the jungle giants were in the poor leafy soil, despite the tall buttresses.

Kees stooped and picked up a brown pod.

'Tamarind,' he said. The thick sticky substance inside the pod was bitingly refreshing, almost like lemon juice, and soon they were all sucking on it. Pereira's eyes were strange, and he sniffed the breeze.

'Watch them,' he told Scaffa. 'I'm going on a little way.'

Scaffa's eyes showed his concern. 'It's not good, Georges, one man to watch six people.'

Pereira looked over at them, gathered around Ginny, feeding her tamarind. 'Just keep your gun on one of the women. Here.' He went over to Attica and pulled her back from the group. 'Listen!' he shouted. 'I'm going ahead to look for food.' He coughed painfully, and went on more quietly. 'Just stay where you are and don't move. If you do, she'll be the first to get it.'

Pereira climbed the trunk of the fallen tree and headed down the incline. It got lighter as he went, and he felt a tightness in his chest as shafts of sunlight – actual yellow sunlight – pierced the mantle above his head. Using the machête he hacked his way forward regardless of the undergrowth as the light got brighter around him. He slithered down a bank and into a shaded *igapó*. The water, red and shallow, was slowly moving: uphill, he noted, back into the forest. The surface was like a red-veined marble floor, reflecting perfectly the floating refuse of the forest – leaves, blooms and seeds. He turned left and splashed along, seeing the scarred bark high up the tree trunks where the waters of *enchente*, the last flood time, had rushed out into the main stream carrying with them a scouring cargo of logs and branches. Twenty metres further on the stream widened and deepened. Pereira worked his way up the bank, and was suddenly standing in bright sunlight looking left and right along the gallery forest of a sizeable river. Disappointment gripped him: it was a backwater river, its current almost non-existent. Again, marks on the trees told him how far the waters still had to rise before they would be able to flow.

A small bank jutted out to his left obscuring the view slightly, and he felt so deflated that at first he didn't see the family of capybara at the river's edge. There were seven of them, the adults following the young ones into the water. Trembling, Pereira raised the gun; his eyes misted and the foresight wavering and blurred. He blinked, looking around desperately for a tree to lean on. By the time he'd arranged himself they were almost in the river. Pereira drew a bead on the female at the back and squeezed the trigger. It wouldn't move. Sweating, he thumbed the safety catch off and re-aligned the shot. The gun kicked in his hands and he saw a spurt of water behind the beast. *Puta*, but his eyes had let him down. No, the animal was over. The bullet had gone clean through its neck. Carefully, Pereira made sure with a second shot to the head. Then he tumbled through the *canarana* towards his kill.

It was only as he was about to descend to the river's edge that he became aware of a different colour in the sky. His new position allowed him to look beyond the small peninsula, and what he saw made him fall to his knees. His clothes steaming in the sunlight, he knelt there and cried aloud for joy. In the misty distance the blue of the sky merged to brown near the horizon, so far away it seemed like cloud. But beneath that indistinct line there was no doubt about what he could see. Brown and broad, extending to the end of sight, there was no other river like it in the world. Pereira was laughing now, tears streaming down his face. Even as he watched, he imagined he could see himself safely on a raft floating sedately, slowly but surely, downstream to civilization. Sober now, he rose, and with a last look west towards the sun, picked his way down to the water's edge.

Turk Bostan heard the shot, and watched Scaffa carefully. But the man didn't move, just kept the gun pointed at Attica's head. Another shot followed, and Scaffa relaxed fractionally. Bostan moved his shoulders, and felt a pain shoot through him from the small of his back. He turned as Kees slid alongside him.

'How are you feeling?'

'So-so. And you?'

The Dutchman's face was serious. 'How long do you think before they shoot us?'

Bostan didn't say anything. It was a hell of a question. Kees went on: 'Pereira's got maps of this whole area, he reckons we're near the river. Did you hear him talking earlier on? I can only think of one reason he'd keep us alive, and that's to build him some sort of boat.

'O.K.,' Bostan said. 'But what the hell can we do? Rod doesn't count, the poor bastard, Cane seems to be in some sort of trance, I can't even straighten my back after yesterday, Ginny's in poor shape: not much of a team, is it? Of course there's always you – why don't you just forget the guns and knife the mothers?' He stopped immediately, contrite. 'Jesus, I'm sorry.' He ran a hand through thick hair. 'I've had it up to here. I know, we all have. When I think of the people on that boat, on the barge, Keith, young Fátima ...'

Kees cut in on him. 'That's the only way to think,' he said. 'Otherwise you'll forget what those two did. You've got to make yourself mad when the time comes, and you won't even feel your back. They're in a worse way than we are; the only advantage they have are the guns. Look,' he said, 'they didn't even take my knife. I buried it over there by the stretcher.'

'Beats me why they didn't shoot Ginny rather than be slowed down.'

Kees considered. 'I think they must have realized that it would push us too far. Or maybe Pereira's a God-fearing man: some killers are. When she came to, he thought he'd seen a miracle.'

Turk looked at the other's familiar profile.

'Reckon he had.' It was funny, Bostan thought, he'd started off by being chary of the blond guy with all the answers, and when he started to get friendly with Attica he'd had physically to restrain himself sometimes from making sour comments. It got all the more difficult as morale sank, and in that respect he could see why Cane had snapped: in a way it was more difficult for him; he'd been a celluloid hero to start with, and there'd been no way for him to go but down. Eventually, though, what the experts said proved to be true: the instinct for survival domi-

nated all others, until there was no room in your head for anything but the aching emptiness in your gut and the recurring,
nightmare question – will I get out of this alive?

'Listen,' Kees was saying, 'you remember the booming?'

'How could I forget?'

'Tonight I'm going to slip away. Before I make a move, I'll
try to make the same noise. Tell the others.' He looked at Scaffa.
'Those two may think it's the Indians again. That could be all
the chance we need. Or maybe one of them will fall asleep:
they can't keep awake all the time. If that happens, make sure
you keep your eyes open.'

'Kees,' Bostan started, but their conversation was interrupted
for at that moment Scaffa turned his head, and the sounds of
Pereira's approach came through the trees. Above the forest
blue sky was visible for the first time in nearly two weeks, a small
welcome interim in the long deluge.

Staggering slightly, Pereira appeared on the other side of the
fallen tamarind. With an immense effort he lifted the pig-shaped
body of the large rodent onto the trunk and gave it a shove. The
seventy pound animal fell heavily to the ground.

'Meat!' he called out triumphantly, and his voice was full of
the knowledge of where they were. He scrambled over the trunk
and caught hold of the animal's back legs. 'Yes!' he said again,
'Meat! So don't say I don't look after you.'

The words held no trace of irony.

Chapter 14

It was ten o'clock and the capybara was the best thing they'd ever tasted. Kees collected some of the dripping and grease and rubbed it methodically into the leather of his shoes. Roasting was the most wasteful of cooking means, but Pereira wasn't bothered, seemingly a changed man as he cut and dispensed the meat. After the previous week's diet the pure flesh was hard to stomach; just a little was enough.

Pereira and Scaffa sat apart wolfing the food, their guns close at hand. But no-one cared for anything except the overpowering smell of cooked meat which lay over them like a blanket, a smell some had never thought to experience again. A sense of false security filled them all, dulling the reality that would have to be faced in the morning. In spite of everything that had happened, all was put aside for the taste of food: such is the power of hunger.

Scaffa ate too much too quickly and brought it up.

'*Lagarto*,' Pereira told him, but his voice lacked its usual flat animosity. The *lagarto* is a lizard that eats too much of anything it can find. Scaffa, undeterred by his sickness, started refilling his stomach. Jack Cane had walked into one of the little balls of ticks that hang on the leaves of some plants, and was covered in them. His revulsion for the crawling parasites was almost as great as his hunger, and he sat there alternately filling his mouth with meat and picking the ticks off one by one, throwing them into the fire where they exploded with a tiny *pssst*! The *pssst*!

seemed to please Cane, and his face would twist slightly at each small assassination.

Scaffa had collected some of the animal's blood and now began to drop it slowly into boiling water; the others watched him, some in distaste, but Scaffa obviously found the process appetizing, draining off the water and eating the dark mass as if it were a real black pudding. Kees started wondering about Scaffa; sometimes his sight seemed to bother him, and he would reach for something and find it not quite there. His eyes were brown, and had the unfixed quality that in some people gives the impression that they are talking to someone else. Kees knew that many people suffered from amblyopia in these areas, a dimness of sight caused by dietary deficiency, but he imagined Scaffa had been well enough fed up to a month ago. He tried to work out what could have happened to the helicopter, and how anyone had survived. And the launch, what had happened to that? Had the men on the launch seen the helicopter come down? Had they caused it to crash? There were too many unknowns in the equation. He would have given a lot to know the reasoning that inspired the river massacre and the identity of the men behind it.

Pereira had relaxed, though his eyes were still watchful. Once he chuckled to himself, a strange sound that mixed badly with the other night sounds of the forest. The fire dimmed, and Kees built it up. The flames covered, it became dark in the clearing, and drying clothes absorbed the light still further. He saw Attica's eyes in the darkness and sat beside her. His hands searched out the knife in the leaves, and he touched her cheek. Then he turned onto his belly and crawled away into the darkness, the familiar earth smell of the vegetation strong in his nostrils, and in his ears the sound of her voice talking with Turk to cover the noise of his departure.

Kees worked his way round the clearing until he was in a position to move quickly against Scaffa and Pereira should they doze off. The two men were nestled impregnably at the base of a tree, Pereira with his rifle angled down at Ginny's body as she lay between him and the fire. His gaze never faltered, though Scaffa slept, and Kees realized that to a sailor who'd spent his days and nights on watch this sort of thing was the habit of a lifetime.

Stray moonlight came down through the trees, and it was then that Pereira suddenly made a count of the figures in front of him. Kees could almost see his mind working, and then he nudged Scaffa; the two men looked around nervously, and silently Kees cursed Cane for his ill-timed move with the gun. But nothing happened; Pereira and Scaffa sat there watching and waiting, and at two o'clock, cold and stiff, Kees moved away to find a nîche secure from both men and the parasites thriving on the forest floor. Propped invisibly in the fork of some raised roots, he fell into a sporadic sleep.

Scaffa woke suddenly after three hours, to the screams of the howlers. Pereira, watchful as ever, caught his eye and nodded. Then he stood up and called out:

'All of you, let's go! *Agora mesmo!* Come on, on your feet!' Standing behind Ginny, he raised his voice still further and yelled '*Escute*, Dutchman, if you can hear me. Don't try anything, or this one will get something from which even you cannot save her.' He looked round the clearing with a baffled, angry expression; privately, he doubted whether they'd ever see the man again. When the others were ready he motioned Scaffa to move them out, and then they all filed off, Pereira and Ginny bringing up the rear.

Kees moved off too, through the trees, keeping the group easily in sight as they cut through the thickening underbrush. Pereira called directions, and they disappeared from sight into an overgrown gully. The sounds dwindled and then there was silence; only toucans in the treetops raided their way noisily through the canopy. He realized they were probably in water. The light was streaming in all around now, and on a jungle floor not one sunbeam is ever wasted. Ferns sprouted thickly, just like the European varieties with their curled edible tops, and small vines and creepers laced the trees. Quickly and quietly Kees followed on a parallel course; within fifteen minutes he came out from under the high crowns of the gallery forest, and found blue sky above his head. In front of him was a wide, almost motionless, body of water, a black river. Humming birds, called *beija flor* or 'flower-kissers' in Brazil, darted by the water as quick as silver, small as dragonflies. But the sun was not yet sufficiently high to light the bank on which he was standing, and the tall shadows of the trees spread solidly across the water, a reminder of what lay behind. It was as he turned to look down-river that he saw what Pereira had seen the day before. Kees stared long and hard at that huge body of brown water perhaps ten miles wide. And he knew that he had almost run out of time.

From his vantage point he watched the others straggle out into the light. They were upstream, maybe a hundred metres. He heard Pereira's voice calling instructions, and saw him waving the rifle. Shortly, the sound of chopping came along the bank as Scaffa wielded the machête, and tall bamboo leant and fell at the river edge. The sun climbed higher and the felled wood took on shape. Kees watched Attica slip and fall trying to drag a length of liana, and Scaffa with his knife kneeling to split it and extract the tough fibres. At the rate they were progressing, a raft wasn't going to take long to build. Bamboo has watertight chambers, and Kees knew that a dozen tall bamboos with a diameter of ten centimetres would take four men comfortably; and here there was no shortage of cane. Palm trunks and hard-wood, which might have seemed an obvious choice, were so dense they just sank.

He lay trying to formulate some sort of plan, but the others were well placed. Gradually he worked his way closer, skirting the forest edge. Now the bamboos were cut to length and lying side by side. Scaffa had discarded the liana in favour of piercing each cane one wall in from either end. Through these holes he was forcing solid saplings, lashing them into place with electrical wire salvaged from the helicopter. Then he started to fix uprights to support what was left of the waterproof cover as a protection against sun and rain.

By eleven o'clock the bulk of the work was done and time was running short. Between the spot where Kees lay and the raft there was plenty of cover; it was the last ten metres that were open. Directly uphill from the raft, rising out of the tall grass, towered a big hardwood. He knew that if he wanted to simulate the noise made by the Indians he had to use that tree, beating the big root membranes with improvised clubs until they vibrated with the sound that carried miles, even in the thickest country. From the tree to the riverbank would take him a good ten seconds: that would leave the ten metres of open ground to cross with no way of knowing what the position would be when he broke cover. He tried to put himself in their position: the first reaction to the booming should be to try to get the raft to water as quickly as possible. And to do that they needed all hands for a lift. So much depended on Bostan and the others, but how much help he could expect from them in their exhausted condition he had no idea.

Down by the river the heat was building up as the sun passed its zenith, and so too was the sense of futility and desperation that Bostan felt as he looked about. The raft was nearly complete, and there was still no sign of Kuyter. Just for a moment it crossed Bostan's mind that he might be far away, making a raft of his own. Then he dismissed the idea as out of the question, and felt guilty for having thought of it. Basically it was up to him in the end, and he had only one trump to play that no-one knew about. He tied off on one of the braces as hard as he could, and stood up. He'd wasted long enough, and his nerves were jangling. If he was going to do anything, now was the time.

He turned towards Pereira, choosing the words in his mind. Behind him the others stopped working, as if they all realized that this was the final confrontation. Before Bostan could say anything, Pereira spoke quietly to Scaffa: together the two men lifted their guns. Sweat poured from Bostan's broad forehead.

'Wait!' he heard himself call. 'There's something you've forgotten!'

Pereira hesitated fractionally and watched Bostan coming towards him, hand outstretched. 'We should have killed them after the Indians attacked,' he thought, 'and been done with it. If I'd known the river was so near ...'

Bostan had stopped in front of him. He held something up between thumb and forefinger, and then lobbed it at Pereira.

The man stepped back, taken off guard, but no-one moved. He looked for the object on the ground, his eyes flickering uncertainly. Then he saw it, like a small piece of glass lying there in the sunlight.

'You,' he said.

'That's right,' Bostan told him. 'Perhaps you'd like to ask Jack how many million cruzeiros he paid for them. That much money must be worth a few lives.'

Pereira took one pace to the side like a chesspiece countering check. He raised the rifle and sighted along it at Ginny's stomach. 'There are ways to die,' he said. 'Tell me where the other stones are, or the girl will bleed. Or maybe we'll shoot your balls off. Take your choice.'

No one moved or spoke. The rifle barrel lifted and steadied. And then, just as before, the strange booming growled out across the forest, vibrating the air as it passed until it seemed to come from all sides at once.

The effect on Scaffa and Pereira was dramatic and instantaneous.

'*Bugres!*' Pereira screamed, and turned on the others. 'Get the raft in the water! Hurry, *bastardos, pronto!*'

Still no-one moved. Scaffa fired the pistol over Attica's head, and she dropped to her knees. He moved to Cane.

'You, Cane, you want to die from curare? Get the raft in the water!'

Jack Cane was not a brave man, though he had played many a brave part. All through their time in the forest he had hated himself for what he was, and even more for what he was not. This morning, seeing the great river that led back to civilization he had felt a strange exhilaration. Strange, because he knew inside himself that what Bostan said was true: if they didn't do something positive, they would never leave this place alive. For the first time since the loss of the ship, Cane felt happy in the knowledge of what he was going to do. But he let nothing except fear show on his face.

'Move!' Scaffa yelled, and his foot lashed out. And Cane turned on him. He caught the man's foot with both hands as it landed on his thigh, and twisted. The next thing he knew was that the two of them were on the ground and he was on top. With an overwhelming sensation of pleasure he felt Scaffa's nose begin to give under the heel of his hand, and his fingers gouged at the man's eyes. He would vindicate himself all right, he vowed, and elation filled him at the thought. But beneath him the pistol barrel turned, wedged between their struggling bodies, and Scaffa pulled the trigger.

At the same moment that Cane unexpectedly retaliated, Bostan seized his chance and leapt for the rifle. But he misjudged, and only got one hand onto it. Pereira jumped backwards, twisting the weapon to break Bostan's grip. Agonizing pain ran the length of the American's arm, and he knew he couldn't hold on. Pereira twisted remorselessly, and with a jerk the rifle came free and Bostan was on his knees looking up at the Brazilian's face. The booming noise stopped and its reverberations died away, but Bostan knew it was too late. It had taken years to get what he wanted out of life, and he'd lost it all in under ten seconds.

Before Kees even reached the edge of the vegetation, the sound of two shots leapt to meet him, first the high-pitched snap of the pistol, then the deeper bark of Pereira's rifle. The sounds mixed, echoing along the river from unseen stands of timber. He spun out of the grass at a run, taking in the sprawled body of Cane and Bostan slumped forward on his knees. In the moment it took him to cross the intervening space, Pereira rounded on the others.

'You're already dead!' he screamed. 'All of you!' He raised the gun, shouting abuse, but by then Kees was on him.

Something warned Pereira of an attack from the rear, because he swung round quickly, and the rifle barrel laid heavily across the Dutchman's chest. Kees brought the knife up hard, but it slid along the wooden stock and sank into nothing between Pereira's arm and body. Pereira tried to back away to give Scaffa a shot, but Kees followed him closely trying to clear his arm and use the blade.

His momentum had been lost, and he pulled away desperately, crouched, and slashed at Pereira's legs. The blade bit and the Brazilian screamed. For a moment the rifle dropped and Kees lunged forward. The blade caught Pereira in the throat, and his weight brought him down onto it. For a second he was held there, arms flailing uselessly, and then his eyes rolled upwards and his mouth blew jewel-red bubbles that burst in spattering blood. Suddenly his body was a dead weight, and Kees caught hold of the rifle, letting go of the knife and staggering slightly as his arm was abruptly relieved of the dead man's weight.

He lifted his head and became aware of Ginny's face; the others hadn't moved, but she was standing there with a piece of wood in her hands and had certainly been on the point of trying to help. But now her eyes were fixed on a point beyond him. Kees turned fast, and a slug tore a hole in the upper part of his right arm. A woman screamed. He tried to bring the rifle to bear, though it was only a reflex, and his arm wouldn't respond. But Scaffa waited too long before firing again, and two large wrists closed on him from below. He kicked out wildly and fired once, but the shot ploughed uselessly into the ground and they all heard the sound of cracking bone as Bostan pulled him down and forward until both men were kneeling. Scaffa screamed once, a high sound, and tried to break free, but the pain from his wrists stopped him. Savagely, Bostan jerked his head across the small space between them. There was a wet crunch as the heavy bone smashed down onto Scaffa's nose. His scream rose piercingly towards the trees, but he couldn't move, and back went the forehead for the second time. Only now there was no strength in it, and Bostan's body stretched out towards the water as if he was thirsty, and lay still. Kees raised the rifle and fired deliberately into the side of Scaffa's head. He jerked sideways and toppled over, rolling off the bank into the river.

Light-headed, Kees walked over to Bostan's prostrate form. He knelt and laid down the gun, and then Attica and Ginny were there beside him and together they turned Bostan over. Pereira's bullet had creased his head along the jawline, taken half his right ear and gouged a trench through his hair. Blood was flowing freely from the ear. Kees felt automatically for the pulse, but Ginny pushed his arm away.

'Go and lie down and let Attica look after you. Rod and I'll look after Turk.'

Gratefully, Kees moved into the shade and sat down. Without

knowing how it happened, he suddenly found that he was flat on his back and the last thing he saw was Attica's face, mouth drawn tight as she used his knife to cut the ripped fabric of his shirt.

When Kees woke up it was dark and he was cold. A small fire burned and Attica sat beside him. He tried to sit up, got halfway and tackled the rest in easy stages. His head was heavy and ached, and he tried to move his arm before he remembered there was a hole in it. He looked at the tight bandage as the throbbing started, but it didn't stop him sniffing the night air which was thick was the smell of cooking meat.

'Welcome back,' Rod said.

Kees grunted and spat into the fire. His mouth felt foul. 'Turk,' he grated. 'How is he?'

'We washed the wound in boiled water,' Ginny said, 'and bandaged it, but you can see the bone and his ear keeps bleeding, and he won't keep still.'

'He's conscious then,' Kees said, starting up.

'Don't move,' Attica told him. 'No, he's not, but he's moving around a lot, and muttering, and his head is very hot. But we've covered him up anyway.'

Kees tried to move his head, but his neck seemed to have siezed up. 'What about the bodies?'

'I put Pereira in the river,' Rod grimaced. 'Jack is behind us. I thought we could bury him in the morning.'

Kees nodded absently. The river to be faced was huge, the raft small. He prayed they would be lucky out on the water.

'What happened,' he said, 'before I came down?'

They all started at once, but Attica and Rod fell silent, leaving Ginny to do the talking.

'Well, I think they decided the time had come to kill us. I could feel it, I think we all could. Anyway, Turk surprised us all. He had Jack's diamonds, and he showed them one and said if they'd leave us in peace they could have the others.' She glanced at their faces, then went on: 'But they just said that if he didn't hand the stones over, they would shoot me in the stomach.' She stopped, close to tears.

'And then?' Kees probed.

'Then your noise started,' Rod went on, 'and Bostan went for Pereira, and Jack went for Scaffa and nearly had the bastard, and I stood there like a bloody vegetable while they both got shot.' His face was white and he drowned Ginny's protests: 'Well, it's true isn't it, for Christ's sake?'

'Poor Rod,' Kees thought, as a heavy silence fell. One day, he supposed, the cause of his disease would be isolated as some insect or other out of the millions in the forest. And maybe years after that a cure would be formulated with a fifty per cent success rate if the victim managed to make the four thousand kilometre trip to Rio within two days.

Rod broke the silence himself. 'It's strange,' he said. 'Now it's over you'd think it would have been easy for us to rush them, or something. But it wasn't, was it?'

Kees shook his head. 'A gun is a powerful argument.' He changed the subject. 'How's that meat doing?' He poked some with his knife, cleaned, he noticed, while he'd been asleep. He skewered a piece and chewed it. Instantly he felt ravenous. 'Five of us left,' he thought, 'and two I wouldn't put money on.' He swallowed and said, 'Who has the diamonds?'

A shaking of heads. 'No-one knew Turk had them,' Attica said. 'The others must be round here somewhere.'

Kees nodded, deep in thought.

'I simply don't understand what Cane was doing wandering round with a case half-full of stones,' Rod commented seriously. 'Crazy risk.'

'Crazier to have left them on the boat,' Ginny said.

'As it turns out. He couldn't have known. Why did he have them with him in the first place?'

Kees ate some more meat, feeling new optimism surge into him as the hot juices scalded his throat and the saliva flowed.

'The strangest thing about those stones,' he said, 'is that they're mine.'

The next day Kees stood on the river's bank in the early chill trying to see through the water, but there was nothing to be seen. When the sun came up a little, he slipped over the bank and waded, but the bottom shelved away deeply, covered with grass and leaves, some of them freshly fallen and still retaining a tinge of green. He had risen at dawn and searched everything and everywhere without success. The only thing he could think was that Bostan, illogical as it seemed, had thrown them into the river or the bush, and Bostan was in no condition to confirm or deny. Even the single diamond that had been on the ground refused to reveal itself. But then, like many things of value, it was so small.

Later they loaded the raft with their belongings and food and rigged the awning over Bostan's inert figure. Clumsily, with makeshift paddles, they set out for the point where black water butted brown. Now that they were afloat their optimism faded slightly; the stretch of water ahead was enormous, more like a huge lake than a river, nor did it seem to be moving. From where they were the forest behind them looked green and inviting, a place of abundant food and shady groves, though they knew differently. The point from which they'd left was indistinguishable now from any other. Only the shallow grave made it a special place.

They reached the confluence, and the water took on a slight turbulence. The raft moved slowly forward until it nosed into brown water. Immediately it started to swing, and they drove as hard as they could with the paddles until half the vessel was afloat on the Amazon. A line of froth and wood delineated the meeting of the waters, and as paddles dug into black water for the last time a floating object turned towards them, and they were reminded that Pereira, like Scaffa, had ended up in the river. Mockingly, the corpse bobbed towards them, one hand raised in greeting. Then a vagrant current spun it in among the other flotsam. There was so much water that the fish had not yet found it, but they would. In the jungle, on land or afloat, nothing was wasted.

They found themselves moving slowly this way and that, and were content to sit and let the water take them. They had no desire to cross the river, but it was important to keep out in the deep water that was navigable to ships and where there was some current to push them downstream.

It was Ginny who found them. She was sitting on the edge of

the raft, toying with one of the bamboo braces, and she slipped her hand inside it. She gave a little shriek as her fingers touched something soft, and pulled them out quickly.

'There's something in there,' she said, and went quite pale before realization dawned. Still, she leant over and looked inside the hollow cane before risking her hand again. She passed the little bag to Kees and he tipped the stones carefully onto his palm.

'Are they really so valuable?' Ginny asked.

Kees looked at them. Somehow they seemed different after all this time, or maybe his values had altered.

'They were never worth it,' he told Ginny. 'Never.'

He gazed south across the endless water and caught Attica's eye; but when he looked at the stones, he could picture only Nigra, his daughter and, for some reason, the deserted mission beneath the cooler heights of the Eagle's Beak with its big view to the west towards Bolivia and the mountains. It was April there, too, a month of pregnant clouds, gutshot by lightning, thunder thrown to the winds, rainfall bleeding on the kneeling hills.

From those mountains streams flowed and swelled till they were rivers. Four thousand miles of waterway, a journey, *hégira*, until the point of it all was lost in the vastness of the Amazon basin, and black waters and brown made uneasy peace with the sea.

Chapter 15

The intense world-wide public interest and press speculation about the fate of the *Mississippi Queen* had barely died away when on April 26 at 5.30 p.m. national radio and TV transmissions in America were interrupted by the following announcement.

'Reports have just come in from sources in Brazil of the miraculous reappearance of four people, who, together with sixty-three others, have been missing, presumed dead, since the vanishing riverboat *Mississippi Queen* was lost with all hands in mysterious circumstances last month. One of the survivors is film star Attica Alloui, whose performances in "Bidonville" and "Pharaoh" won her international acclaim. The others are Tudor Bostan, founder of B.E.C., the owners of the *Mississippi Queen*, Virginia Bailey, an English secretary, and Kees Kuyter, a waiter of Dutch nationality. They were picked up in mid-river from a frail raft by a Russian freighter, the *Odessa*, at 15.30 local time, some eleven hundred and fifty miles upriver. Stay tuned for further news.'

Within an hour the information had been relayed by satellite to dozens of capitals, and all over the world media representatives were driving through the morning, or evening or night, to the nearest airport with a flight out to Brazil. Two days later Bertram's film of the sinking was shown all over the world, and a special programme was compiled to honour the dead.

Far to the south in Buenos Aires, a man sat outside the un-pretentious façade of the Hotel Octavia on the Calle Balcon. In front of him was a pile of newspapers and a cup of white coffee, while opposite a small street ran down to the Japanese vegetable market, its narrow exit framing the hustling morning trade.

At eight o'clock a waiter brought him breakfast, bread rolls, bitter orange jam and more coffee. Halfway through the modest meal a receptionist called to him from the door.

'*Senhor Kuyter? Telephon.*'

Five minutes passed, and then the blond man returned slowly to his table and re-read a report from the previous day's *Herald Tribune*.

'Salvador da Bahia, May 1. A Brazilian Coastguard vessel today found the empty capsized hull of the luxury yacht *Quadalquivir*, belonging to recluse billionaire Viktor Totm, floating fifteen miles off the coast of Bahia. The yacht had sailed from Salvador the previous day bound for Rio, and it's thought that actress Attica Alloui may have been a guest on board, recovering from her recent ordeal in the Amazon jungle. There have been speculations that Totm, who owns large tracts of Brazilian real estate, was a close friend of Tudor Bostan, founder of B.E.C., and may well have helped finance the disastrous voyage of the *Mississippi Queen*. Full story on page three.'

Kees put the paper down and pushed it slowly across the table in front of him. Then he took a flight ticket from his pocket and looked at it: Iberian Airlines; Buenos Aires-Madrid. Madrid-Algiers. Carefully, he folded the ticket and put in in his pocket.

Anger whitened his face, anger and deep sorrow. She had come too far, they all had, to get dealt a hand like that. His mind ran through their names, the names of dead men and women that he had known for such a brief time. Cochran and Cane, Bertram and young Mayall, Fátima ... Rod, whose heart had quietly failed in his sleep three hours before they were picked up, whose body they had sheeted as best they could, and whose corpse they had pushed over the side, where, after painful minutes, it had

216

had the grace to disappear; Ginny, torn with grief, unable to control herself, even when they fired the gun and the rust-streaked, swart, ugly – but beautiful! – Russian freighter hove to and stopped, stopped right there in front of them. Bostan, his head bandaged, thick black hair wet from Attica's ministrations, semi-conscious, had been hoisted aloft like a barrel of Black Sea caviar on a stretcher.

Kees stopped. The process was more painful each time his mind went through it. Attica's Wells of Hope were as distant now as they had ever been in the jungle. More so, in fact, for she was now like a fiction from the past. Perhaps, he thought, it would never have worked in any case. But Christ, we deserved a try.

He drained half a cup of cold coffee and stood up, folding the newspapers as if to take them with him, but then thought better of it and dumped them back on the table. There was nothing to stay for in Buenos Aires. A flurry of movement caught his eye, a girl hurrying out of a cab, and he made his way back into the hotel towards his room. He had in his pocket a certified cheque drawn on a bank in Geneva for the Swiss franc equivalent of 210,000 dollars, but on his mind was a restaurant called Boi nos Ares where he had eaten *churrasco* with Noélia. In the corridor leading to the lift he stopped.

'Señor Kuyter,' a voice was saying. 'Look, I'll write it down for you.'

His mind came back to the present as he registered the long chestnut hair, the voice, the suitcase. She turned, as if she felt his eyes heavy on her back, and for a moment neither of them moved.

'I had to come, Kees.' The words tumbled out of Ginny's mouth. 'I found Pieter Schlater in Manaus and he told me you had rung him from here. I took a chance. I'm broke now. One of Turk's men got me the ticket. Please don't look at me like that, Kees, I'm so lonely.'

He reached her in four strides and held her lightly, smoothing her hair. In a broken voice she said, 'I could do with a little help to get back on my feet – you know – I was so stupid, I thought of you after the trip. I was due to go home the next day,

then the news, and I thought you might be sitting in a bar somewhere feeling like me, and as soon as I thought that I had to
see you. It was a compulsion, I couldn't stop myself.'

Kees looked at the clock on the wall over her shoulder, and
than at the large, sad eyes of the receptionist, obviously moved
by the little drama he was witnessing. Kees caught the man's
attention and watched his expression slip back to normal. A great
surge of affection welled up inside him, and his grip on the girl
tightened.

'Get me reservations at Swissair,' he said, 'and make up my
bill.' And in a half-whisper that only Ginny could catch, 'We're
leaving now.'